POISONED KINGSHIP

JASON BERKOPES

Print Version ISBN: 979-8-9853158-5-1

ISBN: 979-8-9853158-6-8

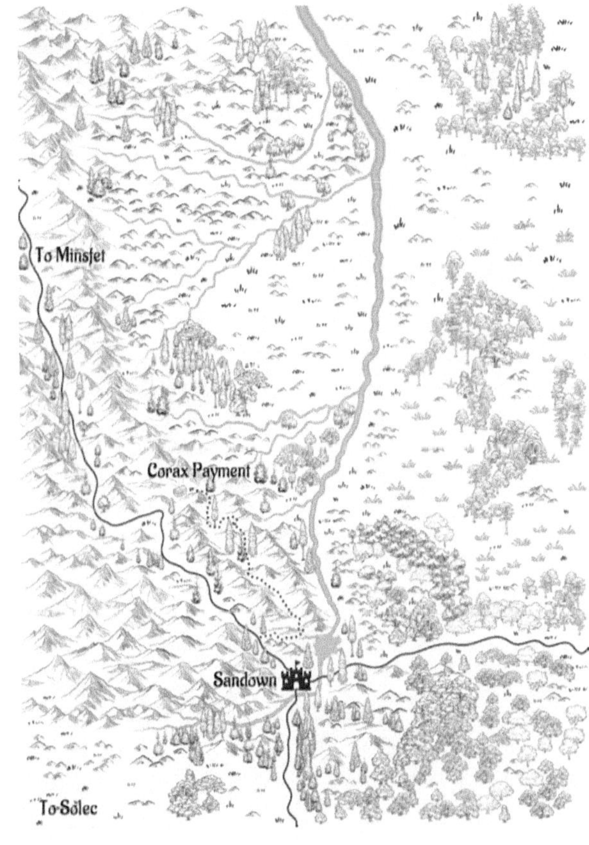

To Minsfet
Corax Payment
Sandown
To Solec

PROLOGUE

Ancient texts reveal that when time and the universe began, it was created by an omniscient being . . . Elohim. Why Elohim decided to make the heavens and this particular world will always remain a mystery.

Elohim created the universe to be in balance. Its entirety is maintained by a perfectly engineered balance based on math. Because of this, a natural opposite to everything came into existence. If there was light, then there had to be dark.

The creation of matter, for example, meant there had to be anti-matter. When the essence of goodness came into existence . . . evil had to follow. The ultimate evil was formed out of necessity near the time of the creation of this world.

He wanted all of His sentient creatures to have free will. The will to make their own decisions during their life on the world He created. To accomplish that, He had to allow the existence of sin and, thus, evil.

So, Elohim made the world and populated it with all manner of creatures. During this period of time, one of his angels, the angel of death, argued that he gave too much power to these new creatures and that his plans for creating even more intelligent creatures should not come to pass.

Grakus, as he was so named, cast away his wings as a sign of rebellion and swore an oath to prove to Elohim that giving these creatures free will would ultimately lead them to evil. He also felt that Elohim was granting them more power than they deserved. In his mind, they should earn that power and the right to pass into Elohim's kingdom of everlasting life and love.

Elohim let him go with great sorrow. Grakus fell from the heavens as a fiery comet that consumed a majority of the creatures on the world. Grakus then populated it with all manner of beings that he twisted from the ones that remained.

Elohim used this moment to bring on the age of elves, his purest and most perfect beings. Elves were born of the forest and had the ability to live in harmony with their surroundings. Grakus saw this as an imbalance where Good held sway over these new lower creatures. He took some of these elves and twisted and corrupted them, bringing forth orcs and even darker version of elves referred to as drow or dark elves.

Orcs lived much shorter lives than the elves but could multiply at a much faster rate. They care for nothing but destruction and conquest. The drow were even more focused on enslaving other beings, and living underground in perpetual darkness only to come to the surface to terrorize those who lived in Elohim's favor.

This shifted the power in favor of Grakus. To

counter this evil, Elohim created dwarves from the earth itself. He formed them straight out of the granite from the mountains of the world.

Along with that, he gifted the elves with magic. He did that to combat the rising tide of evil threatening to destroy and take over the world. The dwarves he made were resistant to magic., countering the gift he imbued upon the elves.

This returned the world to a balance that lasted for a thousand years. Then Grakus twisted the magic of the elves and introduced more evil creatures of his own, once more throwing off the balance in his favor. This is how it stayed until the Dawn of Man started a couple thousand years ago.

Both Elohim and Grakus had made many different creatures. Good and evil, along with neutral creatures, now existed to a lesser degree than the primary races. Elohim made a deal with Grakus. He would create a new race. A short-lived, very intelligent race, that could be twisted to evil or be as pure as an angel. It would be their free will that would determine their path.

Elohim, then made an agreement with Grakus for the two to stop meddling in the affairs of the world and see how things would transpire. Grakus agreed. Now, angels of Heaven where Elohim resides and demons from Hell where Grakus resides meddle for both sides in an everlasting tug-of-war behind the scenes.

When Elohim created this world, he filled it with interesting creatures and flora. He brought forth two massive continents and a third smaller land mass from the watery depths of the oceans, designing them to be drastically different from one another. The Land of the Crescent Moon being one and the other being Ugaria. The name Ugaria was adopted in 4373 After Creation (A.C.) after two magical beings battled there.

Ugar, the high priest of Nimsu, a large city located in the southeastern part of the continent, fought a great demon known only to a few as Gretag. An order of dark priests where manipulated by Gretag into releasing the demon upon the mortal plane. The monster devoured the priests and started releasing terror upon the nearby lands. Ugar heard of the demon and set out to locate and destroy it before the demon unleashed further damage upon the land.

After a great battle between the two powerful beings, Ugar smote Gretag with a holy blast that caused the beast to implode, killing Ugar in the process. The implosion, mixed with Ugar's magical essence, created a powerful anti-magic rift and caused a series of anti-magic pockets to appear around the eastern side of the continent. Anything that entered the magical areas were consumed.

This prevented all magicians, druids, priests, or any other magical beings from entering those areas. Those who were magical and happened to be in the areas when those pockets came into existence were never seen again.

Only the elven tribes existed before the Time of the Gift. Since then, many cities were established, and the primary races have spread across the world, leaving war, peace, cities, and kingdoms in their wake.

One particular city was created to house the elders of magic on the continent known as the Land of the Crescent Moon. Its name originated from the crescent-shaped gorge that borders a mountainous region within. The three primary races selected four mortals that would control the teachings of magic. These four elders would live for one millennium, starting with their induction into their position. Their powers would be passed down to an apprentice who would then take over for another millennium, and so on and so forth.

These four "elders," as they are called, would help spread, teach, and control the use of magic throughout the world.

They made decisions to govern the laws of magic and to keep them in check. A fifth mortal with the power to be a moderator and make a final decision if the Elders could not come to an agreement was also chosen.

The fifth mortal is known as the Constable and is always filled by a current Grand Druid of the known lands.

The era when magic was gifted by Elohim is known as "The Time of the Gift." Scholars of the Crescent Moon highlands documented the Gift back to 1357 A.C. when the elves were first chosen.

It took close to four hundred years for thousands of dwarves and elves to construct the Crescent Moon stronghold where the Elders now live. The two cultures combined to create the greatest conjoined above and below-ground city to ever exist.

The elves built all the above-ground structures to blend in with the land to be almost unnoticeable. Four great towers were designed by the elves within the mountainous region that exists within the gorge that forms the crescent moon shape that the continent is known for. The towers stand above all the land like slender needles pointing to the heavens out of respect for Elohim.

Each tower has its polar opposite. The Ebony Tower sits like a dark dagger stabbing upward into the sky, and the faithful tend to follow the dark arts; death and decay are some of what this tower represents, but not necessarily evil.

The Ivory Tower is the opposite of the Ebony Tower, and the faithful tend to follow the art of protection, healing, and rejuvenation. It stands as a white beacon of purity.

The Granite Tower starts as a dark brown at the base and fades to a bright fiery red at the top. The faithful study the elemental powers of earth and fire as they are born of each other.

Its opposite, the Chromatic Tower, is where the arts of wind and water are studied and mastered. The tower itself seems to shift and change color from white to blue, and every shade in between, with the blowing wind.

Each temple represents one faith of magic. Because even magic has to have balance. Without balance, chaos would reign over the land.

The dwarves, in turn, carved deep into the mountains to link all the temples into one grand metropolis made up of smaller cities, each dedicated to the tower above.

Four primary races make up the majority of humanoids. Humans make up the largest number. They are fragile compared to some of the other more robust species. However, they can be intelligent and reproduce faster than any other above-ground species. By sheer numbers, they have become a force in the world. Considered a "jack of all trades," they are very flexible and quick to pick up a trade but slow to master it.

Elves make up the second-largest group of humanoids. They don't reproduce as fast as humans but can live for thousands of years, and most of them are reclusive and shun outsiders in favor of teaching others and learning about the natural world. Some of the oldest elves still recall the early days of the first millennia.

They produce some of the finest clothing known to the world. They are also renowned for their ranged weapon crafting and skill with any type of bow or thrown weapon. Their ability to be one with nature and the crafting of their dwellings to blend in with or meld with nature is awe-inspiring to the other races and is coveted by humans in particular.

Nobody really knows or cares how many dwarves have come to populate the world—except for the dwarves themselves. Some believe they were a prank played on the elves by Grakus simply because they are almost their polar opposite.

The truth is that they were created by Elohim for maintaining balance. They do not respond well to taunts that say otherwise. Elves are slender, and dwarves are thick. Elves have very little body hair, and dwarves have lots. Elves are very magical in nature, and dwarves resist and reject magic. Being opposites, they tend to disagree a lot, which is the source of the joke.

The dwarves have successfully created a couple of large kingdoms between the two continents.

However, they don't tend to venture far outside their mountainous homes.

In fact, they were chosen to protect and defend the Elders of Magic due to their high resistance to magic and because no dwarves can practice magic. Dwarves are the masters of the earth and stone. They are best known for their armor, weapon craftsmanship, and stone masonry, along with their ability to consume large amounts of their favorite drink, dwarven ale.

The final major species are the minotaurs. Minotaurs look like half man half bull and were created between 4250 and 4700 A.C. when Grakus was corrupting many different beings to counter those Elohim created.

On the northeastern side of Ugaria are many clans of minotaurs that have banded together around a large mountain range. They keep to themselves and, from time to time, make pilgrimages outside their territory. Exiles can be found all over the world.

They are very strong, able to heft two-handed weapons twice the size of most other races'. They are quick-tempered, but they would give up their lives to defend friends and family.

Known for their fighting prowess and little else, not many can say they have tangled with a minotaur and come out on top. Minotaurs tend to get along with dwarves as both are strong, are good fighters, and don't care for magic.

Minotaurs do not have a resistance to magic, so nothing prevents them from practicing magic other than their beliefs. Many are exiled for showing abilities in magic or for practicing the trade.

The rest of the vast expanse is made up of a dangerous mix of grassland, swamps, forests, and mountains that will consume anyone foolish enough to wander alone. Demons, thieves, and monsters of all types have roamed the lands for millennia preying on any passerby that they believe weak. The cities are safe from those dangers. But they have hazards of their own. Politics, power, greed, and corruption await those who live in the cities. This brings us to our story . . .

CHAPTER

ONE

The largest thief's guild lay just under the city of Sandown, surrounded by rough-hewn stone walls and lit with small oil lamps. This thief's den was integrated into the city right under the nose of those who built its defenses.

The guild's existence was no longer in question; however, its location was. Great pains had been taken to keep it secret, including the deaths of fellow guild members, guards, and even the occasional public official. It was a constant thorn in the king's side. As of yet, the city guard had been unable to purge the city of the crime circle.

The guild was open to members as a refuge at all times of the day and night. There was a kitchen, a place to launder stolen goods, and even a secure vault to store items taken from those above.

It was dark, damp, and cramped, but it was home to those who had nowhere else to go. It was so successful that many of the original members had made enough to retire on. They'd since moved to far-off lands, leaving the guild to the one remaining entity.

The person who ran the guild had no identity outside of the guild. He was a ghost, the most sought-after assassin on the continent. He was hunted by those who wanted to bring him to justice and by those who wanted to use his talents.

This night, Corax, the leader of the thief's guild, sat in a meeting with an emissary from Letharia. Whispers in the air carried on it the words of murder that greeted the ears of the veteran dwarf sitting across from the emissary.

Osbur, the emissary from the kingdom of Letharia, sat across from Corax, whose bushy black dwarven beard crawled down his chest like a field of brambles ending at his belly. His black leather jerkin and breeches were snug around his muscled body. His eyes sat behind his thick eyebrows like dark pieces of coal. Corax stared intently at the well-dressed, well-spoken, portly Osbur, who was on the verge of getting himself planted six feet under if he didn't quit asking the same question over and over again.

The two had been discussing a matter of great importance in the master thief's chambers for over an hour. Firelight danced off the chamber's stone walls from the small fireplace nearby. It was cool and damp, with the pungent smell of mildew and the hint of smoke hanging in the air.

"We've been around and around on this," spat Corax. I'm not available for a job like this. Killing the king of Sandown is no simple matter, regardless of how many ways you weave the story. King Stalken is no easy mark, evidenced by the failures of those who tried previously. I have a prosperous guild to maintain in multiple cities, including this one in Sandown. You are asking me to give all of that up to do this one job for your employer." Corax leaned forward while thrusting a thick finger into the polished wooden tabletop they were sitting at.

Osbur's chubby human face frowned as he nodded. "We understand what we are asking you to accomplish. The compensation would be on par with the task you are being asked to perform."

Corax sat back in his mahogany chair for a moment and gathered his thoughts. Killing a king was serious business. And not just any king, one of the most popular and well-known rulers on the continent of the Crescent Moon.

If he took this mission, he could jeopardize everything he'd worked to achieve. If he was successful, it could catapult his plans for his own kingdom to the forefront.

"Hmmm," he grumbled while running his fingers through his thick beard.

Corax stood and walked over to another table that held a variety of rare liquors. He poured himself a brandy and tossed his head back, swallowing the small, potent liquid. Without offering any to his guest, he poured himself another.

"What's the catch?"

Osbur shifted in his seat. "There is no catch. My employer wants the king dead, and I'm being paid to make that happen. Your skills put you at the top of our list, end of story."

Corax walked back to the table with his glass of brandy and slumped back into his chair as if it were no matter to him that he was considered for such a dangerous task as this.

"Why is it that you want the king slain?" Corax asked as he pointed his finger at Osbur.

"That really isn't your concern, master dwarf," Osbur replied. "All you need concern yourself with is that you will be paid handsomely for your efforts. Osbur motioned around the small damp room. "You won't have to hide in a hole and keep running from the authorities like a worm trying to hide from a bird."

Osbur sensed that he might have come on a little too strong as Corax tensed in his seat. Corax tilted his head back and let the brandy trickle into his mouth. He swallowed it and stood back up. He walked over to Osbur and leaned close to his face. Osbur's face wrinkled slightly from the smell of the strong alcohol on the dwarf's breath.

"Don't presume that I'm hiding, stupid, or weak just because I live underground. If you insult me like that again—"

Corax grabbed Osbur by the throat, picked the heavy-set man up out of his chair with just one hand, and pressed him against the wall at eye level, shaking him back and forth a few times as if he were nothing more than a child's rag doll.

"—I'll snap your neck and throw you away like so many others. I don't care who you are or about the kingdom to the west I know you represent."

With that, he tossed Osbur back into his chair and walked over to peer into the fire. Osbur gasped for air and clutched his neck with his hand, shaking from the adrenaline surging through his system after the sudden aggression shown by Corax. Realizing he was in someone else's backyard for the moment and needed to mind his manners, he cleared his throat before speaking.

"I apologize for the insult. I simply meant that the money we can reward you with will be more than you can dream of."

"Will be?" said Corax, leaning forward to stoke the fire with a nearby poker. "If I accept this mission, I will demand half payment up front for even attempting such a task."

"That sounds reasonable," Osbur replied while rearranging his clothing.

Corax started playing with his beard again as his mind churned through his options. He knew if Letharia had the means to give him as large of a payment as he was going to demand, then that would mean his actions would escalate the conflict between Letharia and Sandown. If Letharia were to take possession of Sandown, then his guild would be on the chopping block. If he failed in this task, then his very life would be on the line. Even if he escaped, he would be hunted by both sides for the rest of his life.

Corax turned his head just a bit and peered at Osbur out of the corner of his eye. His dark vision gave him the ability to see in low light. He could see the face of the man before him, plump like a ripe tomato from eating too much food. The man didn't look like he could fight his way out from under a blanket. The skin around his eyes was tight and drawn up, but Osbur's eyes were cold and heartless, just like his own.

Corax had to admit he didn't like hiding like a mole to make a living. He had grand plans in store for the world, and this could give him a great start on the next stage of that plan. But he didn't trust this man. Of course, he didn't trust any man or beast, just as he couldn't be trusted. Many fools had already made that mistake.

No matter. If the man could back him with the money he was implying, it would be worth attempting—even if it did mean having his head stuck on a pike on top of Skull Gate. A few of his previous employees were stuck up there at this very moment. He shook the scene out of his mind. It was time to see how desperate Letharia was over their current predicament.

Corax smirked and looked over at Osbur for just a moment. "I'm going to require one hundred and fifty thousand with half the payment in advance," he said while looking back at the fire.

"That would be a considerable amount of gold," Osbur commented.

A chuckle escaped the dwarf's bearded face. "I think you have underestimated the importance of this mission. The price is in platinum, not gold."

Osbur scoffed and then squinted at the dwarf for a moment. "That seems like a lot to slip a dagger in someone's back. I don't believe my employer will like that request. The other names on the list will likely be of better value. They—"

Corax jumped in. "It isn't a request. It is a demand." Corax turned to face Osbur.

"The mistake you made is letting me know an assassination attempt on the king will happen. My guild gets the blame for every wrongdoing in the city, whether or not it's warranted. The city will be torn to pieces if the attempt succeeds, destroying my guild in the process. There will be a mark on every known member of the guild for the rest of their days. Therefore, to protect my investments from the slip-ups of another assassin, I will have no choice but to kill them before they kill the king. Three assassination attempts have been tried on the king, and now their skulls are baking under the sun on Skull Gate. That leaves me as the only option on your precious list."

Osbur slid away from the table and stood up. He adjusted his clothes a bit more from the earlier engagement with the dwarf. "This will not go over well. That much platinum will put a considerable drain on the wealth of my employer."

"Your employer has no choice. If memory serves, they aren't fairing too well in this conflict after laying siege to this city before and failing. Obviously, they have learned that it is better to weaken your adversary prior to any future engagement. War is here, and if they want the wealth stored in this mountain, they need every advantage they can get."

"I see . . . I will have an answer for you within twenty-four hours."

"Very well," replied Corax. "Contact me through the normal channels."

Corax dismissed him, had him escorted back to his bodyguards, and released back onto the streets of Sandown through one of the guild's many secret entrances.

Osbur walked the streets back toward the inn he was staying at. The ego of this dwarf was like none he had ever experienced. He hoped he would have the opportunity to be there when the dwarf bit off more than he could chew, preferably during the handoff should the council determine this was the best course of action.

CHAPTER

TWO

It was early evening, and The Slab, a popular watering hole in Sandown, was just starting to fill up. Tegin and Thena sat across from each other at their usual table in a corner near one of the many fireplaces of the tavern. Tegin was enjoying some of his favorite lager while he watched the patrons coming into his tavern from the cool mountain air. He'd built the place with the help of some local carpenters who'd settled in Sandown when the town wasn't much bigger than a hamlet.

The Slab was one of Sandown's favorites and always drew a large crowd. The tavern had been enlarged twice since opening. The original bar crafted of pine was now used as a food and drink station after the new extension was added, and a giant hard oak bar was built to resist the treatment from the patrons and occasional brawls that would break out. The original bar had been hastily built when the place was nothing more than a small village, and most people referred to it as Stalken's mine. The hand-hewn original timbers stood out from the sanded and polished wood used in the expansions. Tegin never changed it because he liked to be reminded of where they started, and it brought questions from visiting travelers, giving him an excuse to tell the origin story over and over.

Coming to The Slab always made him feel better, even on the worst days. It was like a warm blanket was thrown over him as soon as he stepped inside.

Tegin discovered at an early age that studying a fire calmed him. Watching the flames dance and intertwine with the red, orange, blue, and occasional flecks of green while letting the day's stress flitter around in the back of his mind.

His tavern was unlike the others in the city. The smaller fire pits scattered around created more comfortable areas instead of just a few larger ones that forced patrons to crowd around. Tegin had shaped the smoky-blue granite foundations for the fire pits and the circular vents made from iron with his own two hands. The iron vents were suspended above the fire pits, allowing the heat to permeate the tavern in all directions yet preventing the smoke from choking the patrons on windy days. They took on a nice brown rusty patina that accentuated the bucolic feel of the tavern.

Near the fire pits, he'd put small tables with individual chairs that utilized leather straps for back and leg support. Though more expensive to keep than solid wood, leather allowed the person's body to be more comfortable and maintain a more natural shape.

Every night patrons would fall asleep watching the fires and listening to the yarns being woven around them. Instead of jostling those sleeping comfortably in their chairs at closing time, Tegin installed small bells on a contraption he invented. They were rigged to ring more or less of them the harder a rope was pulled. He could control the amplitude of the ringing bells, allowing the sleeping patrons to wake up gently.

The effort he'd put into The Slab to make it a pleasant place to rest was why the tavern was a favorite. Some owners would take offense at patrons falling asleep in their establishment, but Tegin didn't mind at all. A hard-working minor dozing in front of a fire was no concern of his. Even Tegin could be found napping in front of a fire more often than not.

Years previous, he had turned over the tavern's management to someone else so he could work for the king as captain of the city guard. He still retained ownership and was known to visit almost every day.

The warm summer days had started to wane as autumn settled in on the mountain town. Autumn was short-lived in this part of the world, which meant winter storms would soon be coming to dump loads of snow on the region. Tegin's tavern would be a common spot for those wanting to warm their bones with fire and a hardy drink.

Next to Tegin sat Thena, a high elf maiden turned warrior. Everyone knew that a dwarf and an elf were unlikely friends. Though Thena was older than Tegin, he treated her like his little sister.

Tegin was a rough-looking dwarf covered in scars with a well-groomed bushy brown beard and a handful of small braids adorning it. Small gold and silver clasps kept the braids intact during the hustle and bustle of his workday.

Thena, a fair-skinned elf with bright green eyes and golden blonde hair that ended just past her neck, was the definition of beauty. The two of them couldn't be more different.

They were bound by an unbreakable friendship forged years before when Thena was saved by Tegin while he was working as an aspiring mercenary.

Just a week previous, she had returned from her trials at one of the many academies found throughout Crescent Moon. It had been over thirty years since they met, not that either of them looked much older; benefits of dwarven and elven longevity.

Thena sat with her back to the door and sipped her favorite cinnamon butter rum tea that Tegin always kept stocked just for her. She wore her usual dark grey pants, black knee-high mountain boots, a long-sleeved blouse, and a shimmering black cloak that hung from her slender frame. The blouse changed colors on a regular basis, but her boots and pants never seemed to change, which was rare among elves.

Thena's Elven background made her look thin and frail compared to humans and especially dwarves. On more than one occasion, she'd surprised would-be suitors who didn't know the meaning of "no."

The mage wasn't in charge of protecting the king for nothing. At five feet tall, she towered over the dwarf by ten inches, but his bearded face and dark, hairy body couldn't hide the power he possessed in his wide frame. His strength had helped defend the city he had loved so much for many years. The two of them would risk their lives to protect Sandown, and most citizens knew it.

Thena and Tegin were lost in memory as they stared into the nearby fire. It had been almost a decade since she and Tegin had settled here. The king had persuaded them to take up the positions that they now held.

Thena became captain of his personal guard, and Tegin became captain of the city guard. Their task was to keep the king and the city safe at all times, and they relied much on each other to do both.

Both of them had grown up as only children, and they saw each other as an odd brother and sister. Many nights they could be seen here relaxing after a long day, drinking their favorite beverages. They would spend hours just staring at the fire dancing in the fireplaces, enjoying each other's company in silence.

Tegin was nursing his ale and staring at the fire that was getting low. The embers were still hot and red with little blue flames sprouting from them occasionally. He slid out of his seat, grunting as he hefted his weight onto his tree trunk-like legs. He grabbed another log out of the wood rack he had built into the tavern's walls and slipped it into the fire pit. He sat back down with a sigh and glanced over at Thena.

"Any leads following that latest robbery?" asked Thena, not looking away from the fire recently disturbed by the fresh log.

"Not yet," said Tegin. "We can't seem to get any information on the guild's location. If we can't locate the guild, we will never lower the crime rate in this town. Suicide seems to be the better alternative to being captured. I can't imagine wanting to work for a guild that requires suicide over being caught."

Tegin watched some more patrons drift into the tavern.

Thena put her cup of tea down on the table. "This damn crime problem is the last thing we need while this war is going on. We don't have a clue to go on, and we have to report to Stalken in the morning. I'm guessing he won't be too pleased, and I hate giving him bad news."

"Yeah, well, I gave him the bad news last time, so don't be tryin' to sweet talk me into doing it twice in a row," Tegin chimed in.

"If I didn't know any better, I'd say you were glad I'm giving the report instead of you," Thena replied.

"Oh, don't give me that! He never gives you as hard of a time as he does me . . . I'm a gruff ol' dwarf full of piss and vinegar, and you are a beautiful elf. If I were him, I'd let you off easy too."

A tinge of pink showed on her cheeks as she blushed. Then, she sighed and leaned back into her chair. "We wouldn't have to take turns getting yelled at by Stalken if we could just catch a break," she hissed as she brushed away a bit of golden hair that fell over her eyes.

Tegin raised an eyebrow and mumbled something incoherent as he took another big gulp of his ale.

She poked at him. "What's that, mumbles?"

He put down his mug. "I said, it sounds to me

like you need a vacation." He grinned through his beard.

"I wasn't expecting to return to a city undermined by a thief's guild bent on robbing every citizen and merchant who lives or visits."

Tegin waved to the waitress for a refill on his ale as Thena picked up her tea for another sip. They both went back to staring at the fire and wishing their problems would all disappear.

The small log Tegin had dropped into the fire pit was already burning with orange and red flames licking up from under the log in a fiery embrace. It was hypnotic to watch. They both returned to thinking about everything but saying nothing.

THREE

Evening wore on in the bustling mountain town of Sandown, which had started settling for the night. Most of the businesses had closed, save for the taverns, who remained open into the late hours.

The town was carved right out of the mountain about five hundred feet below where a mine entrance was located. That mine was the reason for the prosperity, and it was the reason for the war.

The king was a sound strategist. He knew that once word spread about the wealth of the mine, trouble would come knocking. He was able to keep it a secret for many years by slowly mining it with just his friends until they had enough wealth to establish a proper mine and join the regional mining guild. But, once word spread, so did the trouble. Luckily, the king had built the city with defense in mind, and it had proven its worth in the days since the war started. The thief's guild, however, was becoming a major concern.

. . .

IN THE SHADOWS, three cloaked figures moved down side streets and passages to avoid being noticed by any passers-by. They made their way to an alley in the corner of town near the market area, where a fourth cloaked figure waited.

"I have my employer's answer to your price, master dwarf," whispered Osbur from beneath the hood of his cloak as he and his guards approached.

The massive dwarf crossed his arms but said nothing.

"He has agreed to your price and payment in advance as you requested. However, he does request a memento as evidence of the deed."

"What is it that your master wants?" growled Corax.

"My master would like the two long swords he carries as proof. If no swords are delivered, then the second half will not be paid . . . agreed?"

"Agreed," replied Corax. "I will deliver as promised. Just make sure the first payment is placed two days up the old mining road where this map shows."

Corax tossed a folded piece of parchment toward Osbur, who stooped down and picked the parchment up off the ground where it landed.

"Oh, we'll be ready," Osbur replied. "And good luck to you."

Corax squinted at the chubby fellow from the shadows of his cloak. "I'll be ready too, fat man," he muttered under his breath.

FOUR

Gregory Stalken, the king, stood in front of his mirror as he did every morning, staring at his reflection above the wash-bowl in his royal chambers. Over the past few years, his hair and well-groomed beard had started to grey. He still had a full head of hair and the body of a man half his age, but the stress of protecting his capital city and kingdom was starting to take its toll.

He wished that Letharia would quit trying to destroy his kingdom and let him live in peace. But Letharia's greed would never allow that to happen. The mountain full of precious metals and gems his capital city was built on had also caused him to lead this stressful life.

It seemed like yesterday that he took shelter in the small cave where he first discovered the veins of gold and platinum. Now he was in command of one of the most elite armies in the known world. Unfortunately, the army he fought was very powerful and much larger than his own.

He sighed as he turned on his heel to walk over

to where his attendant had laid out his clothes for the day. On the wall near his bed, a canvas caught his eye. It was a painting of him looking out over the southern lowlands, a gift from Thena. It reminded him of the day she painted it, which brought a smile to his face. He'd placed it near his bed so he could start every day with a good memory.

He had come from a simpler life. Even though he was now royalty, he preferred his living quarters to be comfortable and small. His room was nothing more than his bed, a wash area, a small hallway that led to a closet, and a balcony he liked to stand or sit on to look out over the rolling hills leading down to the fertile fields of the south.

Two small fireplaces flanked either side of his room, along with a wood stove that sat near the wall in front of his bed. Though the size was bigger than he'd ever had growing up, it was not adorned in anything that was not functional. Anyone brought to this room blindfolded would never know he was a king. He was a simple man, and no amount of riches was going to change that.

After dressing in light leather armor, he attached his two magical long swords to his hips and proceeded down the hall with his bodyguards to what he'd nicknamed the War Room. The swords were gifts from the elves to the south. When he took power over the region, they came to make introductions. The swords they gifted him were light, perfectly balanced, and simple in style. He'd fallen in love with them immediately. A silver pommel and black leather-wrapped handles blended into both classic straight blades.

Simple and effective. They were pure and unsoiled, and he hoped to never have to use them to take a life.

He still practiced with the swords regularly. But in recent years, he relied more on his personal guards for protection rather than his own skill. *How times have changed,* he thought to himself. He used to be a guard for the VIP. Not the other way around.

The War Room used to be part of an indoor garden that was converted to its current state after the initial siege by Letharia some years back. It was a rectangular room with hanging plants around the edge of the ceiling, and a large ring of ferns and flowering plants lined the walls. Light was let in through openings in the walls, and the room was heated by an expansive fireplace at each end. Three large square tables were placed around the room for planning strategy. A small magical orb hovered above each of the three tables to provide light when natural light wasn't enough.

The smallest of the three tables was used to create miniature battlefields for use in upcoming conflicts, one was for general strategy and meetings for current issues in the kingdom and in the city, and the third was always cluttered with maps, papers, and the like used for reference on the other tables.

The plotting table was about the size of a small wagon and was filled with about four inches of sand. An interesting enchantment had been placed on the table that allowed a person to create a detailed map based on their thoughts and mental images. The magic would shape the sand into whatever shape or design they could imagine. It had proved quite useful when their counterattack against Letharia had started.

The table used for meetings and general discussion filled up a large portion of the room. It was only four feet wide but almost stretched from one end of the room to the other. It had been crafted out of iron oak wood provided by the elven kingdom to the south.

The elves there occasionally traded with the humans, who were kind enough to offer up some wood that they harvested for their own purposes. The wood was gifted to the Stalken as a peace offering at a small ceremony. He had it fashioned into this table as a reminder of the peace he worked hard to keep with the elves.

Once the table had been completed, a free trade agreement was also signed on the table that showed the ongoing peace between the two kingdoms. It had taken ten master carpenters working with a small team of elves that knew how to work the wood to finish the table. The seasoned wood still retained a greenish hue, and it took on its name well.

Iron oak was not some cliché. It was as difficult to work as iron. It took an edge like metal did and was impervious to insects. That was why the elves planted and nurtured the trees nearest their borders. They made an amazing deterrent to an approaching army. It had held the Letharian troops at bay for over a hundred years. It was very difficult to cut, just as difficult to work into something useful, and almost fireproof. Its presence in the War Room reminded everyone of the peace between the elves and the kingdom of Stalken. More importantly, it reminded everyone that anything was possible given the right tools, effort, and enough time to think things through.

In stark contrast, the maps and information table looked as though it had been dragged out of a trash pile. It was sturdy, but it looked as if it was owned by a pauper. Rumor had it that Stalken himself owned the table, and it was a possible hand-me-down from his father.

As the king entered the room, he was greeted by his two highest-ranking military officers, his personal security officer, captain of the guard, and a master mage. The mage wasn't on the king's payroll. She was there because she wanted to be, and her counsel was always welcome.

She came and went as she pleased and had nearly as much authority as the king. The group was made of an odd assortment to be certain: a dwarf, an elf, a few humans, and a dark elf.

"Good morning, everyone!" greeted Stalken as he entered the room.

"Good morning, sire," almost everyone replied. Lelanda, the resident mage, just nodded.

"Okay, let's get straight to business. Anything new on the location of the thief's guild?" asked Stalken.

"Nothing good to report yet," Thena hesitantly replied. "We just can't seem to catch a break with that situation. Whoever is running that guild knows how to keep their employees under a tight rein."

"Well, keep on it, Thena. I need your very best on this one. I can't have problems at home with so much at risk. I'm sure you know that, so I won't bother beating a dead horse. Same goes for you, Tegin. I trust both of you, so work the magic that you do and keep this city safe. Now let's get to the heart of the matter. What is the current situation around Solec?"

Solec was the name of the city that Stalken had just taken control of from Letharia during the counterattack a few weeks earlier.

Tegin poked Thena in the ribs with a thick finger. "See, I told you it was much nicer when you gave the report than when I did," he whispered with a sly smile and a wink.

Thena pretended to not hear anything he said, but a slight smirk appeared on her lips. She alone knew why the king was easier on her than the rest of the group—or at least she hoped she was the only one in on the secret.

The general, a big fiery red-haired human who went by the name of Gunner, stood up from the main table and said, "Sire, let me show you some things on the plotting table."

The king nodded, and the group followed the general to the table. One only had to grasp the metal post at the base of the table and picture the layout in their mind.

Everyone stood around the table as the general pointed to areas of Solec laid out in detail prior to the king's arrival. His loud, boisterous voice echoed off the granite walls of the large room.

"As of now, Colonel McLeod and I have subdued the city and its inhabitants. We are in a state of lockdown until we can get some laws in place and secure all non-essential areas," stated the general. "We have repaired the walls with the help of

Sandown craftsmen and mages. Most of the damage was caused by a wingless dragon Letharia had forced to do its bidding. The rest of the damage to the city is superficial and can wait to be repaired once we get settled in a little more. All positions have been fortified in case of a counterattack, which is long overdue. At this point, we are simply reinforcing the defenses and preparing for our next offensive move to take Saldanah to the north."

"Sounds very encouraging, Gunner. I hope our good luck continues for the foreseeable future. You and Colonel McLeod have done a wonderful job. I want to thank you for your loyalty and dedication to pushing back Letharia from our borders." Both Colonel McLeod and General Gunner bowed their heads to the king.

Stalken turned toward his two security officers. "You two . . . feel free to leave the briefing if you wish. We are just going to discuss some possible scenarios for Saldanah."

Tegin and Thena nodded in agreement and left the meeting to attend to their own agendas. That left the king, Gunner, McLeod, and Lelanda, who hadn't said a word since the meeting started, to start laying possible attack points for Saldanah. That didn't count the usual group of attendants that took notes, ran errands, or pulled reference material for the meetings. It was a beehive of activity. The four of them managed to not notice.

Lelanda was always quiet, and that disturbed most people around her. Her appearance didn't do anything to ease people's minds either.

Mages were secretive types anyway. One look into her eyes would chill most people to the bone.

Lelanda and the king went way back to when he was entangled in a mess during a caravan journey that neared the edge of the Pit, a desolate place north of the kingdom of the Crescent Moon. That was where Stalken first met Lelanda and Tegin.

Next to Tegin, Lelanda was the king's closest friend and confidant. Stalken rarely knew what she was thinking. Lelanda only said what she felt was important for others to hear, which wasn't much. Her actions spoke for themselves.

Lelanda was a dark elf. This is to say she was out of her environment on the surface. Dark elves lived almost exclusively in the earth's dark depths, where sunlight never shines. Yet here she was sitting at a table with three humans above ground. Nothing tended to end well when dark elves were encountered. She dealt with a lot of discrimination as all of the primary races of the surface world greatly despised dark elves.

Compared to humans, she was small at five feet tall and around one hundred and thirty pounds. But those extra pounds were not fat. She was as in shape as an elf could be. In fact, compared to other elves, she was very muscular and hid that fact under robes and cloaks.

She was a long-time practitioner of magic but was never seen without her two scimitars. She also wore most of her combat gear when away from her secluded mountain home. Stalken couldn't re-member the last time he had seen her wear much of anything else. She even wore them at the annual ball he threw at the castle.

Most of the time, she wore a hooded cloak that she would have up to not frighten people by her appearance. Silver hair and ebony skin were not the only oddities this one possessed. One faintly glowing red eye and the other glowing blue, high-lighted by the dark hood shading her sensitive eyes, were the first things anyone noticed about her. She carried her two swords or, on occasion, a large thick silvery metal staff.

Today she wore her swords, but they were not for decoration. Everyone in the room knew she was a very accomplished swordswoman. In fact, she had never been beaten by any of them when they sparred together.

Both swords were very powerful scimitars. One scimitar had two gems in the hilt. One gem would glow a fiery red, and one would have a transparent sheen to it with a faint bluish glow. The stones never glowed at the same time.

A whip, which she also kept on her person at all times, remained coiled and snapped on a belt around her waist. Even her closest friends didn't know the nature of the whip or why she kept it with her, just that she'd had the whip ever since Tegin or the king had met her. Her talents had become legend after she killed the wingless dragon at the battle of Solec.

She was known as a Battle Mage, a rarely trained art even in these magical times. Most mages failed to comprehend why time should be spent on physical training and the art of melee weapons. To become great, it took mental training of the highest caliber to learn all that was needed to be a specialized mage.

Lelanda proved over and over again that a Battle Mage definitely brought a whole new angle to the table. It was an easy compromise for her to make because of her long lifespan. At 441 years old, she was still quite young for her race. Yet, that was quite a few human lifetimes and, by account, plenty of time for a dedicated elf such as herself to learn the arts that she had up to this point.

The small group settled in for a long day discussing troop movements, artillery placements, defensive plans, offensive plans, and anything else they could think of.

They knew they were outnumbered. The only way to balance the sides was to be a step ahead in strategy and talent. Letharia would stop at nothing to kill anyone and everyone who stood in their way of taking the wealth of Sandown as their own.

FIVE

orax made his way through the broken landscape littered with boulders and large pine trees. He could feel the difference in the air as he climbed higher and higher into the mountains.

The area here looked like Elohim had taken a handful of huge stones and scattered them about. It gave Corax great cover. It also made moving across the countryside much more difficult than sticking to the road, which he dare not attempt.

He had been making his way to the drop point for five days now, making sure to move at night and stay in the shadows. He frowned as he thought about what Osbur said in the alley. His tone was not right, and it implied a hidden agenda.

Corax was good at picking out traitors and liars. It was a gift he learned at an early age. It served him well growing up in the mountains below the towers of the Crescent Moon. It saved him on more than one occasion while leading a guild of thieves and rogues that he couldn't trust at all.

One thing he knew for certain was that Osbur

was a bad liar and a traitor in the making. Corax expected the down payment to be too much for Osbur to let slip through his grasp without attempting to take it for himself.

Sending any of his men to pick up the payment would be the last time he ever saw them, even if they did escape the trap he expected Osbur to have waiting. He could never have trusted anyone but himself to take delivery of the largest deposit on any job he had ever heard of. Of course, the payment was warranted, considering his target.

He could kill any number of commoners without even breaking a sweat, but a member of royalty was a completely different story. They were always surrounded by walls and guards. Everything about a castle is there to make potential assassins like him think twice about taking a job like this.

In the fifty-plus years he had been in the business, Corax had never even been scratched. He wasn't going to start changing things now by delegating errands or not doing something himself, no matter how powerful he becam—though part of him yearned for someone to trust when he couldn't be in two places at once.

He knew his enemy and how they thought. They would assume he would arrive with a few others and a wagon to load the money onto. It was such a large amount that any other way wouldn't be possible. Well, any way *they* would expect.

He patted his vest and smiled to himself as he slipped through the rocks. That is where he had them. Years ago, he commissioned a mage to make him a little something special just for an occasion like this.

CHAPTER

SIX

Corax had made a good deal of progress in the six hours he ran during the night. His axe thumped his back as he leaped over rocks. In his right hand, he carried his trusty blowgun, which was already loaded with a poisoned dart. Two daggers were strapped to either side of his waist. His finishing touch was the bracers he wore. Those were his prized possessions.

He wasn't a fan of magical weapons. He didn't see the need considering he had never encountered anybody that resisted his poisons. However, he did have a liking for magical armor and clothing; those he could secure to his body and were not easy to steal or destroy. His bracers of strength gave him that extra edge. It allowed him to achieve moments like these when he ran for six hours straight and barely broke a sweat.

He guessed there would be around five to ten soldiers, not including Osbur, who would try and take the drop they had placed there for him. A larger contingent would bring attention. How accurate his guess would be, time would tell.

At his current speed, he expected to make it to the drop area by the next night. Osbur would probably have lookouts in place in an attempt to see his approach. They would be expecting a small group with a cart or wagon, not a lone dwarf with nothing on him but weapons.

The rocky terrain would be perfect for a silent approach. That was unfortunate for them. He smiled under his beard as he hurdled over a small boulder and skipped un-dwarf-like off the face of a rock out-cropping. The chess game had been started, and he intended to not let a pawn prevent him from checkmating the king.

SEVEN

Osbur and his seven men had entrenched themselves in a semi-circle around the cache of platinum coins sitting in the chest on the ground. Torches and a large fire were placed to light up the area during the night. The men arrived three days before the scheduled drop-off to set a trap for what they hoped was a couple of peons the assassin would send to collect the deposit. However, it wasn't unexpected if the dwarf were to show up himself.

Osbur contemplated the scenario. He expected at least two men to tag along with Corax to help bring the payment back. This amount of platinum could only be carried on a wagon. The chest weighed hundreds of pounds, and it had taken three of his men just to put it on the cart and take it off.

Osbur had the chest taken off the cart and put in a clearing with as few rock outcroppings as possible near the chest. Since the ground wouldn't permit pits to be dug, he had his men drop caltrops on the ground and disguise them with twigs and leaves.

Caltrops were little triangle-shaped spikes that, when thrown, always landed with a spike pointing up. He had the men put them in an arrangement left just enough room between each section of caltops to permit his quarry to enter and his men to block the exits. That way, they could trap the small group in the middle with the only way out through the caltrops.

He had three men with bows posted atop nearby rock outcroppings to scout and assist in taking down any guild members once the trap was sprung. Two guards stood near the chest, and two were stationed at the wagon. Osbur sat in the back of the wagon with a bow nearby in case it was needed.

He scratched at his fat, grizzled chin as he thought. As long as the group stayed cool, the dwarf and his comrades wouldn't be the wiser until it was too late.

He had the men set up a watch schedule where three men rested while four set watch. All were awake and in place for the scheduled time of pickup. All they had to do was wait for the arrival of his targets and spring the trap.

He couldn't wait to gloat in the dwarf's face for being rough with him at the negotiation. He didn't dare take on the dwarf single-handedly, but he didn't mind taking him on with a few strong lads at his side. Assassins were notorious for being cowards and running from a straight fight. They were just good at surprise tactics. If the coin was flipped, they would go down just as easily as any normal person.

After taking down Corax, he and his men would make their way to the town of Minsfet to the north and catch the first boat out of port to leave behind these lands forever. He would set sail for the continent of Ugaria and put an ocean between him and this wretched life.

While he was busy daydreaming about his future wealth, he failed to notice that they were being watched by some shadowy figure on a cliff a hundred yards away to the northwest.

EIGHT

It was well past midnight when Corax started to catch the faint smell of smoke coming downwind from the ridge to the north near the trail to Minsfet.

"Looks like this is the place," he muttered to himself.

He went into a crouching walk that made almost no sound as he worked his way through the rocks, taking care to not make a silhouette or jar any stones loose.

As he peered over the edge of the ridge, his eyes were met with a bonfire and a dozen torches lighting the area around a large chest sitting on the ground. Two guards stood to either side of the chest.

He watched the scene for about an hour from the ridge, marking men as they made themselves known by visual cues or sounds.

Corax could tell they were not veterans of subterfuge by the way the trap was set up. He spotted the caltrops gleaming in the firelight from the ridge, and it became quite obvious how they planned to take him down.

What a bunch of pathetic imbeciles, he thought to himself.

His low-light vision allowed him to see the archers on the other outcroppings overlooking the chest. He decided those would be his first targets. No need to get shot in the back if at all possible.

He located Osbur's heavy frame sitting on the cart just outside the fire's light, looking over his long sword with two other guards. Corax glanced at the night sky and realized he'd better get a move on. First light was in about three hours, and it would take time for him to get into position and take out the archers.

Osbur slid out of the cart, took a big stretch, and yawned. He looked at the setting moon and realized it would be a little over an hour before daylight started to show on the horizon.

"I wish that damned dwarf would show up already."

Initially, Osbur thought this task was just a fool's errand. He came to realize that it was the final gasp of a kingdom ruled by fear and greed.

It was never enough for his masters. They couldn't be content with what they had. The elves to the south would never allow trade through their lands after Letharia tried to force its will upon them. The iron wood barrier around their kingdom thwarted any major offensive Letharia could ever hope to muster against them.

With the kingdom of Stalken rumored to have

a free trade agreement with the elves and free passage through their lands to the rest of the continent, it was just a matter of time before these lands had power over the whole northern region. Trade had already started to shift east to the Minsfet port of call, taking away imports from Letharia's cities.

Even the rank he'd obtained within the hierarchy kept him in constant fear and paranoia. He just wanted to kill off the crew that came to pick up the chest and be off this continent by this time next week with enough riches to live on for the rest of his days.

Just as he was about to give up for the night, he noticed movement over by the trail leading from the road. He looked over to see the two men at the chest peering ahead into the flickering shadows. Corax strode into the firelight. Osbur glanced back up into the rocks and couldn't see any of his bowmen. He hoped they weren't sleeping on the job. He felt a bead of sweat on his forehead as what he was about to attempt set in.

He hailed the dwarf, which was the signal for the archers to prepare for the ambush, and the two guards at the cart approached the dwarf. One guard took a position to either side of Corax while the two others at the chest stood their ground. Osbur grinned because the stupid dwarf had walked right into his trap.

"Ho there, my dwarven friend," said Osbur as he walked toward the dwarf.

"Interesting situation we have here," commented Corax. "I come here for half my payment only to find seven soldiers and a huge bonfire going when subtlety should have been the better approach."

Osbur stopped walking as quickly as he started. His hands started sweating as he realized Corax knew how many men he had, including the ones hidden in the rocks.

"You have miscounted, Corax. I don't have seven men. As you can see, I only have four."

"Correction, *now* you only have four," replied Corax. "I already killed the other three hidden in the rocks when I realized you intended to betray our deal!"

Before Osbur could react, he watched the dwarf raise something to his mouth, and the guard to the left clutched his throat and dropped like a stone to the ground.

In a fluid, seasoned move, the dwarf dropped what looked like a blowgun and swung a battle-axe from his back. He rolled under the wild swipe from the guard to his right and back to his feet in an instant.

Before the guard could even react, he buried the axe into the side of his thigh. With a twirl, he wrenched the axe free and brought it up and around just under the chin of the guard, severing his head.

Osbur couldn't believe his eyes. "Kill him!" he yelled as he stumbled back toward his horse, away from the fighting. He turned and grabbed a bow from his saddle.

He looked back just in time to see Corax turn to face the other two guards rushing him. Osbur grabbed an arrow from his quiver in the cart. He tried to nock the arrow but realized the bowstring had been cut. He couldn't believe it. The dwarf had snuck right up to him and cut the bowstring, and he didn't even know it. That sent a very real shiver down his spine.

Meanwhile, Corax parried a blow from the first guard wearing an eye patch that almost took the weapon from the guard's grasp.

Osbur climbed up on his horse and realized he had greatly underestimated the assassin. If he lived past this night, he would not make that mistake again. Osbur just stared slack-jawed. Never in his days had he seen men taken out this fast by a single combatant.

C orax glanced over his shoulder to see Osbur climbing onto his horse. In front of him, two men prodded in his direction with their long swords. Neither man wanted to commit to an attack after seeing their fellow men-at-arms fall so fast to the dwarf.

Corax feigned an attack at the guard on his right, then whipped one of his daggers into the foot of the guard on the left. That guard dropped his sword and fell screaming to the ground as Corax parried a swipe from the remaining guard.

Then he jumped back about three feet, kicked up some loose rock and dirt in the direction of the remaining guard with the eye patch, and hurled his axe at him at the same instant. The axe embedded into the guard's chest, tearing through his chain-mail armor and almost penetrating through the other side.

When he looked back at Osbur, he saw that he

was trying to flee on his horse. Corax walked over to the blowgun he had dropped at the start of the fight. He located a freshly poisoned dart, pushed it into the blowgun, and fired a quick shot toward Osbur as he attempted to flee.

Corax tucked the blowgun into his belt. He retrieved his axe from the guard's chest and wiped it clean with the shirttail of the dead guard. He turned to the last remaining guard, who was still grimacing in agony with the dagger lodged into his foot.

"Tsk . . . tsk . . . tsk . . . looks like your leader ran off to leave you all by your lonesome."

Corax knelt down by the guard and wrenched the dagger out of his foot. The guard gave a short scream in pain and looked into Corax's eyes.

"Please, please don't kill me!" begged the guard. "I have a family back home . . . I'm just trying to feed them and earn a living!"

"Well, I guess you should have thought about that before you listened to an idiot like Osbur."

Corax brought the dagger up to the guard's chest and pushed it an inch at a time through his armor; all the while, the guard was screaming and fighting to prevent the dagger from entering his chest. Just before the dagger made it to the hilt, the guard stopped struggling and went limp. Corax pulled the dagger back out and wiped it off on the pants of the dead guard, then looked around just to make certain everything was quiet.

None of them noticed the shadowy figure watching everything from a distance. The figure moved back away from the ledge as Corax went about cleaning up.

.   .   .

THE CLOAKED figure knelt inside a small cave and pulled out three white scrying crystals. In a natural depression on the stone floor, he poured some water and then let it settle. He took each crystal and muttered a small incantation to each one and placed them an equal distance from each other to form a triangle around the pool. He muttered another spell, and the small pool shimmered to life. A face appeared in the pool.

"Status?"

"The assassin has received payment, master, even though Osbur tried to betray him just as you predicted," replied the cloaked figure.

"Good."

"If Osbur still lives, I think it is time I washed my hands of him."

"Contact me when the deed is done." The image faded, and the crystals went dark.

OSBUR HAD MADE it about a quarter of a mile away before his horse started acting weird. It stopped galloping and then started walking. He could hear it gasping for breath as it came to a stop. No matter how hard he prodded, it wouldn't move. He slid off the horse, and it immediately kneeled down and lay on its side. Its breathing had become ragged.

Osbur noticed something about two inches long protruding from the horse's hindquarters. He went over and pulled the object from the horse, recognizing it as a blowgun dart. He threw it away and glanced around. He had about a third of a mile head start over the dwarf. Osbur looked into the sky. It wasn't as dark now; dawn was approaching. He needed to make the most of his head start and get moving.

He grabbed his pack from the horse that was in its final stages of death as far as he could tell. He was lucky the dart didn't hit him. The horse weighed hundreds of pounds more than him, and hadn't made it half a mile before being brought down by the poison. He swung his pack onto his back and moved as quickly and quietly as his feet would carry him to the north.

CORAX STARED in the direction that Osbur rode off. He was certain he had hit the horse. It was an easy target.

"Damn it," he hissed. "I'll find you again, Osbur, that I promise you," he said out loud.

Corax walked back to the chest he came for. He picked his way back through the caltrop field by shuffling his feet instead of taking steps, kicking away any caltrops he came upon. He made one last scan of the area and listened for a few minutes as he sat on the chest. He didn't want to be shot in the back while unloading the crate after all the nonsense he just went through to acquire it.

After sitting still for a few minutes, he was confident nothing threatening was nearby. He knew Osbur wouldn't return and figured once his horse died, he would continue on toward Minsfet to board the first boat off the continent. Corax would make certain to send word to his men in Minsfet after returning to the guild. They would be waiting for Osbur, and revenge would be his. *It was only fair,* he thought.

He slid off the chest and completed a thorough inspection of the lock and chest to make sure it wasn't trapped. He grabbed the lock in his hands and twisted hard until he heard the lock break. Those magical bracers came in handy.

Corax cracked open the strongbox and stared at the largest amount of platinum he had ever seen in his life. A grin escaped his bearded lips as he ran his hands through the coins, then pulled out a folded flap of cloth from the inner pocket of his vest. He knelt down and unfolded the cloth on the ground beside the chest of platinum, taking care to keep it nice and flat. The cloth he unfolded was acquired from a mage he had killed years ago after making an order for the mage to create it.

Once the cloth was unfolded, Corax muttered a command word, and it shimmered and became an inter-dimensional storage compartment. The weight of the contents was negated, so the carrier only felt the weight of the cloth no matter how much was in it. The space varied depending on the size the creator made it when it was enchanted. This hole was about four feet in diameter and about five feet deep.

Platinum was rare to see, used by kings and the wealthy to save space in their treasure holds. The pieces were usually only about as big as a finger-nail. Depending on the city, one platinum coin could be exchanged for nine to ten gold pieces.

Corax dug down to the bottom of the chest and made sure everything was as it should be. With the ease of a giant, he tipped the chest up on its side and poured the contents into the portable hole. He tossed the chest aside and picked up the few hundred pieces that didn't make it into the hole on the first try, tossing them in as well. Corax repeated his command word again to deactivate the hole. He folded the cloth up and tucked it back into his vest pocket.

He glanced one last time in the direction Osbur rode off toward and frowned. He didn't have time to chase him down and kill him this day. He had to get back and prepare for his mission. However, Osbur wouldn't make it any farther than Minsfet. That he knew for certain.

CHAPTER

NINE

Osbur traveled two days across the country and decided on the second night that he couldn't go on any longer without a decent amount of rest and a bite to eat. He found a good spot in a ravine surrounded by heavy woods. It looked to give him the best cover and shield the light from his fire. He mounded up some stones in a semi-circle and started a small fire to warm himself.

While settling in by the fire, he kept replaying the ambush in his head, trying to figure out where he had gone wrong. *Damn*, he thought to himself. *If Taslar knew what I had attempted, it would be my head on a pike ... or worse.* As if on cue, a cloaked figure stepped from behind a tree into the firelight, almost knocking Osbur off his stone seat in surprise.

"Hello, brother Osbur."

Osbur tensed up at the sound of his brother's voice.

"Wh-What are you doing here, Dosan? You scared the wits out of me," murmured Osbur.

"There is no need for your presence; the delivery was made."

"It was not I who decided to check up on you, my brother. Our master requested it, so here I stand."

Dosan looked around expectantly. "What happened to your men? You left with seven, and I did not see any as I approached your fire."

"I sent them on ahead, so it was harder to detect our presence in enemy territory."

Does he know? Osbur thought to himself.

"I see. Good thinking, my brother. But why make a fire? You know it can be smelled for miles downwind even if you hide its light and keep it small."

Osbur looked up at Dosan from his seat near the fire. "I haven't eaten much in two days, so I decided to take a chance on it."

Dosan knelt down and put his hands over the fire. "I know. I've been watching you the whole time. Our master is pleased that the mission was a success. However, he was not pleased that you tried to ambush our newest ally while making the payment."

Osbur moved as fast as he could and whipped a small thin dagger at Dosan. Dosan's cloak parted, and a blur of steel slipped out to deflect the small projectile from reaching its target.

Without skipping a beat, Dosan continued. "You know . . . when we were younger, I always looked up to you because you were my older brother. But as time went on, I realized you only cared about yourself. You never embraced the throne, even when you swore your oath to it. You used it as a stepping stone to gain more power.

"After everything you have been given, you go and try and ruin it all by only thinking of yourself yet again. Long ago, I stopped looking up to you and started looking down on you. Now, it looks as though your time is up, brother . . . long overdue, in my opinion."

Dosan said that last part as he stood up. Osbur tried to reach for his longsword, but again, Dosan's cloak parted, and another flash of steel separated Osbur's head from the rest of his body.

"You're welcome, brother, for killing you quickly. I don't think the dwarf you tried to rob would have been quite as pleasant as I."

Dosan wiped off his sword with a handkerchief he pulled out of a vest pocket. Then he tossed it into the fire and prepared the scrying pool to report his success to his master.

His master's face appeared in the magical pool shortly after activating the scrying device.

"Osbur has been dispatched as requested."

"Excellent news. The empire will no longer have to worry about Osbur stabbing us in the back. Now head back to Sandown and monitor the assassin's success or failure. If he tries to take the money and run, it will be up to you to retrieve payment in full, along with reparations for not attempting the mission."

Dosan leaned forward. "I will do as you say, but I do not believe the dwarf to be in that state of mind. I think he revels in the idea of showing off his skills. He will make the attempt. If it goes awry, he may try and take the money and flee. But with the enchantment on the platinum, I'll be able to track him down."

"Actually, we want the payment back regardless. We will need it back to support the war against the kingdom of Stalken. The offer had to be legitimate; otherwise, we would have had to use a lesser tool to remove the king."

"I understand. I do what the empire requires of me."

"And that is why we need you and not your brother. You are our best, and it would have been you we sent to take care of this issue with the king, but we need anonymity. Do your duty and keep me posted as to the events so we can time our attack at the right moment."

Dosan nodded. "I will contact you once I'm in position in Sandown."

The face faded away. Dosan doused the fire, took what valuables Osbur had on him, and left the body for the scavengers. He had no love for his brother and was happy to end his life.

It served him right after betraying everything he had pledged to do for the empire. Osbur's repeated failures and excuses lowered the value of their family in the royal hierarchy.

Dosan's successes were the only thing countering Osbur's failures and keeping their family with enough honor to retain the power they had. It would take time to reverse the black mark Osbur had put on their family name. Every time Dosan did something to bring honor to their name and recognition of their family in a positive light, Osbur would do something to smear that honor into the mud, like robbing and killing the assassin they needed to help topple Stalken's small kingdom to the east.

That is why it had to be him to kill Osbur. He had to show he was loyal to the empire, even over family, if he were to remove all suspicion and regain the honor originally brought to their family by his father. He took one last look at his brother's decapitated body and turned toward Sandown.

TEN

Corax made his way through the rough countryside until he could see the white granite walls of the city looming ahead. It had taken him a bit longer to get back because he wasn't in such a hurry. He'd had the luxury of cooking warm meals a few times on his return trip.

He made his way to a rock outcropping about three hundred feet outside the city walls. After glancing around to make sure no one was watching, he traced an outline on the face of the tallest rock, and the rock slid apart to show a secret entrance to a tunnel that led to his guild below the city.

Corax slipped inside the shadowy entrance and down a steep incline to a wooden ladder that led down to a tunnel below. The pitch-black tunnel was about two men wide or one and a half dwarves at the ladder.

It expanded quickly until it was comfortable enough to wield a weapon. His dark vision allowed him to navigate the tunnel with little issue. This tunnel had been created after the exterior walls were put in place, and it allowed the guild to export stolen goods during the cover of darkness without notice from the city guard.

As Corax approached the entrance to the guild, two lookouts appeared from hidden alcoves, weapons at the ready.

"Password," hissed one of them from the shadows.

Since the guild was being sought so vigorously by the city guard, it was imperative that safeguards be put in place to prevent infiltration. Once Corax had given the appropriate code, the guards let him pass through a small, darkened passage to reveal two more guards and a door that led to a man-sized hole chiseled through one of the city's outer walls.

Corax made sure that was as difficult as possible to determine how to enter the guild. He had the passage made to look like a finished hallway that led to a room with no visible exits. As he entered, he stopped to marvel at his own handiwork. The room always stayed brightly lit so that any light escaping from the secret doorway would not give away the location.

Corax slid his hand over to the corner just to the right of the entrance to the little room and pulled on a sconce. That allowed him to step on a combination of raised pegs that sprouted out of the floor when the sconce was pulled.

A stone panel hissed and slid back and to the side. Corax stepped into a small alcove that was dark except for the light from the outer room. He pulled two rings on either side of the entrance at the exact same time, and the disguised stone door slide back into place, plunging him into almost complete darkness. He could see with his dark vision the walls and the heavy oak door in front of him. This room was designed as a second defense to prevent light from the guild hall from giving away the door's location. The rough oak door required a key to enter from this side, or someone had to open it from the other. Only Corax and a guard stationed inside the door had keys, and that key was changed once every season or as Corax saw fit.

Corax unlocked the door, entered the guild, and motioned for the guard to shut and relock the door behind him. Next to the door hung a large bell about three feet tall and two feet wide at the base. Out of the wall came the rope attached to the ringing arm of the bell. The rope led back into the tunnel. It was a quick and effective way to alert the guild hall to an unwanted presence in area of the complex. Contingencies had to be put in place so the guild could evacuate in case it was discovered. Corax was always thorough and looked at every scenario from all angles.

The main hall was a large square cut out of the bedrock. Heavy wooden tables and chairs decorated this area, which was used for eating and guild meetings. Support pillars were scattered here and there to keep the ceiling from falling in. It wasn't the best-looking stonework, but Corax had to depend on lesser hands to do the work.

On one end was an alcove where everything stolen was brought to be fenced. A reasonable amount of coin was given in trade. The items were either sold for a small profit to traveling merchants frequenting the city through business fronts that the guild owned or snuck out of town and smuggled to other cities for sale. The more sought-after items were exported to the guild location in Minsfet to be sold outside the kingdom or even overseas.

The other end contained the kitchen, which was open most of the day. To hide the exhaust from cooking, it had vents that led to a tavern and a bakery. In the mornings, when the bakery was running, the vent was switched to their chimney. Once the tavern opened, the vent was switched over to that chimney. That left just a few hours a day that the kitchen wasn't running.

On the far end, away from the door Corax just entered from, were two separate hallways. One led to the general sleeping quarters, where stacks of bunk beds lined the walls, and the other to Corax's chambers.

Life in the guild didn't seem to have changed since he went to collect his payment. With the constant investigation into the whereabouts of the guild, the guild was almost always on high alert. Most of the time, the guild was quite empty except for the guards or guild members between jobs or just taking a break from the pressures of being caught plying their trade in the city. About fifty members made up the guild split between Sandown and Minsfet.

After Corax disarmed his traps in the entry to his hallway, he walked up to his room door and pushed or pulled on a multitude of stone shafts that stuck out of the wall next to the door. Entering the wrong combination of movements would result in a spray of acid and poison into the intruder's face.

Once inside, he reactivated his traps with another group of stone levers next to the door. He lit a couple of oil lamps and stoked his fireplace with an armful of slender logs.

Though small, his room was decorated and adorned with comfort in mind. Tapestries hung from the stone walls, and expensive liquors sat on a mahogany table wedged between the wall and his bed. He had a small work area for his trade. One of the walls near the work area contained armor, weapons, and tools he needed for various jobs. Chains hung from the wall for the occasional torture session he enjoyed doling out.

Corax was as cold-hearted as he was intelligent and would do anything to reach his goals. With this successful mission, he could change most of his dreams into reality. Right now, all he wanted to do was look at the platinum again.

He pulled out the magical cloth that contained all the platinum, unfolded it on the bed, and drew up a chair. Uttering the command word, a king's ransom glittered from the firelight. Corax took off his gloves and tossed them to the side while his eyes never left the glittering platinum. Its liquid silver luster almost seemed to flow like water. It made silver look dull and uninteresting.

He slid his arm deep into the cache of platinum until his elbow was just above the surface. Pulling his arm back out, he let the platinum coins trickle through his thick, calloused fingers. Corax chuckled to himself, and a rare smile appeared on his bearded face. These lands would regret him getting his hands on this much wealth. They just didn't know it yet.

Corax quietly gave the command to close the

portal, folded the cloth back up, and tucked it into a small slit in the nearby wall that looked nothing more than a groove to the untrained eye.

He took off most of his gear and hung it in his work area, then sat down in a large hand-carved oak chair. Reaching over, he poured a glass of wine he had grown a taste for. The wine wasn't strong, but it did calm his nerves. He never drank in excess anymore. That was how mistakes were made.

He closed his eyes and stroked his frizzy black beard, mentally revising all the steps he would be able to skip with his newfound wealth. Another grin appeared on his bearded face.

This brewing conflict had brought him so much fortune, and now this . . . enough riches to forge his own kingdom. He looked up at a map he had mounted on the wall above his desk. It showed the whole of the continent.

All the major cities and kingdoms were noted, but he had circled an area of wildlands east of Sandown. The terrain was nigh impassable with deep lakes, tall mountains, and all manner of creatures that would enjoy dining on a person's innards.

"One day, your kingdom will have more to worry about than your enemy to the west, Stalken. That is, if your kingdom doesn't crumble after I slay you," Corax said out loud. He gulped down the last of the wine in his glass and set it aside.

Corax left the confines of his room and made the first person he ran into find Lieutenant Mulf.

Mulf took care of things when Corax was away, and he would be needed for the upcoming assassination. He was a human and not so clean. However, he was almost as vicious as Corax when it came to running things, and he never disobeyed an order. That was the part Corax was going to need now.

Corax had disarmed his traps and was looking over the most recent map of the castle he had in his quarters when there was a hard knock on the door.

"Enter," he said.

Mulf opened the door and strode in with his six-foot frame and muscular hundred and ninety-five pounds. Corax glanced up at him. Mulf's hair was its typical greasy mess. It was matted to his head and shiny with oil.

"Sit."

Mulf took a seat at the small table where Corax had sat with Osbur. Corax picked up the map he was looking over and brought it to the table, showing it to Mulf.

"I have a mission for you. It's going to be dangerous. If you live, you can take over possession of the guild."

Mulf eyed the map. Though he recognized the castle's layout, nobody was ever allowed to try and infiltrate it.

He studied the map for a minute and then looked over at Corax, who stood about an arm's reach away. Mulf knew if he said he wasn't interested, he would be dead a second later. This was an ultimatum, not a request. Fortunately, ownership of the guild was something he would definitely risk his life for.

"Of course I'm in," answered Mulf. "I live for this kind of excitement."

"Good. The mission is simple." Corax leaned in close and whispered, "I'm going to kill the king."

His nose wrinkled at the pungent odor coming from Mulf but said nothing about it.

Mulf looked into his eyes and offered a devilish grin. "And you need a decoy mission to pull the heat away for the best chance of getting the king alone."

Corax smirked and took a seat across from Mulf. "See, that is why I like you. You have a talent for tactics. Let's start going over what I'm going to need."

ELEVEN

Tegin's body was slick with sweat from the battle raging in the wet underground cavern. He stood with his back to Lelanda as kobolds, a semi-intelligent short rat-like creature, swarmed all around them.

"What have we gotten ourselves into!?" shouted Tegin. "This was just supposed to house about twenty or thirty kobold—not two or three *hundred!*"

Lelanda deflected a small torch thrown at them with a scimitar in her left hand and skewered a kobold with the one in her right.

She made no sounds other than an occasional grunt and the splashing of her feet in the bloody, ankle-deep water. A trail of dead kobold bodies led from the entrance of the cave to where they stood now, about two hundred feet further in.

Tegin peered through the gloom with his dark vision and noticed a small band of kobolds huddled away from the others that seemed to be organizing the defense.

"We need to take them out over there!" roared

Tegin. Lelanda glanced that way as she kicked a kobold in the face and spotted the trio of larger kobolds pointing at them as another wave of reinforcements rushed from their location to replace the dozen they just slew.

"Well, there is no way we'll be able to fight our way there . . . so that leaves two choices!" she screamed back. "We cut a path to the entrance and come back with others, or I fly your hairy ass over their heads so you can kill them. Hopefully, that will cause the others to panic and retreat!"

"Well, dwarves don't retreat," bellowed Tegin over the echoes of battle.

"That settles it!"

She flipped her scimitars back into their sheaths and muttered a spell that hastened her movements. Just as she finished, a kobold hit her in the face with a lit torch. She struck out blindly, catching the rat-like creature in the throat with her knee, and then picked it up. Blinking through tears and soot, she threw it into some of the others near her.

Tegin bellowed a challenge and charged toward the trio about 150 feet away, slamming and slicing his way toward them. Lelanda whipped out her scimitars just in time to cut the heads off two charging kobolds. Then, using her magically enhanced speed, she killed five kobolds nearest her in a blink of an eye to give herself a bit of breathing room.

Seeing their kind killed so fast by the dark-skinned elf held up the rest of the mob for a few moments. She stabbed her swords down into a dead body and muttered words of power as her hands formed a triangle that she twisted into a ball that began to glow blue, enveloping her right hand.

Just as the next wave of kobolds decided to charge the weaponless elf, she jumped about two feet straight up and inverted her hand so it was palm down, then slammed the glowing hand into the ground, causing an explosion of blue flame in a radius around her and killing a dozen of the horrid little vermin. She did all this before Tegin had managed to hack and slice his way thirty feet.

He was taking on as many as he could and was paying for it. He felt a rib break, a slice on his right thigh, and to make matters worse, his beard had been partially burned away.

The kobolds were starting to overrun him, and he staggered under the sudden onslaught. Suddenly the stone under him was torn from the ground by some invisible magic and lifted into the air. The jarring shift in movement caused him to almost let go of his axe.

He plopped onto his stomach on top of the stone Lelanda had ripped out of the ground with a spell and was flying it toward the trio of larger kobolds.

Hanging on to the boulder, he was flying with great speed toward them when he suddenly slammed hard to the floor, then off a stalagmite, and then back fifteen feet into the air, where the spell gave out with him flying right at the largest kobold. He roared as he hefted his axe over his head.

He awoke from the vivid dream, roaring his challenge while throwing a hand axe he left on the table next to him straight into the far wall. He blinked a few times as he realized he was sitting in his bed.

Once he took the moment in, he gave a chuckle. He slid his hands over his sweaty face and checked his beard to make certain it wasn't half gone, like in his dream. Then he sensed he wasn't alone. He snapped his head over and looked into the glowing blue and red eyes of Lelanda sitting over by the door to his room.

"It's good to see you still have that killer instinct, my friend," she said.

"Aye, funny you should say that. I was dreamin' about that time you and I got trapped in that kobold lair some thirty years ago."

"Yes, it seems like yesterday that we were getting into all kinds of trouble."

"What do ya mean, it seems like yesterday?" he asked. "We've been in trouble since the first time we met! I can't believe how many times we've cheated death. I'm barely middle-aged, and I've done and seen more than whole families of my kin combined."

Tegin slid out of bed and pulled his trousers on. He tromped over to his hand axe and yanked it out of the wall across from his bed.

"Not a bad throw if I do say so myself," he quipped.

He turned and walked over to the fireplace next to Lelanda, laid the axe on the stone hearth, and stoked the hot coals with a poker nearby to bring the fire back to life.

"So, what brings you to my quarters at such an early hour?" Tegin asked as he turned and sat on a nearby stool.

"I suspect another attempt on the king is about to happen," replied Lelanda.

Tegin looked over at Lelanda. She and Tegin had known each other for almost forty years. In all that time, he never remembered her bringing him good news.

Somehow, stranger than that was the fact he was friends with two elves—both beautiful for their races, he suspected, but neither seemed that interested in finding love. Maybe it was due to their long life expectancy, though he had his suspicions about Thena. She was aloof when she was home from her breaks at the academy and has disappeared a couple of times since returning to her duties full-time. He dismissed the thought. No regal elf was going to woo her over. She was too much like Lelanda—probably because of Lelanda.

Tegin couldn't say much for himself, either. He was past the point in a dwarf's life when they typically took a wife. He wouldn't mind finding a mate, but dwarves didn't stray far from their lands, and those were far away to the south and east of Sandown. The area where Sandown had sprung up was human lands. He could count the number of dwarves in the city other than himself on one hand, maybe two.

The elven kingdom of Erilia bordered to the south, but they kept to themselves. That was the one thing that both races could agree on—keeping to themselves . . .

All the surface-dwelling elven races either hated or looked down on the dark elves. Having your kin slaughtered by dark elves tends to create grudges. He shook himself out of his thoughts as what Lelanda said started to sink in.

"I'm sorry. I'm still a bit groggy. Did you say another attempt might be made on the king?"

Lelanda nodded at him.

Tegin glanced down, thinking over the last few times an attempt was made on the king's life. He looked back up at Lelanda. She was wearing her dark cloak and leather armor. Tonight she had a staff with her, along with her swords.

Lelanda had her hood down since she was in good company. Her hair was originally a silvery white, but she long ago concocted some sort of spell that turned and kept her hair black whenever she wanted it. Not to blend in like a surface dweller but to be able to hide her white hair in a dangerous situation.

Her natural hair had gotten them noticed on more than a few occasions in the past when they didn't need or want the added attention. She hid her hair because she saw tactical advantages in it being dark.

She saw advantages in having dark skin as well. Thus, she didn't bother to hide it much anymore, even though she was well-versed in spells that could do just that.

She never seemed to rest and was always doing things behind the scenes that helped her friends. She was ever vigilant and responsible for sniffing out the other attempts on the king's life that had been orchestrated by some unsavory characters.

"What brings you to that conclusion?" Tegin queried.

"One of my contacts came to me when he was questioned about the goings on in the castle. It seems like someone is probing the defenses and scoping out the castle grounds. It wasn't necessarily out of the ordinary, but the person who came to my contact matched the description of one of the officers of the thief's guild. I'm not sure what this means. Everything in my being says to be cautious. We've also not seen a counterattack from Letharia yet or any sign of their forces. They seem to be waiting for something."

Tegin thought over what she said for a moment.

"Aye, it doesn't sound right. We'll meet with Stalken about it as soon as the sun rises. Let's head downstairs and have some breakfast before we head over—unless you think the danger is imminent?"

"No, I don't think Stalken is in imminent danger," replied Lelanda. "Let's go ahead and head down to the common area. It has been a while since we've caught up on things," she said with a smile.

"Aye, that be true," chuckled Tegin.

TWELVE

Stalken woke to the rays of the sun creeping over the eastern hills. He stretched and gave a big yawn, rolling himself onto his feet with the edge of the bed. He paused a moment to stare at the painting near the bed and smiled.

Walking over to the plain-looking porcelain washbowl, he splashed some water onto his face. As he wiped his face with a soft cloth hanging off the wall, a teenage attendant came in with his fresh linens for the bed and undergarments for the king to change into.

His bed was the only thing in the room that looked like it should belong to royalty. It had nice silk draperies and was deep and soft. He swore that he would have a proper bed after he left his mercenary days behind. Little did he know that he would become a king.

After changing and getting into his light armor, the king walked out onto the balcony off the bedroom and surveyed the city. The balcony was made of stone and protruded from the smooth granite walls of the castle.

The castle was constructed of dark grey granite, and the city walls were of lighter granite with flecks of grey and brown. Both types of stone had been quarried nearby and stood out in stark contrast to each other. That was his intent when he had them built.

This was his favorite routine of the day. His balcony overlooked the southwestern side of the city. He could see Skull Gate and smell the bakeries' fresh bread wafting up into the morning air. The rocky grasslands and deep ravines that led up to the gate for miles were also visible from his perch. It was an awe-inspiring view that he never tired of.

Not a cloud showed in the sky this day, and for the first time in a long time, the king felt a twinge of a smile cross his lips.

The attendant busied himself with changing the sheets on the bed.

"Very calm morning, wouldn't you say, Pete?" asked Stalken.

"Yes, it is, sire. Mother says it feels like the calm before the storm."

That removed the hint of smile from Stalken's face.

"That very well could be, but let's pretend for a moment we aren't in the middle of a conflict with our neighbor, and it is just the start of another peaceful day."

"As you wish, sire," replied the young boy.

Just as the king finished dressing, a messenger came in and bowed before the king.

"Sire, your presence is requested in the war room by Captain Tegin."

The king turned and looked over at Pete. "I

guess the peace was short-lived. It looks like business as usual in Sandown."

He looked back at the messenger. "Tell him I will be down in a few moments."

Stalken turned and walked to his swords in his weapon rack near the foot of his bed and started lashing them to his waist.

THIRTEEN

When Stalken made it to the war room, he found both Tegin and Lelanda leaning over a castle map.

"Well, this can't be good. Two of my friends request my immediate presence, and I find them scouring a map of the castle grounds."

Tegin turned to him. "Well, maybe if you would quit painting a target on your forehead," Tegin said while drawing a circle with his finger in the air. The two clasped each other's forearms in a gesture of friendship. Lelanda never looked up from the map.

"It looks like someone is after your head again."

"Oh, is that so? Another attempt on my life? What is that, three or four times now?"

"This would be number four, I believe," said Lelanda, leaning closer to the map.

"Well, I don't have any public appearances planned. What information do you have on the attempt?"

"Rumors and gut feelings at this point," Tegin answered. "It's all pretty thin, but you know how this one gets when she's caught a whiff of something unpleasant."

Lelanda looked out the corner of her eye. "Should I review the win count in duels between you and me, Captain Tegin?" she quipped.

Tegin cleared his throat and motioned over to the map.

"The lack of information is why we are going over the map of the castle grounds and the castle itself. We believe this attempt will happen here. None of the previous assassination attempts have ever been attempted on these grounds, probably due to our security. Since you no longer leave the premises very often, it makes it very difficult for any attempt to be made other than here."

Lelanda looked up from the map for a moment. "Plus, the war has been going in our favor. We have taken one of Letharia's cities, and they will be grasping for anything to turn the tide back in their favor."

"As your friends and as your loyal servants, we request that you keep four of your elite guards at your side at all times. Stay fully armored and armed as often as you can until we can uncover this plot or until the attempt happens and is thwarted." Tegin turned and walked back to the map.

"Besides, I'd hate to see an old friend of mine caught with his pants down and not given a chance to at least fight for the last moments of his life," said Tegin.

Stalken stroked his cleanshaven chin for a moment. "Is it okay if I take off my armor to sleep?" he said with a smirk.

His face grew serious. "Listen, I know that you

and Thena are currently up to your necks in the thief's guild investigation. I would like to request that Lelanda continue to pursue this investigation and report to us with any new information. Since we can't rule out the guild's possible involvement in this attempt, work together and share any information with each other that you know or discover in both of your pursuits."

Both Lelanda and Tegin nodded their agreement.

Stalken sighed. "I would really like to sit here and talk about my potential death. Alas, I must get in communication with General Gunner for a status update. I will talk with you two again soon."

He turned on his heel and headed out through the door of the War room. Just as he was walking out, he cocked his head back over his shoulder.

"Remember when I wasn't king, and we lived from tavern to tavern?"

His voice faded as he exited the room.

Tegin watched him leave. "I think it's starting to wear on him, being king."

He turned back to Lelanda.

"This whole scenario feels wrong. It is suicide to attack the castle grounds."

"No argument here," she replied.

"We need to move with haste to find out what we can and bolster the defenses of the grounds. I will get with Thena on that," said Tegin.

"I'll run some checks on the elite guards set in place to protect the king and make sure that they are one hundred percent loyal to us. We should put those with families under the castle's protection to make sure that they are not used to turn any of them," replied Lelanda.

Tegin nodded. "Sounds good."

Tegin started out of the room when Lelanda grabbed him by the arm.

"Take this crystal. If you need to communicate with me no matter where I am, just hold it to your throat and speak these three words; umani, supitri, lan. Just put the crystal to your throat and speak normally, and I will hear you."

Tegin tucked it into his inner vest pocket. "Aye, lass . . . I hope I don't need it."

Tegin's eyebrows raised as an idea came to him. "It could come in handy. Maybe if I need you to get me some ale or some food," he said.

Lelanda smiled at him. "If you do, it might slip out that you've been bested repeatedly by an elf in a sparring match." She uttered a word of magic before he could respond, and in a blink of an eye, she disappeared.

Tegin looked around to see if anyone was around. "Why does she keep holding that over my head?"

He thought about it for a moment and then shrugged. "Bah, like anyone would believe her."

He turned and headed off to find Thena and inform her of the new situation.

FOURTEEN

Stalken and his personal guards meandered through the castle's smooth granite halls in the general direction of the northwest tower. Stalken mulled over the new information.

Three times they've come for me, Stalken thought to himself.

His hands drifted to the hand grips on his swords that clinked lightly as he walked down the long corridor.

Stalken frowned at the thought of his dream of uniting the lands and finally bringing peace to this part of the continent being shattered by his death.

He decided it was time to have a little talk with Gunner. He needed to prepare for the worst.

Stalken was so deep in thought that he barely realized he had made it to the communications tower. The tower was turned into a small communications room run by apprentice mages from the mage guild.

They played a vital role in the conflict and allowed almost instant communication to remote locations with their magical trinkets. Plus, a few of the more experienced apprentices could teleport individuals from prepared locations around the kingdom.

The room wasn't large by any means. It went skyward for several stories with a stairwell that followed the curved shape of the outside wall. The bottom floor was all white marble like the rest of the castle. Redwood was used for the levels above, giving the room a nice woody smell.

About five to ten apprentices could run the flow of information to and from the front. They could double that number to help the king stay informed up to the minute during battles or skirmishes.

Stalken tapped his chin while looking through the door at the scribes and mages preparing for another eventful day.

"How are we today?" asked Stalken as he stepped through the doorway.

A young lieutenant looked up from writing and jumped to his feet.

"Nothing to report, sire. Just the normal morning communications. I was just finishing up the morning report. We also received word that General Gunner is ready for your communication."

The king smiled at the lieutenant. "Actually, I need to speak with the general in person today. Please inform him that I need to meet him in the war room in a couple of hours and have a scribe sent to my chambers immediately."

"It will be done," replied the lieutenant.

"Excellent."

He headed back toward his chambers to think about what he would say to the general.

The guards fell in behind him as he went. He

had grown accustomed to them being around him over the years and barely even noticed that they were near him. He had become friends with all of them and even kept track of their birthdays and the birthdays of their families.

He liked to surprise them with gifts and treats for them and their families. He knew they were there to lay down their lives for him, and he respected that on a level few understood.

He wanted to make certain they knew that he respected them for their service and genuinely cared for them as much as he would his own family . . . if he had any. His mother and father died when he was very young, but he did care for someone on a romantic level. As much as it pained them both, their relationship was kept a tight secret from even his closest friends. But the kingdom couldn't be left to her at this time.

FIFTEEN

Meanwhile, Tegin headed toward the city guard's headquarters to find Thena. Some thought it strange that she often stayed at the city guard's barracks. She had a place there the same as Tegin had quarters in the castle.

They worked together often, so it only made sense that they be able to stay and get to know each other's teams.

He made his way through the morning crowd of refugees and city folk. The city was busting at the seams with all the people finding safe refuge here in Sandown, though keeping them safe from the thief's guild had been impossible. The war taxed the city guard to the limit, allowing the guild to run rampant on those just trying to survive.

The city guard was made up of almost all humans, which matched the majority of the city's population.

Years ago, Tegin had a hard time getting respect from some of the citizens of Sandown. Over time, he became a common sight, and nobody questioned his authority or that of Thena. They had both been integral in protecting the city in the past and had earned the respect of the citizens during that time. Plus, his tavern was such a hit that most people were eager to greet him on the street.

Tegin turned the street corner and walked into the courtyard of the city guard headquarters. The HQ for the city guard was fenced and gated near the city's center. This allowed it to be a defensive position if the need should arise.

It was centrally located, so the guard could get to any part of the city in the same amount of time. The walls and gate were made from redwood trees that grew thick on the nearby mountain slopes. There was even a small jail built to house drunkards who needed to sleep off too much alcohol from the previous night's festivities.

Tegin found Thena standing outside talking with a small cluster of plainclothes guardsmen. She noticed him as he approached and dismissed the group to their tasks.

"Morning, my friend. You have a grim look about you today."

"That is because I carry grim news," said Tegin. "Lelanda seems to think another attempt is going to be made on the king soon."

Thena's slight smile faded as she took in the news. She sighed.

"Great, is the Letharian army at our gates today, too?"

She turned and opened the door to her quarters. "Let me hear all the details, and we'll see what we can do about this. I don't plan on losing the king on my watch."

"Aye, lass, I agree," said Tegin. He stepped past

Thena and through the door. Thena's quarters appeared very basic. It was a small two-story dwelling with her sleeping quarters upstairs and her office on the main floor. It was maybe three hundred square feet.

She made good use of the small space. Her desk was at the far wall so she could see anybody who entered. No windows were located on this main level, which passively increased security and the defense of the building.

Everyone knew the king had a price on his head, but it was well known that every one of his main officers had bounties on them as well. It was wise to stay prepared during this time.

A small desk shaped to fit the corner of the room was located to the right of the entrance when they came in. It was covered with various maps lit by oil lamps. Thena walked in past Tegin and shut the door. She walked over and took a seat at her desk.

"What information has Lelanda provided?" she asked.

Tegin took a seat in front of her desk.

"Our mutual friend has come across some information that is leading her to believe another attempt is coming. Though it seems more of a gut feeling at this point."

Thena shifted in her seat. "I would believe her if she told me the world was going to end tomorrow."

"That's why I came to talk to you," replied Tegin. "Stalken has put it on the three of us to solve this problem along with squashing the guild's influence on the city. I've looked at the reports, some information corroborate these rumors of assassination. For some reason, the guild's activity the past few days has dwindled to almost nothing."

Tegin ran his fingers through his well-groomed beard in thought. His silver and gold clasps twinkled in the light from the lamps.

"They may have inadvertently given us a peek at their hand. This lack of activity could be a warning of something big coming."

Thena nodded, stood up, and motioned Tegin over to the table with the maps. She paused for a moment when she eyed a painting that hung above the table. It was almost identical to the one in the king's quarters.

Tegin noticed the pause but said nothing. She continued to the table and shuffled through a few of the maps before stopping at one and laying it before Tegin.

"Those plainclothes guards I was talking to this morning have been assigned to exploring the nearby area around Sandown. I have a larger crew working the city from west to east, then starting over from north to south. I tasked them with locating the entrance to the guild. They will notify us of any shady figures they spot, locations for the guard to check out, and establishments for us to audit."

"Where did you find the manpower to do this?" Tegin asked.

"We just got that new batch of recruits from Minsfet you requested. I didn't want to put them into uniforms just yet. I decided since they were new and not marked by the guild, they could be useful in this task instead."

Tegin slapped the table lightly. "Well done, lass,

well done! Maybe with some luck, we can at least snag one to interrogate. Lelanda would have a field day with one of those little vermin."

Thena laughed at the comment as she walked back to her seat and sat down. "Do you think this is the first time the guild was involved in an attempt on Stalken's life?"

Tegin's brow furrowed. "I don't know, but I would be willing to bet they have brokered information to those responsible.

"Let's see, the first time was on the mining road headed back to town. Though . . ." He chuckled to himself. "I would barely call that an attempt. By the time Stalken even knew they were under attack, his bodyguards had dispatched four of the five would-be assassins, and the last one gave up—well, until he poisoned himself a moment later. It didn't take long to determine who sent them. Letharia laid siege to the city a week later.

"Then they sent the dragonling to attack his main tent in the middle of the night on the plains to the west. That time we lucked out because Lelanda happened to be meeting with him at the time, and just before the initial attack, she sensed its approach somehow and teleported both of them a safe distance away. Since then, he hasn't left the city.

"The third one happened by Skull Gate during our fall festival. That time he was actually injured. I can almost guarantee that the guild was in on that one. They would have been the only ones to have the means to get access to that information."

Thena leaned forward to say something when

there was a light knock at the door. She stood up and said, "Come in."

The door opened, and Lelanda strode in with her cloak billowing around her.

"Ahh, good timing. We were just discussing our current situation and about to go over some options."

Thena motioned at the maps on the table. Lelanda reached up and pulled the hood of her cloak back to reveal her now pitch-black hair and glowing blue and red eyes. Every now and then, her staff crackled with arcing electricity.

"I have news," said Lelanda. "Our spy network in Letharia has confirmed that an attempt is going to be made. An assassin of some repute has been selected for the attempt, but we have no identifying information on him. The information provided is that he is a master of the art with fifteen known high-profile kills and maybe more undocumented ones. Their records indicate that he has never failed a mission. Five of those kills were ordered and paid for by Letharia. Over the past couple of decades, I've tracked only one assassin that is equal to what their records state. The only information I was able to dig up is that he is definitely a 'he,' and his call sign is a poison blowgun dart. Now, this poison is very toxic and very rare. In fact, it isn't even found on this plane of existence."

"What?" puffed Tegin. "That would mean he is either a mage, knows a mage, or worse yet, is a planar being. Tampering with planar travel is completely forbidden by the ruling council."

"As all three of us are plainly aware of," replied Lelanda. "I am guessing that he has a mage getting him the poison. I've had the mage's guild looking for signs of a rogue mage with enough power to do this. We have come up with no contacts in the vicinity of Sandown or nearby regions. There is a slight chance we have just failed to detect a magical presence of that magnitude, but the odds of that are very unlikely. I'm betting that he either has contracted a mage or forced a mage to do his bidding. That means he has powerful contacts and that this attempt is going to be one we need to worry about. Even if we knew the location of the mage, it would be improbable that the mage would even know the whereabouts of the assassin anyway."

"GAH!" grumbled Tegin. "My head is starting to hurt. I need a drink before I start punchin' holes in the wall."

Thena stood up from her chair. "I think we need to double the security detachments on the castle grounds. I know it will thin the ranks of the Minsfet guard, but we should pull about fifty guards from there to secure the castle grounds and fortify the ranks of the city guard. Tegin, can you send word to Minsfet after this meeting so we can get those resources moved here as quickly as possible?"

Tegin nodded in agreement as he stroked his temples with his thick fingers. "I'll also let the military detachment there know of this move so they can lend a hand if needed," Tegin responded.

Lelanda took a couple of steps toward the door and turned back toward the two. "I will continue scouring any records for an identity of the assassin. If you happen to acquire a guild member during your attempt to find the entrance to the guild, please let me know. I will question them on any knowledge they may have."

Tegin stood up from his chair. "All right then, let's try and turn the tables and go on the offensive for once."

He got up and stomped his way out the door. Lelanda nodded her goodbyes, closed her eyes, and muttered her teleportation spell before disappearing. Thena was left alone to gather her thoughts. She walked over to her desk and reached to touch a cross that had been given to her. She whispered a silent prayer to protect her friends and loved ones. Her eyes drifted to the painting and the figure within. It was a good day.

SIXTEEN

General Gunner was sitting in the makeshift communication tent near a part of the keep's walls that they had breached during the counterattack on Solec. He was waiting on one of the mages to come and teleport him to Sandown.

The city's walls and most of the main structures had been rebuilt since they had captured the city, and construction on the main keep had begun in earnest. With limited access to woodlands for lumber, most of the walls and poorer communities were built with dirt, clay, and gravel similar to a poor man's concrete enhanced with magic so it didn't deteriorate in the rain or cold. Imported lumber from the north and west was limited to the higher class buildings. The city was largely devoid of color with earthy colors being commonplace around the city.

With Solec devoid of quarries nearby, granite was carted in from Sandown to reinforce the walls and some of the main keep. It didn't blend well with the original construction design, but nothing much did.

The keep was of an interesting design. Gunner had never encountered anything like it. The stone they used was as black as a moonless night. He overheard one of the construction workers talking about it. They called it midnight glass. Apparently, only a few locations in the world had that type of stone, though it could be created magically at great expense. Rumor had it that the ebony tower in Crescent Moon was built from it and that it was mined from deep in the mountain. Tegin mentioned another location in his homeland to the south.

Gunner picked up a shattered piece of it that lay near his feet and turned it over in his hands, noting its sheen and smoothness along the fragmented edges. It did seem like dark glass to the touch, which would explain why it was so easy to breach. It wasn't used for defense. It was typically used for showing off wealth due to how rare it was. Tactically, it was useless because it was so brittle, easily shattering under catapult and trebuchet attack. It didn't make sense to him to create a keep out of it, let alone defensive walls.

Gunner looked up at the keep while he twiddled the stone fragment in his hands. He had to admit, the stronghold did capture one's attention. The pitch-black walls ringed the keep in an octagonal shape, which the keep mimicked in its outer walls.

Sitting on top of the structure was a large dome made of the same material and then inlaid with gold accents with bands of silver that created intricate designs leading to the center.

It seemed to him a massive waste of resources on something that couldn't be fully seen by anyone on the ground. Only the birds and Elohim himself could appreciate the splendor of the building. But maybe that was who it was for.

Gunner looked around at the construction going on here. The longer it took for Letharia to re-group, the easier it would be to defend the city from counterattack. As Gunner listened to the sounds of construction going on around him, one of the two apprentice mages assigned to him walked up.

"Sir, I am ready to teleport you to Sandown to meet with the king."

"Okay, let's get this over with," he said.

The mage motioned for him to stand still. He started making magical gestures and symbols with his hands while muttering words of magic.

A familiar sickening feeling washed over Gunner as his vision blurred. Everything looked like a washed-out painting, with colors rushing past him to finally slow and come back into focus, and he found himself standing in the communication tower of the castle.

A human lieutenant stepped forward and mo-tioned him toward the exit. "Glad to see you again, general."

Gunner shook his head to remove the dizzy feeling he had. He never liked magic, let alone being teleported. It always sent a chill up his spine.

"The king will be waiting for you in the war room, general," the lieutenant said as they walked into the hallway.

"I'll be on my way then." Two elite guards took up positions on either side and just behind the general as he started down the hall, leaving the lieutenant to his duties.

The king was standing at the main table in the war room and reading when the general walked in. The king looked up from the parchment to meet Gunner's gaze and smiled.

"I'm glad you're here," the king said as he opened his arms in a welcoming gesture. Gunner walked up, and they clasped each other's forearms. "I'm sorry I had to pull you away from your duties at Solec."

Stalken motioned for Gunner to take a seat, and he attempted to find a comfortable position on a bench nearby—no easy task due to the armor he had to wear at all waking hours. Gunner leaned forward and smiled.

"It's great to see you, William. It's been too long."

Stalken smiled in response. "It has. We've not shared a calm moment in many months, but I'm grateful you're leading my forces to victory. My only regret is that I was not able to do it myself. As you may or may not have heard by now, there are rumors of another assassination attempt on my life."

Gunner's smile faded with this news, but he kept quiet as Stalken continued.

"Since I don't have a queen or any children to speak of, my highest-ranking general would assume my duties if I were to fall. As you know, that general is you, and I just wanted to make it official. As the leader of my armies and one of my oldest friends, if my life is taken, I want you to lead this kingdom and its people into the future."

A scribe who had been standing motionless in

the corner startled the general when he stepped forward and laid some documents on the table along with a quill and ink.

"If you'll sign these few documents, general," the scribe requested. "Then I can take these down to the archive, where we will have a record of your acceptance of this request."

Gunner stared at the scribe for a moment then he looked over and met the king's eyes, trying to determine what he was thinking since his facial expression showed no emotion.

"It will be an honor, sire." He took the quill and dipped it in the ink. Gunner scratched his name into the area designated at the bottom of the document next to the royal seal. He noticed that the king's signature was already there. The scribe nimbly rolled up the parchment and slid it into a scroll tube.

The scribe looked up. "Your majesty, General Gunner, the final task will be to have you both seal the scroll. Then I'll take it down to the royal vault for storage." Minutes later, the scribe walked out of the room with the double-sealed scroll.

The king watched the scribe walk out of the room and then turned to the general and said with a smile, "Phew, I am glad that's over!"

Gunner chuckled as he took a seat near the map table. "You had me going there, William. I didn't know what to think with you acting all proper. I thought you'd lost your mind!"

The king let out a hearty laugh. "I thought it would be great to try and act proper around you. But it's hard to fool someone I've known almost my entire life. But, hey, you can't blame me for trying!"

the king said as he walked over and slapped his old friend on the shoulder.

Stalken adjusted his armor and took a seat next to Gunner, whose smile faded as he became serious. "So, what are you planning to do about the rumored assassination attempt?"

"Thena, Tegin, and Lelanda are working that angle as we speak. As you know, this isn't the first time someone's tried to take my life, and if I survive, it won't be the last," he said. "I'm just glad I have a friend like you that even if it comes to the worst . . . my dream . . . our dream will live on."

The king stood up and walked over to the maps. He glanced idly at the city map of Sandown, then looked up as if he were peering through a thick fog.

"I remember years ago when this was just a fledgling little town. Wealthy . . . but fledgling just the same. The odds for us to grow into a city, let alone for me to establish this kingdom and the town of Minsfet, were so small that I probably had a better chance of being born into royalty as a child."

"What? And in all this time I thought you enjoyed growing up as an orphan!" exclaimed Gunner with a hearty laugh. Gunner pulled himself out of his seat and walked over to the king, putting his hand on Stalken's shoulder.

"I'll say this, you are like a brother to me, and I would do anything for you. Even take your place should the worst comes to pass. I truly hope it doesn't. But in the end, all we can hope for is that good triumphs over evil. They may win a battle or two, but I promise you they won't win the war."

The king and the general stood in silence as

they accepted the paths before them. Gunner turned and headed toward the door. He looked back over his shoulder. "William, if that is all, then I'll be heading back to the front. We've got a lot of work to do, rumored assassination attempt or not."

Stalken gave him a knowing nod and turned back to the map of Sandown.

SEVENTEEN

Tegin trudged down the street from his office at the guard headquarters. Dust kicked up off the cobblestones as he walked toward his tavern after a long and frustrating day.

The sun was low in the sky as dusk settled on the city. The light from the sun made the city a hazy orange in the evenings as it bounced off the white granite walls and reflected into the city. Today, the haze matched his mood.

The twin moons were already forcing their way into the sky as though they were pushing out the sunlight. The brothers white, as they were known in this part of the world, provided enough light to throw a shadow when they were in the night sky. The bigger of the two, Alexander, was about twice the size of Tegin's thumb when he held it to the sky.

Tegin's thumb just about covered Alistair, the smaller moon. Alexander led Alistair by about one hand's breadth through the night until they plunged into the horizon a couple of hours before dawn when a deep darkness would fall upon the land. The twin moons were named after two brothers who died during the construction of the Tower of White in the city of the Crescent Moon ages before.

Tegin's attention returned to the dust coming off the street as trudged toward his tavern. The past two days had been quite troublesome for him. He clenched and unclenched his hands in frustration. The weather had been bright and sunny the past few days, not that he noticed it much.

He could feel a storm brewing on the horizon. It was like a dull ache in the back of his head that gave him an uneasy feeling. He had never had an adversary like the guild give him so much trouble in all his life.

He came across a loose cobblestone and kicked it as he walked, watching it skitter past the opening to a shadowed alleyway.

A quick movement in the alley caught his eye, and he stopped in his tracks as he peered closer. He ran his fingers through his bushy beard as he always did when thinking.

He could feel the hair starting to stand on the back of his neck, and he knew from experience that something wasn't right.

Though he couldn't see very far down the alley, he could hear some rustling and muffled sounds further back. He detached his battle ax that hung from his back with one hand.

He kept it low to his side to avoid drawing attention to it and walked calmly into the alley. He paused at the entry to give his eyes time to adjust, knowing this alley was a dead-end. As he walked further back, he discovered the cause of the rustling sound.

Two hooded figures stood on either side of a third who was pulling a slender dagger from the back of what looked like a runner used by wealthy houses to ferry messages around town or to complete other menial tasks. The runner didn't look much older than sixteen or seventeen years of age.

Just as Tegin finished looking them over, they noticed him.

The boy slumped to the ground, eyes open, without a sound. The two flanking hooded figures drew short swords. The third stooped down and pulled a small envelope from the hands of the dead boy and wiped his dagger off on the boy's trousers.

"I think you wandered into the wrong alley, dwarf," the cloaked figure said as he stood up and slid the envelope into a pocket.

"Actually, I helped build the city. Do you realize how drunk I would have to be to not know where I am in this part of town? But the better question is, what the hell do you think you're doing killing an innocent boy on my city streets?" replied Tegin.

The hooded figure that took the note paused and peered at the dwarf. "Shit, that's the captain of the guard! You two hold him off while I get this back to the boss."

Tegin swung his axe up and laid it on his shoulder. The twin edges gleamed in the gloom of the alleyway. With his free hand, he grabbed a throwing hatchet from his waist belt and whipped it at the middle figure, but the cloaked figure parried the small hatchet away with ease. The two larger figures moved forward while whipping back their hoods so that they could see better in the coming fight.

Unable to keep the obvious leader from getting away without further endangering his own life, Tegin grasped his battle ax with both hands and shifted his stance so that his back was to the wall.

The two figures were almost as different as night and day. The shorter of the two was a dirty-looking young man that couldn't be much older than the boy they had just killed.

Tegin could see he was shaking from the adrenaline coursing through his veins. The look on his face was not fear but excitement. It was apparent he was looking forward to taking on a battle-hardened dwarf.

The taller figure was a much older man. He was clean, well-groomed, and looked rather normal. One of his eyes looked dull and grey. Yet, the other eye looked alert. Tegin had been in many battles throughout his life, and he took every encounter seriously. That was the only way to survive. The two men were brandishing nothing more than short swords favored by guild members.

The young man's sword was dull, dirty, and looked like it was picked out of a rummage heap. Though blunt, it could still be used as a weapon. The older man's short sword was gleaming and sharp. He also pulled a dagger out with the other hand. Tegin had both men on reach with his battle ax. He twirled it in his hands in anticipation of their first move.

· · ·

ANTOINE EYED the dwarf with his good eye. This was no child with a note or even a fellow guild mate. Few in his guild could stand a chance against the captain of the guard in a fair fight.

At least he had this little runt of a pickpocket to throw between himself and that wicked battle ax the dwarf was brandishing. The axe had a much better reach than their short swords. Antoine just hoped the hulking dwarf was slower with it than they were with their swords.

Antoine looked over at Peter. His dirty little companion was shaking with excitement. Peter's short sword looked as if he'd used it to cut wood. At best, it would gash the dwarf even if he had a free shot.

Antoine caught Peter's eye and nodded toward the dwarf's far side while he started creeping to Tegin's nearest flank.

TEGIN KNEW the two men would try and flank him. He quickly closed the distance between him and the frail-looking boy. He brought his axe up in a slow but powerful swing that started low at his ankles and to the left side of the boy in an attempt to stop the flanking maneuver.

PETER, not anticipating the dwarf could close so quickly, was barely able to sidestep the attack to the left. This move prevented him from getting a flanking position on Tegin. As the blow swept past Peter's head, Tegin spun with the swing and brought it from high to low in a wide sweep toward

Antoine's legs. Antoine anticipated the attack and jumped over the axe as it came in low, but he was unable to answer with an attack of his own. The reach of the axe proved difficult to counter.

The maneuver brought Tegin back around into a defensive stance. This movement had assisted him countless times before in battle when fighting multiple opponents.

Neither the men nor the dwarf was wearing much armor. Tegin wore simple leather breeches and a long shirt with the sleeves rolled up to the elbows. He had retired his plate mail long ago. Neither rogue was wearing anything more than cloth. Common clothing kept them nimble and easier to blend into a crowd.

TEGIN SPUN the handle of his axe in his hands while thrusting it toward One Eye's direction, who slapped it away with his short sword. The younger guild member sensed he had an opening and stepped into a full swing with the sword aimed at the dwarf's head. He was surprised when his face was met with the butt of Tegin's axe coming back at him, breaking his nose and blinding him with tears.

Tegin would have loved to follow the strike up with something more life-threatening than the butt of his axe. However, One Eye was pressing the attack now with quick defensive strikes meant to keep him from doing just that. Clearly, the older guild member was starting to realize that they were no match for the dwarf.

· · ·

Antoine could care less if Peter lived or died. Having two blades against the dwarf was keeping him alive just as much as it was keeping Peter alive. While Peter was attempting to recover from the dwarf's strike to his face, Antoine kept Tegin busy enough to force him to block his own attacks and keep his attention away from Peter.

Tegin decided that it was more important to focus on the stronger fighter for now and let the lesser opponent have time to recover.

He feigned as if he was going to swing on the younger boy. He brought the axe back to his right and stepped toward the younger assailant, who was still blinking back tears and blood.

Tegin swung his axe to his left from about chest height down toward the boy's legs. One Eye, thinking the dwarf left an opening, started a thrust meant to gut the dwarf.

Unfortunately, he realized too late that Tegin never meant to strike the boy and was luring him to do exactly what he did.

His blade turned, and he followed it into a powerful spin back toward One Eye. The only thing One Eye could do in time was take the full brunt of the powerful swing on to the dagger in his offhand braced against his forearm. He could feel his forearm break and the dagger fly free from the power of the blow.

The boy had recovered enough, and with sword in hand, he rushed at Tegin in a rage. Tegin spun away from One Eye while evading the boy's wild thrust with the short sword. He brought the flat of his axe straight into the boy's back, who gasped as he fell face-first into the alley wall. He fell limp at Tegin's feet.

One Eye turned toward the entrance to the alley. By the time he took three steps, Tegin had closed the distance and put himself between the older man and the exit. One Eye stared at him in disbelief.

The dwarf should not have been able to close the distance in that amount of time. Something was unnatural about his speed of movement. One Eye turned again toward the back of the alley where his partner had disappeared over the wall. He sprinted as fast as he could and leaped up to grab the edge of the wall with one hand. He felt a strong hand grab his ankle in the middle of his leap and yank him back to the ground. One Eye lay on his butt with Tegin standing back a ways, holding his axe with both hands across his chest.

"So, you give up yet?" chirped Tegin.

One Eye knew he couldn't afford to be caught. He scanned the ground near him and slipped a pebble into his hand as he stood up.

"I guess there's only one thing left for me to do."

One Eye slipped the stone into his mouth. Tegin, fearing poison, brought the butt of his axe hard into One Eye's gut in an attempt to prevent him from activating the poison. He heard a sharp crack come from One Eye's mouth as he crumpled under his blow. Tegin stooped down and wrenched open the man's mouth with his thick fingers.

One Eye gurgled as his life faded away. Tegin could see that he had a hollow tooth, which he used the stone to crack open when he bit down. Tegin paused in frustration.

He looked over at the boy, who he had smashed face-first into a wall. He got up and rushed over to him, only to find out that he was dead, too. Tegin sighed as he stood up.

"Damn it!" he growled.

He kicked One Eye's lifeless body a few times in anger.

EIGHTEEN

Lelanda stood completely nude in her darkened training room with nothing but her two scimitars. In the middle of the round thirty by thirty chamber stood a wooden practice dummy she could see as clearly as if it were the middle of the day with her dark vision.

Her ebony skin blended into the dark room, contrasting her silver hair streaming midway down her back. Her muscular body rippled as she moved into her well-practiced combat pose.

Lelanda's right-hand blade set just above her head with tip pointed forward and slightly down. The left blade she held horizontally about waist-high.

This stance was her favorite when she entered most conflicts, due to its balanced nature. These blades were her favorite possession. She acquired them during her earlier years running as a mercenary with Tegin. She didn't even know how to wield the blades at first. Their beauty and power persuaded her to take up the art of swordplay to add to her sorcery.

The blade she held in her right hand was a traditional scimitar shape just over three feet long. The handle was long enough to grasp two-handed, and the hilt contained two gems.

A deep blue sapphire and a blood-red ruby straddled the blade. Both gems were about the size of the tip of her finger. One or the other glowed, depending on what evoked power she was commanding from the sword.

The other scimitar was much slimmer and not as elegant. The blade was no wider than two inches at the hilt, but it still had the traditional curve of the scimitar that ended in a sharp point.

The odd thing about this particular blade was that both edges were sharp. It was about four inches longer than her other sword. The handle was black with white pearls embedded in it. While the offhand scimitar was longer than the gemmed scimitar, it was just as light.

Lelanda started to move in a very slow, almost dance-like manner, moving the swords this way and that. Her movements were precise and effortless in appearance. She started on the outside of the room, slowly moving in a circle orbiting the wooden training dummy mounted in the center. She sped up her pace bit by bit as she moved closer to the training dummy. With every orbit of the room, her speed increased. By the time she reached her fourth rotation, her hand and feet movements were almost a blur. At the end of her fourth orbit, she was within melee range of the wooden dummy.

At the last moment, she turned all of her focus into three lightning-fast strikes that cleaved an arm, a leg, and the head from the training dummy.

She paused to look over her results and inspected her blades for damage.

As she walked over and slid her blades back into their scabbards, she heard a familiar chirping from the nearby room. She grabbed her robe from a wooden hook on the wall as she made her way to the door.

There she saw a messenger bird from the castle sitting on the perch made for them. They were used to ferry messages from the castle or her network of informants. She walked over to the perch and held out her hand. The bird didn't hesitate to jump onto her fingers.

"You aren't scared of me, are you, little one?" she quipped. Lelanda un-clasped the small note from the bird's leg.

The note read, "Please return to castle Sandown. We need your immediate assistance." — Tegin

She let the bird climb into a nearby cage, where it was rewarded with fresh water and seeds. She turned and headed to her bed chambers to change for her trip to the castle.

CHAPTER

NINETEEN

Tegin summoned the city guard and had the alleyway scoured for clues while he sent a messenger bird to Lelanda. Meanwhile, he had the bodies brought to an examination room in the castle. Tegin had the means to communicate with her magically, but he wanted to reserve that for emergencies.

Tegin and Thena waited for Lelanda outside of the examination room. Lelanda came walking from the direction of the war room, where she'd teleported into the castle. Her eyes were glowing from within the shadows of her hooded cloak.

"What do you have for me?" she asked as she approached the two.

"Well, our hairy friend here got himself into a tussle in one of the alleys near his tavern," said Thena.

"Easy there, lass. They jumped me first, and I did my best to try and keep the bastards alive. One was more fragile than I thought, and the other was rather sneaky. I was busy keeping a sword out of my gut to think a thug may have a hollow tooth filled with poison in his mouth. I'm hoping you . . ." he said as he turned to look at Lelanda, "can find some clues from the bodies. I had all three bodies brought to this room. The boy is an innocent bystander, as far as I can tell. I know he's a runner by his clothes. He was the primary focus of the other two who covered a third's retreat."

Lelanda nodded at what he said. "Well, let's see what we can find out."

The three of them entered the small room. In the center of the makeshift room, three wooden tables were set side by side with space to walk between them. Above each table, three lanterns hung with a thin metal shield over the top of each lantern that deflected light down at the tables like a spotlight.

Lelanda walked over to the counter against the wall and pulled back her hood. She opened a small bag she carried and closed her eyes for a moment. She then opened them again, snapped her fingers, and a small pair of thin leather gloves leaped from the bag. After tying the bag back to her waist belt, she slipped on the gloves.

"Help me get these three stripped down so that we can inspect their clothing and bodies for any clues. Thena, go ahead and start on that runner. Tegin, you get the honor of that smelly thin little fellow in the middle," Lelanda said.

"Great, he smelled bad enough when I was fighting him. Here I thought the two of us were just going to watch you do all the work," he jabbed back at her, his beard curling into a smile. "Why we are at it, why do you have gloves and we don't get any?"

"I didn't know what to expect when I got here, so I'm using my pair of riding gloves. Besides, you are a dwarf. Aren't your hands always filthy anyway?"

That got a giggle out of Thena.

"Wha . . .?" Tegin held up his hands and looked at them. They were calloused and rough, and his fingernails had dirt under them. He glanced back and forth between the two beautiful elves. He had no retort for what Lelanda said, so he just got to work on the body in front of him.

Thena shook her head. She could never figure out how the two of them stayed in such high spirits, no matter the situation.

The three of them went to work on the task at hand, and soon a small piles of clothing was mounded up at the foot of each table.

"Thena, can you please go through the clothing and look for any clues while Tegin and I inspect the bodies?"

Thena nodded and started with the runner's clothes, carefully going through each pocket and inspecting the clothing for any clues.

"Tegin, I'll need you to assist me in inspecting the bodies."

"Aye, and here I thought the fun was over." he remarked while holding his hands up and feigning disdain.

Lelanda instructed him to move the bodies around as she needed for her inspection while she took notes on what she found. When the three were finished, they took all their notes and clues down the hall to the war room to go over what they found.

"These guys didn't have much on them," Thena said as she sat in a chair at the main table and continued. "The runner has 'for house Brenkan' sewn on the cuff of his shirt. They were one of the first mining families to establish their base of operations here once the town was founded. They also own one of the quarries that provided the stone for the castle. To my knowledge, they are an honorable house with no debt or corruption to speak of, but we can do some digging to confirm that. We will notify them that their runner was murdered first thing in the morning. They would have a lot to lose if they were ever linked to a thief's guild."

"They would indeed," Tegin responded, nodding in agreement.

"The dirty fellow," she continued, "had two silvers and three copper pieces along with that extremely ragged short sword that looks more effective as a club. I can't see why the thief's guild would even employ a person such as him unless they were in dire need of muscle, of which he didn't have much.

The largest of the three had nothing on him except his dagger and short sword. He left no clues behind in his personal items. This leaves us with very little to go on."

Lelanda nodded. "Other than the causes of death, I didn't find much to help us either. The runner was killed in a professional manner. A dagger blade slipped into his lungs between two bones in his rib cage. The dirty one died when a bone from his nose was shoved up into his skull. The older man died from self-inflicted poisoning. A hollow tooth provided enough poison to kill him within seconds. The dirty one also had one of these in his mouth.

"This is a recent development. I have not found hollow teeth in any of the previous bodies I inspected. It's quite dangerous as even a little bit of leakage from the tooth would mean premature death. This might give us a lead, or it could be a waste of time. I suspect it is all done internally. I will chase this particular clue."

"Nothing explains why they killed a runner. The rogue that got away took some paper or an envelope from the runner's hand. He said something about getting that back to the boss. I guess we'll never know what was on that paper," Tegin said.

"If it was a communication to the guild, then it was encoded anyway," replied Thena.

"Let's get back to our normal duties," Lelanda said. "Let me know if either of you needs anything."

Lelanda teleported away while Thena and Tegin went to get some rest before another long day came calling.

TWENTY

Tegin decided to make a detour to pick up some of his personal belongings that the king allowed him to store in the treasury.

He made his way into the castle's depths and past four guards that watched the entrance. He pulled a magical key from his pocket. Only three of these keys existed.

He had one, as did the king and Lelanda. He slid the slender key into the keyhole of the large gold inlaid mahogany door and turned it clockwise three times, pushed it in further to a resounding click, and turned counterclockwise three times.

The door popped open an inch. Tegin retrieved his key and entered the room, shutting the door behind him.

This room contained the personal wealth of the king. The wealth of the kingdom resided in the mountain. It was much easier and safer to store and safeguard the treasure vault there than it did in the castle. This room was about one hundred feet square, with some chests set around the perimeter and shelves above those to hold various precious baubles.

Tegin's chest, made of mahogany and banded in silver, required the same key it took to get into the room to open. However, only his key would open his chest. He slid the slender key into the chest and turned a quarter turn. The chest made an audible click.

His most prized possessions were stored here. He didn't have need for them on a day-to-day basis, but times were dire, and the fight in the alleyway reminded him that he should take every advantage.

The chest held his life savings, his suit of full plate armor, his shield, and two very powerful weapons. The first was a magical war hammer that had saved his life from an iron golem that almost killed Lelanda.

He was unlikely to come into contact with heavily armored individuals from the thief's guild, so he didn't have much interest in the hammer.

He reached in and grabbed the weapon out of the chest anyway. The war hammer was quite heavy and took considerable strength to wield. It was a slow but powerful weapon made for foes that wore heavy armor or creatures that were resistant to damage by other means.

The thieves he would be encountering in the days or weeks to come would be agile and wearing little or no armor. It still felt good in his hands, and he was pleased that it didn't feel heavier to him than it did the first time he wielded it.

The face of the hammer was slightly rounded, with the back half of the hammer coming to a point for piercing armor.

He slid the hammer back into the chest and moved his eyes to the reason he came. His double-headed war axe. Made from a rare metal that fell from the heavens, the creator of the axe called the metal Titaine. Tegin acquired the axe during his travels in Ugaria, another continent east of the Crescent Moon.

He reached out and grasped the handle. The entire weapon was cast in Titaine, which had a melting point much higher than iron or steel. It took the crafter months to create and was nigh unbreakable.

He had been in many battles with it, yet it didn't have a scratch on it. The weapon, unlike his hammer, was near the weight of a dagger in his hand. A similar-sized axe could weigh as much as fifteen pounds. The leather-wrapped handle was loose and worn. He would need to replace that before use.

Just then, a familiar voice entered his head. "It has been many years, Tegin. Am I to assume you are in need of me once again?" said the voice.

"Aye," replied Tegin. "I'm sorry I haven't visited more often. I had hoped my days of war were behind me."

Tegin always felt weird talking to his axe. The axe contained an intelligent spirit, and he could hear it speaking in his head. He, however, had to speak out loud when he responded to the axe. It always looked as if he was talking to himself.

He chuckled. "People are going to start thinking I'm crazy again."

"Is that not part of the fun of having me around?" replied the axe.

Tegin recalled the first time he ever heard the axe talk to him. What a crazy time that was. It was hard for him to believe the soul of the axe's craftsman was sealed forever within its blade.

Rothan Hammerblade was a weaponsmith whose lineage went all the way back to the first generation of dwarves. His family forged some of the first iron weapons, and from that point on, the family was obsessed with crafting the deadliest melee weapons the lands had ever heard of. At times that obsession went horribly wrong. The crafting of a soul weapon was invented by a dwarven priest in the Hammerblade family. A willing soul was required to forge the weapon properly.

It wasn't long before other darker-minded smiths took unwilling souls, and some of the most powerful weapons ever created were brought into existence with that dark craft. After a few near-catastrophic events by those wielding these artifacts, the technique was outlawed by the elders who managed the laws of magic—though the process wasn't technically magical in nature as it required a priest's holy power to work the soul into the weapon. Due to the danger, it was deemed a potential world-breaker or something that could bring about a cataclysm similar to the one in Ugaria between Ugar and Gretag.

Rothan's involvement came hundreds of years after the technique was lost to the ravages of time. Rothan, a priest for many years, collected historical artifacts and came upon an ancient chest of the Hammerblade family. Among the myriad of relics within the chest, the ancient book on crafting a soul blade brought him the most excitement.

He knew the dangers and the punishment for crafting a soul blade. He had no intention of attempting the technique until he learned of his father's health suddenly took a turn for the worse. Rothan determined his father was cursed. There were many suspects, but no evidence could be produced to accuse any of them of the deed.

In an attempt to keep his father alive, he came to him on his deathbed in secret and asked him if he would submit his soul to the technique. His father agreed take his soul and embed it in a specially crafted axe.

Unbeknownst to Rothan, the book he discovered was not an incomplete draft, and the reason it survived was that some of the incantations were incorrect. As Rothan attempted to insert his father's soul into the axe after crafting it, he inadvertently inserted his own soul.

The family buried the axe with Rothan's father, and Rothan spent over a century in the darkness of a tomb until tomb raiders unearthed him. Rothan successfully dominated the mind of the human that had taken him. Unfortunately, the human was a thief, not a warrior, and it wasn't long before he was killed. Rothan was then carted around for years as a treasure cache, eventually ending up in the hands of a very dark battle mage whom he could not dominate.

It was then that Rothan learned of the powers his soul had bestowed upon the axe. Every soul imparts random powers on a soul blade—it's what makes every soul blade unique. Some soul blades are cursed. In an effort to create more powerful weapons, the souls used for the weapons were ripped from unwilling victims. Those weapons can be as dangerous to the wielder as they are to the wielder's intended target. Insanity or even death can come about by just touching a cursed soul blade.

Rothan's soul was a special case, as it was taken by accident and not taken willingly or unwillingly, allowing Rothan to attempt to dominate the wielder. If he was successful, he could persuade and, in some cases, even control the wielder's decisions like a puppet on a string.

Those he could not dominate had full control of all the powers his soul bestowed on the axe, including being able to communicate with him. It wasn't until an unlikely meeting with Tegin and his band of misfits that he came into contact with someone well-versed in the art of battle with a mind powerful enough to resist his domination.

Tegin experienced some of Rothan's powers first-hand and had the scars to prove it. After Tegin, Lelanda, and Stalken killed the battle mage, Tegin took hold of the weapon, and Rothan attempted to dominate him. After a short and painful mind meld, Tegin was able to wrestle his mind away from Rothan's control, and after days of Rothan attempting to persuade Tegin that he was no longer in any danger from Rothan, they came to an understanding.

Rothan and Tegin spent the rest of the adventure getting used to each other. Rothan learned about Tegin's battle tendencies, his family history, and most of his other internal secrets, while Tegin learned the powers Rothan's soul brought to the blade. Those powers had aided Tegin many times in the past.

Tegin gave the axe a few practice swings and then uttered a command word that electrified the head of the axe.

Tegin always wondered and never fully understood why he wasn't electrocuted whenever he enabled this power of the axe. Rothan tried to explain that he was a part of the axe when he grasped the handle. That never made complete sense to him. He just took it on faith.

"I am assuming that you have need of my abilities again?" Rothan echoed in Tegin's head.

"I can only hope that I do not need to use you. It's better to have you at my side and not need you than to need you and not have you at my side," Tegin said as he stooped down to grab his well-used steel plate shield from his chest.

He decided to leave his plate armor since mobility and vision would be important if he were trudging below ground in a thief's den.

He slipped Rothan into a loop on his belt, unhooked his battle ax from his back, and placed it in the chest, then put his shield in place. He was now bristling with weapons. Rothan in one hand, a short sword in the other, two small throwing axes, and a dagger constituted his offensive capabilities. His shield guarded his back. Now he was ready to bring the fight to the enemy should they show themselves.

CHAPTER
TWENTY-ONE

It was a dreary, wet, and stormy day that Stalken observed from the balcony of his room. The balcony hovered 160 feet from the base of the castle.

A storm front had come in from the northwest overnight, dumping buckets of rain down on the city.

He had just finished suiting up the armor he'd wear until the rumored threat of an assassin was reconciled. As he looked down and to his left on the city of Sandown, he thought about how long it had been since he had peace in his life.

He could only count a few years of his life that he didn't encounter some sort of strife. He understood the role Elohim had given him. He lived the life of a warrior so that others could live in peace. Many of his friends did the same so that the prosperous little city could remain.

It seemed like a distant dream when he and Gunner were kids. Orphaned and alone, all they had was each other. Now he was a king, and Gunner was second in line to be king, but conflict remained in their lives. Alas, some things never changed.

He sighed, turned away from the view, and started walking to his briefing with his old friend about the status at the front.

He wished he could find a way to end the war. One way would be to crush Letharia. The biggest problem with that wasn't the skill of his men or tactics. He didn't have enough men to take over even one more city, let alone the whole of Letharia.

Planning on expanding the kingdom was never a concern until the war started.

The goal was to train the men in such a way that he could defend his land and his city along with the coastal town of Minsfet. Highly trained men were cheaper in the long run for defense than thousands more that were poorly trained.

On the behest of Gunner, he had counterattacked Letharia instead of letting them regroup and lay siege to the city once again.

They were well-equipped to withstand a siege. They couldn't hold out forever against repeated sieges on the city.

Eventually, the enemy would either get lucky, find a weakness Stalken hadn't thought of, or finally thin his ranks enough to break through.

Even the general knew they were pushing the limit of their effectiveness. It would take months to bolster the ranks of men they had lost up to this point and even longer to train them up as well as the men they were replacing.

Money was not scarce for his kingdom. The mines were the richest he had ever seen or heard of on this continent. The mines could run dry tomorrow.

Being prepared and working hard to create other products that could be exported or traded was the number one goal on this list after the defense of his kingdom.

Before the war started, Minsfet started making a name for itself in the fishing and shipping industries. Now all the sailors were busy building warships or patrolling the nearby waters from attack. This crippled the industry and the economy of Minsfet.

The elves to the south never ventured very far outside their forest kingdom, and that was just to trade with the small towns that skirted the border between the human lands and theirs.

Stalken had long ago forged a lasting peace between the two kingdoms and had prospered because of it. Elves even helped him establish a mages' academy in Sandown. Yet, they couldn't be persuaded to join the war in the west.

He needed a way to get them to join him in the war. Their relationship with Letharia was not a peaceful one. But the elves didn't want conflict outside of their borders. He hoped that taking and holding the city of Solec from Letharia would show that his kingdom was strong.

Maybe that would be enough to show the elves they could win if they would form an alliance with his kingdom. If he controlled all of the lands of Letharia, the elves would have nothing to fear to the north, and he would have nothing to fear from the south. They could both prosper from that situation. That all seemed like just a glimmer of hope at this point.

All this thinking almost made him walk past the entrance to his war room. As he entered, he saw General Gunner and Colonel Barrett Mcleod, a stocky tree stump of a man who the king had never seen without a shield—even during dinners where no weapons or armor were required—standing together near one of the tables.

As odd as that seemed, he was a brilliant tactician and as good a fighter as himself or the general. Yet he was a good fifteen years younger than them. A polished steel Gin sword hung at his side. It looked similar to an oversized double-edged straight dagger that was about as long as a scimitar.

He was a moving wall in battle that could lash out and snuff the life out of anything he touched. He had come to Sandown as a mercenary of a trade convoy that had been attacked by rogues on the road between Minsfet and Sandown.

He made a name for himself after he helped Tegin break up a brawl that started in Tegin's Tavern. He was hired and promoted to Sergeant in the city guard and quickly moved up the ranks.

When he could go no higher in the city guard, he was transferred under General Gunner and given a field commission to lieutenant. After the fighting started with Letharia, he again moved up the ranks due to the deaths of his superiors during the siege and the push out west. Now he was third in command after the king and Gunner.

The general and colonel were discussing some things on the map in front of them when the king walked in. They both looked up, with the colonel snapping to attention as Stalken approached. He returned the salute, and the general greeted him.

"Sire."

The general always kept things formal when anyone outside his inner circle was present.

"What have you got for me, general? Good news, I hope."

The colonel raised an eyebrow as he glanced at the general. Gunner motioned the king over to the map table.

"I don't know if this qualifies as good news, but things are pretty quiet on the front. Scouts have not come in contact with the enemy for many days. We know for a fact that the enemy is not within three days' march from Solec. Though the colonel and I agree they are not finished with us, it makes me believe due to recent events that they are waiting on something, but that is speculation."

"Show me what progress you've made on the defenses of the city."

Gunner looked to the colonel, "Colonel Mcleod, run us through what your group has done in recent weeks."

Mcleod nodded. "Yes, sir."

He situated himself between the general and the king in front of the magical sand table.

"If you look here to the east, where a majority of the damage was located, you will see we have reinforced the damaged walls to the best of our abilities for the short term. The good news is that the northern and western walls were largely untouched by our siege on the city, which would be the most likely direction of the counterattack.

"We haven't ruled out the possibility of them trying to flank us to the south, but we have scouts hiding out in areas south of us within sight of the southern border. We've also laid out kill pits from the northeast to the southwest to defend and or channel ogres and giants into kill zones for our catapults, ballista, and the very few trebuchets stationed in the city.

"As you know, the city lies on a very flat plain open for miles in every direction. This makes it difficult to approach without being noticed and almost impossible with a force large enough to take back the city. Letharia's use of magic, magical beings, and conjuration of beings from other planes looks to have made them arrogant when it came to settling the city. The city's wall is not even wide enough to hold archers. They never used them and instead made use of flying creatures and even young dragons for aerial assaults or counterattacks.

"We have modified most of the walls to accept archers now. Also, we know that their other cities have much better defenses with proper walls, moats, and anti-siege weapons. Lelanda and her team haven't figured out how they are getting dragons to do their bidding. We assume they have some sort of agreement or have blackmailed the dragons into compliance. Dragons are solitary and don't even like being around their own kind once they hit maturity. Yet they were used in defense of the city. We hope they do not use them in the counterattack. If they do, it won't go well for us."

Stalken scratched his chin. "What are our numbers currently stationed in the area?"

The general spoke up. "Approximately five hundred archers, one thousand phalanx soldiers, three thousand foot soldiers, and around one hundred heavy horsemen remain. I would say 60 percent of the entire battalion is seasoned troops."

The king sighed. "I didn't realize we had lost so many heavy horse."

"Tactically, the defense of the city doesn't require heavy horsemen, so even though they had the highest casualties, they did their job in helping us take the city. We did lose a lot of good men in the primary attack, but the city's defenses are not going to suffer due to lack of heavy horse," chimed in the colonel.

"The colonel and I are in agreement on this, sire. I plan on holding the heavy horse back as a reserve."

The king paced back and forth in front of the map, thinking. "What reserves do we have in case they break through?"

"Well, not counting the city guard, I'd say what we have about three times the foot soldiers, five times the archers, and ten times the heavy horse. We are expecting to be outmanned three to one in their counterattack, maybe even four to one. However, that was the case when we took the city," said Gunner.

The king stopped pacing and leaned over the map. He placed his hands on the edge of the table so as to not disturb the sand.

"What if we were to pull back and consolidate our forces within the kingdom's borders and let them take the city back?"

The colonel started to speak up, but the general cut him off.

"I think that would be most unwise, sire. Having seen their forces firsthand on the battlefield throughout the past months, I believe they would see that as a sign of weakness and push forward until they caught our army in the open field. We would be at a huge disadvantage on a level playing ground. They could surround us with their greater numbers. Even if we made the trip back, they would push forward until they lay siege to our city again. Either way leads to us being at a disadvantage."

Colonel Mcleod nodded in agreement. "This is our best position, sire. We have our primary forces within the walls of three cities. We couldn't ask for a better situation. If they do not use dragons against us, then we will have a very good chance of repelling the attack."

Stalken stood up straight and crossed his arms over his chest while staring down at the map.

"Thank you both for coming on such short notice. I know you have many things to do. I agree that we are putting ourselves in the best possible position. The reinforcements are on their way, as you requested, and should be there soon. I'll let you both get back to your duties."

The colonel saluted, the general nodded, and they both headed for the door. The king walked over to a liquor cart against the wall and poured a healthy amount of wine into a goblet, and walked back over to the map.

Stalken took a deep drink from the cup, knowing the outcome of this battle would determine who pressed the advantage going forward. He was coming to the realization that Letharia was going to have to be destroyed to end this war.

His small kingdom was not going to be able to do that alone. His only hope for the future was to press the elves in the south to side with him. The only way to do that was to show that he could take and hold one of his enemy's cities. This coming battle would determine the fate of his kingdom going forward.

TWENTY-TWO

Corax stood in his quarters in front of his equipment wall that contained his weapons, gadgets, potions, poisons, armor, and many other equipment items he might need on a job.

He always did the same routine before a job, selecting each piece he would use for his mission. It was like piecing together a puzzle for him. He didn't want to carry too much and didn't want to leave something behind that may be of use.

This was a night job, so his blacked-out leather armor and darkest cloak were necessities. He laid out each piece on his table. He checked them for tears, light or shiny areas, and cleanliness. Nothing was overlooked. His life depended on it.

Once completed, he pulled his favorite mahogany blowgun from the wall and inspected it for cracks and shine. He also gave it a few shots against a practice target in his room to make sure everything was in working order. Mahogany, being a dense wood, gave the two-and-a-half-foot-long blowgun some weight, but it also imparted strength.

A loop of dark leather allowed the blowgun to be slung under his shoulder and hidden from sight. Yet, it was easy to get to when needed. The effective range for a blowgun such as this was around fifty feet in calm weather.

However, with years of practice and being a master of the weapon, Corax could dependably squeeze out another twenty feet, hitting his mark eight times out of ten from seventy feet away.

Many hours were spent familiarizing himself with this type of weapon. He even custom-made his own darts so they would consistently perform the same way. Though, environmental conditions had a large effect on accuracy at almost any distance.

He pulled a dagger and short sword from the wall along with a set of iron knuckles that he used as a backup when all else failed. Black soot coated every surface, including the sharp edges, to prevent any glint of metal that might be noticed while lurking around in the shadows, waiting for a mark to let their guard down.

Corax had run across a few magical weapons in his occupation, but he refused to get attached to any specific weapon other than his trusty blowgun. It was easy to replace a non-magical weapon. Though magical weapons had many benefits, he enjoyed not having any attachment to his weapons in case they were lost in a fight. He did enjoy wearing his leather bracers of strength and boots of agility. They had saved his life on more than one occasion. Those items were able to be secured on his person. Weapons could be stolen or lost a lot easier.

Corax held the sword in his hand and gripped it with his mighty strength. The tricky thing about magical items that granted abnormal strength was the user needed to take into account that their body's ability to handle that type of strength. Magical as those items were, they didn't grant a person's bones and tendons the ability to hold up against extreme feats of strength.

He ran his callused fingers over one of his bracers, feeling the hard leather, and thought back to a story he'd heard about a man gifted with a set of bracers that granted the equivalent strength of a giant. The man was so excited he tried to pull a tree out of the ground with his bare hands. To his dismay, he pulled his arms out of their sockets.

Corax had learned by hearing about the follies of another that doing stupid feats of strength could cripple a person for life. Much care and practice had to be taken when wearing such a magical item.

After hours of practice, he could safely use them to make him more dangerous as an assassin. He may not be able to safely punch through a solid stone wall with his bare hands, but he could easily throw a rock the size of his hand hard enough to kill a person or swing a weapon hard enough to cleave a grown man in two.

The bracers were the reason he could get the extra distance out of the blowgun. The extra power in his diaphragm allowed for a more powerful exhalation. A blowgun made from less dense material would crack under the repeated pressure during use.

Corax finished laying out his gear. He walked over to a small shelf protruding from his equipment wall and opened a small chest about the size of his hand. Inside rested a half dozen small pyramid-shaped vials glittering like little jewels in the firelight. He slipped on a pair of tight white leather gloves he had just for this dangerous chore.

After he squeezed each of his thick hands into the white gloves, he pulled out one of the small vials that were no larger than his pinky finger and used a pair of tweezers to pull the small little cork out of the top of the vial.

The vial was placed in a small metal holder that it slid down into. This allowed him to clamp the vial in place so it would not move. He retrieved five custom-made darts from a bag that he kept next to the small chest. He dipped the tip of each dart into the vial, coating them in a sticky dark liquid. After dipping each one, he placed them in a hanger to dry.

His brow was beaded with sweat as he put the cork back into the vial and placed it back in the case from where he retrieved it. He pulled off the white gloves so that they were inside out and tossed them into the roaring fireplace. He secured the chest's lid and wiped off his brow with a rag from the table that his equipment was on. He took a deep breath and relaxed.

Working with poisons was a hazard of the job and something he never took lightly. This poison he had gotten from a rogue wizard that used outlawed magic to retrieve the poison from another plane of existence. It was one of the deadliest poisons known in the land and was untraceable. No wizard would ever admit to using outlawed magic to acquire it. Nor was there any use for it other than as a poison.

The first time Corax tested it was on a mountain deer. It had died in less than ten minutes and could barely move after one minute. There was no chance this batch could ever be traced as Corax tested it a second time on the very same wizard he purchased it from, with even better results.

As the darts dried, he dressed in his leather armor and secured his weapons into their proper places. The five darts were placed in a specially made leather holder that Corax had designed to fit his blowgun, both securing the darts in place for easy access and protecting the tips from being exposed to moisture or inadvertent contact with himself or someone else.

There were no cures for the poison he was utilizing, and even the smallest amount would kill a person. The amount of poison used only affected how long it took to kill, not whether or not a person could survive it.

That was the reason he went out of his way to get it. Dwarves and a few other races were quite resistant to plane-bound poisons created on the primal plane. This particular poison ensured that he didn't have to change his tactics based on any specific target due to their resistance to some other poison he utilized.

As he made some final adjustments to his armor in the mirror, he thought about what he had in store for his future if he was to succeed and live through the night. If the plan was executed without error, the king would be dead, and he would be out of Sandown before anyone was the wiser. If he failed, then he would be dead, and nothing but the dark emptiness of whatever hell he was destined for awaited.

Even unarmed and unarmored, the king would be a handful if he discovered Corax's presence before he was able to deliver a fatal shot from his blowgun. Not to mention that Corax was less familiar with the layout of the king's quarters than any other place in the palace.

He paid a lot of gold for a rough layout of that wing of the castle from a contact within one of the families that provided the stone for the castle. His lieutenant had no choice but to kill the runner when the runner recognized him. They were fortunate the guard captain was not able to pull any information from the two rogues he'd killed in the alley upon the lieutenant's escape.

The information he purchased gave him the location of the room and its generic layout from a construction point of view. Still, traps or a failsafe could be in place to protect the king if he were alerted in advance that an assassin was approaching. Getting the king's swords as proof could prove harder than killing the king.

Corax could feel the excitement starting to get his heart rate up. He hadn't felt excitement like this since he first took up assassination as an occupation. He smirked at himself in the mirror; he was ready. The effects of tonight would echo throughout the land for years to come.

TWENTY-THREE

Stalken sat at the head of the table in the War Room of his castle, surrounded by his usual entourage of officers and heads of state along with Thena, Lelanda, General Gunner, Captain Mcleod, and of course, Tegin.

The king was starting to look weary as of late. The war, along with everything else in the monarchy, was enough to frazzle anybody. Add to that a top-shelf assassin that could strike at any time, and it could push a lesser man over the edge. The king trusted his inner core leaders and friends with his life, but stress was still stress.

He stared at the flame of one of the large candles on the table as the meeting was letting out. The flame was so calm and unwavering, seeming so strong and steadfast until someone walked by. Then it flickered about in the slightest draft, almost going out at times. This was how he felt about his kingdom.

From the outside, it seemed so solid and unwavering, yet it was being weakened from within by a corruption he couldn't weed out. It could cost him his life and even the loss of the kingdom. He felt it could be snuffed out in the blink of an eye.

Suddenly he felt very tired. He glanced over toward Tegin, who was sitting on a bench with his back against the wall, puffing on his pipe and staring at the king.

Stalken met his gaze and gave a weak smile. The last of the attendees had left, and just Tegin and Stalken were left in the room. Stalken stretched his arms wide, then high up over his head. His leather cuirass rubbed against itself.

"I think it's time I get out of this confounded armor and catch a few winks. Care to walk me to my room, my friend?" Stalken asked as he rose from his chair.

"Aye," said Tegin as he tapped out his pipe in a goblet next to him and tucked it away in his vest.

They both strode into the hallway toward the king's chambers. "I see you pulled Rothan out of storage. Are you expecting a fight?" asked Stalken.

"I just want to be prepared for whatever the future brings. If danger comes knocking, I don't want to be caught with an empty mug if you catch my meaning."

"I don't know if I feel more uneasy with you bringing out weapons that you hoped to never use again or better because you are embracing what you know you are and will always be . . . a warrior."

Tegin grunted at the comment. He wasn't certain how he felt about the situation either, but Stalken was right. Ignoring his past was about as smart as putting a dress on a pig. He wasn't going to change himself by ignoring his past or what it made him into. It was time to embrace the past and use it in the present to thwart the current threat and any others that came his way.

"I told you it was a mistake to try and hide me away," Rothan whispered in his head.

"Seems like everyone knew what was best for me. It just took time for me to come to grips with it," said Tegin.

Stalken looked over at him as they walked on.

"Don't be hard on yourself. You aren't the only one who regrets their past. Sometimes I wish I'd never found that damn cave but just died. Knowing that my friends have problems with their own skeletons shows me that I'm not alone. Great things can only be accomplished by making sacrifices. You and I have sacrificed a lot. It makes my hair stand up on my neck to think about what Lelanda has sacrificed. I think she is a good example for us to accept our past and embrace how it defines us."

They approached his honor guards outside his chambers. A guard stood with his back to the wall on either side of the large wooden door inlaid with polished steel designs that also worked to strengthen the door. Stalken turned and clasped his hand on Tegin's shoulder and gave it a firm squeeze.

"No matter what the future brings for me, I want you to continue to hold this place together. If the worst should happen, then the general will take it from that point on, and he will depend on your strength just as I do. You are a true friend, and I hold you in the highest regard."

Tegin clasped Stalken's forearm and looked

deep into his eyes, and said with a grin, "You keep talkin' like that, and I'm gonna get all misty!"

Stalken leaned his head back and gave a hearty laugh. Tegin chuckled as they bid each other good night, and he turned and walked back down the hallway the way they had come.

Stalken entered his abode by way of the two guards in the hallway. Typically he wore a chain-mail shirt under armor for some protection and comfort, but lately, he had been wearing a light suit of leather armor that he had worn in his youth for extra protection.

He stood in front of his armor stand, and his assistant helped him start removing the pieces of armor. The armor was lighter and more comfortable to wear than his plate mail or scale mail set.

Still, it was not designed to wear every day all day. It was like a breath of fresh air to get out of it. Things like this made him wonder if he would do it all again knowing what it would cost him.

He scratched at the stubble of his whiskers. "Yes . . . I'd do it all again," he mumbled to himself. His assistant looked up at him with a questioning glance as he helped him with his leather reinforced boots.

TWENTY-FOUR

After leaving the king's side, Tegin stopped by the kitchen on his way out to grab himself a flask of ale from the castle stores.

He popped the cork on the flask and took a big swig as he snatched an apple from a fruit bowl on his way out. He took a side exit from the castle and nodded to the two guards as he passed them into the orchard that lay just inside the iron fence surrounding the front of the castle estate.

While knocking back a swig of ale, he failed to notice a couple shapes in his peripheral vision making a move toward the entrance he had just left. He was biting into his apple when he heard shouts erupt from the guards behind him. Tegin spun around to see four cloaked individuals cut down the surprised guards and run inside.

Instead of trying to catch up to the infiltrators from behind, he decided to head for the front entrance of the castle to head them off. He dropped his apple and looked at his flask.

He tucked it into a pouch on his belt and sprinted for the main entry as fast as his enchanted boots would allow. He yelled for the city guard as he made his way to the main door. He could hear clashes of metal on metal from inside the castle, two wings away from the king's quarters.

He told the front guards to stay at their posts until the city guard arrived to relieve them, then follow him in.,

He swung Rothan off its catch on his belt with his right hand and his short sword off his right hip with his left hand and sprinted up the front entry stairs and ripped open the front doors just as six cloaked intruders came running down the foyer stairs.

"Kill the dwarf and bar that door before others come," the shortest of the six shouted.

A big brutish-looking fellow pointed at him and said, "Dibs on the axe!"

A dagger sprouted from his mouth a moment later, and he went down with a gurgle, blood spouting into the air in a frothy mist.

"You boys are lucky. Any other day, and I'd be tryin' to take you alive!" shouted Tegin.

He pulled his axe back out after having killed the biggest threat with a lucky throw of his dagger. The five men came down the stairs at him.

One of them spit at him. "We're gonna kill you, dwarf!"

All five men carried daggers and short swords, giving them a slight speed advantage over Tegin. He knew he needed to get to the king as fast as he could. Spending time on this lot was not an option.

The five men started to flank him. He backed up, parrying a couple of probing attacks by the ex-perienced attackers until he was just inside the open doorway to the courtyard. The guards outside could see him, but at his orders, stayed put.

The largest of the men to his left came at him with a thrust of his short sword meant to lead while a killing blow from the dagger held off-hand followed. Tegin brought the flat of his axe across his body to slap the sword away and his short sword up into the armpit of the attacker. The tip of his sword sprouted from the man's shoulder.

The man on his far-right used the opening to bring down his sword onto Tegin's back. A re-sounding clang came in return as it bounced harm-lessly off the shield hidden beneath his cloak.

The dagger dropped from the impaled man's grasp. Tegin parried another limp attack from the man's sword with his axe, then brought the axe tip into the man's gut with a powerful thrust. Tegin heard the man gasp as he drove the axe home and, with a swooping motion, picked him off the ground.

Tegin's muscles rippled as he picked him off the floor with nothing but his axe and threw him at two of the attackers to his right.

Tegin could hear the echoes of weapons on weapons and shouts from the direction of the kitchen. He knew the castle guard had been rousted and would hopefully be making short work of the infiltrators.

Tegin knew that this was his best opportunity to attack. He threw himself at his foes while they were still gathering themselves. Rushing the closest man to his right, he thrust at the man's face with his axe and then went into a counter-clockwise spin and came around with his sword that was parried up and away.

At the same time, he muttered the command word for Rothan to electrify. Without warning, the entrance to the castle was filled with the bright blue glow of crackling electricity of his axe. Surprised by the sudden light, the axe made its way past the rogue's defenses and cleaved deeply into his neck at a forty-five degree angle, killing him.

That left three healthy combatants and one wounded one. Tegin knew that precious seconds were ticking away. Not knowing what to do next, the rogues kept their distance. They still pressured Tegin with feints and quick stabs to keep him away. An idea came to him. He whispered his command word, which made the axe cut off the electricity effect.

Tegin looked at the axe in disbelief and grunted, "huh?"

He shook the axe like whatever powered it was shorting out. One of the men, suspecting treachery, was about to tell his men to hold fast, but it was too late. The others jumped to what seemed like an opening in Tegin's defense.

Muttering the command phrase once again, he swung the axe in an uppercut as he jumped to the left of the other two assailants. He caught the man to his left just under the chin, splitting his face open from bottom to top as the lightning boiled away his flesh and burst his eyes in their sockets. The man fell to the marble floor with a gurgling scream.

Rothan soon crackled back to life again as the axe regenerated the electricity it had discharged into the man's face.

"Maybe it's time we make the most of this and head on out the back?" said the rogue that took Tegin's sword to his armpit.

One of the other men turned to him and thrust his sword into his neck.

As he slid it back out, he replied, "There is no turning back. The king dies, or we die!"

He locked eyes with Tegin. "Maybe I'll just keep you alive long enough to pull your arms and legs off," said Tegin with a snort.

"Whatever you do to us is nothing compared to what our master will do if we come back without the king's head. You may not know his name now, but in time, all will fear him."

"Says the lacky that was sent to his death," replied Tegin.

The other rogue, not knowing what to do or say, just stood his ground. He was afraid to attack the lightning-wielding dwarf. But just as afraid to meet the fate of his counterpart for speaking up.

Tegin, sensing his indecisiveness, shoulder-rushed him and connected with his elbow into the unprotected groin of the surprised rogue. He crumpled to the ground, coughing and groaning. Tegin spun to parry a slash from the leader with his short sword. He came at Tegin with a cry, feinting again and again until seeing what he thought was an opening.

His sword connected with the lightning-powered axe. All that could be heard was his echoing scream in the foyer. The axe electrified his sword and turned his arm to brisket up to the elbow. Tegin followed that up with a quick stab to the chest with his short sword. The rogue free fell to the floor, landing face-first, the life gone from his body.

As for the rogue he'd elbowed in the groin, Tegin kicked his face with the bottom of his boot and heard his head smack the marble floor with a high-pitched cracking sound. Blood started pouring from the rogue's split skull. Tegin turned and sprinted up the stairs while giving the command word to extinguish his axe.

Right about then, the front guards came to secure the entrance, along with half a dozen city guards.

"Secure the entrance and assist the others in need near the kitchen wing! I'm headed to the king's chambers!" Tegin yelled over his shoulder.

He saw a couple of dead castle guards and a half dozen dead of what he was certain now was thief's guild members in the hallway that led to the Royal Wing. He ran into five of the king's personal guard, yelling for two of them to follow him and the rest to hold the hallway.

TWENTY-FIVE

Corax spent over half the day working his way around the base of the castle, making sure to leave no trace. He wore his black cloak splotched with mud on one side for his movement through the forest and countryside, and then he could flip it to the gray side while he climbed the canyon wall at dusk. That could be shed after the canyon wall climb to reveal his black armor during his nighttime climb of the castle.

He knew climbing the vertical cliff wouldn't be a challenge. It would take two or three hours to reach the base of the castle.

The time-consuming part was climbing the smooth castle wall. Even with his climbing skills, he would not be able to secure his grip on the smooth surface. One slip could end his life unless he used his magical trinket to invoke a slow fall, and he needed that for his escape.

That meant that he had to utilize special climbing knives he invented to wedge between the thin gaps in the heavy granite blocks of the castle walls. Even then, they required his extreme strength to push into the thin crevices. If he didn't take care, he could snap off the blade, and the mission would be over.

The balcony loomed around two hundred feet above the base of the castle and around eight hundred feet to the canyon floor where he was starting his climb.

His augmented strength would allow him to hang in place all night if he needed to. He had to be in place before the raid started against the castle and city guard. If the raid was squashed ahead of schedule or if the king left his abode, that could complicate things.

He felt nothing for the men he was sacrificing—they were pawns in his strategic game of power. He had his use of them, and now it was time to bet everything on this single move.

Corax's body tingled from the feeling of adrenaline he had not felt in some time. He adjusted some of his gear and started his ascent up the canyon wall. He had to be careful not to make noise or dislodge rocks that could alert any patrols to his presence.

He made quick work of the canyon wall, leaping from ledges and holding on to perches that no human, let alone a dwarf, would consider.

He smiled at the thought that the king had no idea what would be waiting for him. It was a shame that the poison would work so quick to paralyze his diaphragm and his heart. He would have to take pleasure in watching the life fade from his eyes.

Corax made it to the base of the castle tower

wall. He peered over the canyon edge and was surprised to see a two-man patrol standing guard near the spot he intended to start his climb from.

Torches had been embedded into the ground for a bit of light while the guards scanned the area around them.

Lucky for Corax, the torches made it more difficult for them to see outside of the firelight. He slipped up into the grass on the canyon's edge and dug out a small stone from the ground. He slipped on a pair of steel knuckles he favored when hand-to-hand. Soot concealed them from the firelight. He would have to be perfect on his strikes.

He took a deep breath and tossed the stone so that it skittered off the wall and into the grass close enough to get the guard's attention.

Just as they turned their heads toward the sound, he moved quickly and silently, straight at the nearest guard standing to the left of the other. As he entered the firelight, he burst into a sprint.

The guard never saw him coming as he connected a left hook into the guard's knee, taking his feet out from under him, followed by an almost instantaneous hammer-like blow from his right. The force hit the guard in the face so hard it bent the steel helm onto the guard's head and broke most of the bones in his face, splintering them and forcing them into the man's brain, killing him before his body slumped to the floor.

The commotion brought the attention of the other guard back toward him. Their eyes met just as Corax leaped up and brought the power of his right arm encased in steel into the man's neck, almost ripping his head from his body. All that was heard was a gasp of air and the snap of bone.

Corax secured the area, snuffed the torches, and tossed the bodies of the guards over the cliff. He took the chance that they would be harder to find at the bottom of the ravine than where they were standing moments before. A faint clank and thud could be heard from each as they landed.

Not his cleanest, but he didn't have time to hide the bodies before the next climb. Dealing with them took up any time he saved during the first climb up the canyon wall.

He took position near the wall and adjusted his gear so that he could reach an oil skin filled with a mixture of grease, pig fat, and oil.

He put away his steel knuckles and unsheathed his climbing daggers. He dipped each into the skin at his side and coated the blades with the slick mixture.

He designed the blades to slide into the vertical seams between the stone blocks. Ninety percent of the blade was designed to be forced between the seams. Then the blade's hilt was broad, thick, and flat.

He shoved the thin part of the blade into the nearest vertical seam in the stone wall until the hilt pressed up against the stone, creating a small perch for him to stand on while he worked the blade of the other dagger into the seam above.

Then, clutching the handle of the dagger above, he could pull out the dagger below, dip it into the fatty mixture, and pull himself up to the next dagger. It was slow work and would be impossible without his augmented strength. That is what made coming this way such a surprise.

Up he went, a dark cockroach, working its way up the side of the main tower toward the balcony that sprouted from the smooth castle walls close to two hundred feet up.

CHAPTER

TWENTY-SIX

Stalken finished removing the last of his armor and had finished getting his shave from his assistant.

"Let me dispose of this water sire, and I'll bring in a fresh bowl."

Stalken nodded as he felt the drain of the day's activities finally come over him. He closed his eyes and was listening to the quiet of the night and thinking of a fair-skinned maiden he hadn't found any time to sneak off with lately. The vision was disturbed a moment later when he heard some faint clanking sounds from outside his door. He disregarded them as the night shift adjusting their armor, and it grinding up against the stone wall.

Suddenly, all his mental alarms started going off. He normally couldn't hear the guards outside unless they yelled or knocked on the door. The normal movement shouldn't have been heard from his room.

He got up and walked to his door. When he pulled on the latch, he found that the door had been barred from the other side.

He jerked hard, and it didn't budge. He heard his assistant coming back from the adjacent room with fresh water. He walked over to his weapon stand and pulled his swords free just as his assistant entered his field of view. He saw a quick movement from the balcony.

"Down!" he screamed at his assistant.

It was too late. The young lad fell to the floor with a small dart protruding from his temple.

Stalken's adrenaline surged as he yanked the curtain from the awning around the master bed. Another dart shot forth, ripping through the curtain past his head. He grabbed the boy and half hurled him across the bed, away from the balcony as another dart nicked his shoulder and embedded into the bedpost.

He knew it was a poison dart as soon as it hit him. What would have been a minor scratch erupted in a burning sensation that started to spread into his shoulder. From the shadows of the balcony slipped a dwarf in all-black leather armor.

He wielded a short sword and a parrying dagger with three blades like a person holding up three fingers.

It was a pointed middle blade with a flat blade protruding from either side to catch an opponent's weapon. It was made for counter-attacking an opponent with slashing weapons. Both weapons were covered in soot to prevent the reflection of light.

Stalken could feel the poison moving down his arm and into his chest. He could barely raise his left arm let alone grip his sword. It clattered to the ground. He would have to work fast to try and dispatch the intruder. Stalken growled at Corax as he lunged at him with his sword that remained in his good hand.

Corax sidestepped the attack and smiled.

"Looks like I got you! I thought I had missed all three times. I would have had you on the first shot if not for your little shit-stain boy that walked into my shot. No matter. You'll be dead soon and will have a terrible time moving even sooner than that. So . . . let's make this quick. How about you just give me those swords, and I'll be on my way."

"To hell with you!" spat Stalken. He twirled to his right and came in low with his sword. Corax flicked his wrist to the left, catching the blade of the sword with his parrying dagger.

Corax spun left, bringing him in close to the king. He thrust his thick elbow into Stalken's ribs, sending him reeling end over end from the blow. At the same time, he wrenched the sword from Stalken's grasp.

The resounding snap of ribs sounded like a bull-whip. Stalken landed hard, and his strength was being sapped by the poison coursing through his veins. His whole arm was on fire and hung almost lifeless at his side.

He managed to stand, but his broken ribs made it difficult to breathe—or was it the poison? He couldn't tell. He gasped for breath. He had never been hit that hard in his life.

Corax picked up the first blade that he had wrenched from Stalken's good hand and walked over to the other blade. He stared at Stalken for a moment.

"I have no care to fight you further unless you

insist. You are a dead man standing, and I have what I came for."

He lifted the second blade off the floor where it had slipped from the king's grasp. Time slowed for Stalken. He knew this was the end.

The burning had made it to his head, and his vision was starting to blur. He wasn't afraid of death; he was just sorry that he couldn't put up a better fight. All he could think about was his friends, his people, and . . . Thena. He failed them all.

His eyes drifted to the painting on the wall near his bed. He tried to take a step. But his strength gave out, and he collapsed face-first onto the bed near the already dead servant boy.

TWENTY-SEVEN

Tegin had gathered a few men and headed for the king's chambers. He remembered the item that Lelanda had given him, cursing himself for not remembering earlier to alert and summon her. He put his wrist up to his throat and whispered the phrase she had taught him.

Dwarves were the opposite of elves. Elves had been ingrained with magic since the time when Elohim had gifted them with it. Dwarves, on the other hand, had no magical talent at all. They were very resistant to all magic, and any attempt to practice magic ended in disaster.

Their resistance to it prevented them from channeling the energy or even tapping into those planes of existence—but it did not prevent them from using devices imbued with magic. Lelanda had given him a gem that he had sewn into his bracer that had a simple incantation scribed into it. It would channel the spell for him when he uttered the phrase.

As he finished saying *"argoth vocatus,"* he saw the gem start to glow a dull bluish color. When the color faded, Tegin found himself tripping over Lelanda as she popped into existence right in front of him. In a cloud of shimmering smoke, Lelanda stood there in nothing but her undergarments, cloak, and her scimitars gleaming in each hand. Her ebony skin looked soft and smooth in the torchlight of the hallway.

The guards couldn't help but gawk at first sight of this beautiful ebony battle-mage standing before them.

"He's in trouble," is all the Tegin grunted out before he moved down the hall toward the end of the castle where Stalken's boudoir was located.

Lelanda fell in behind him, with the two guards following behind her. They rounded the final corner and found two dead guards perched outside of Stalken's room.

Tegin motioned for the two guards to secure the hallway. The door had a coil of wire connecting the door's handle to the wall, preventing it from opening from the inside.

Tegin and Lelanda made eye contact and nodded. They shifted stances. Tegin positioned himself to the right of the doorway with Lelanda to the left. Lelanda sheathed one of her swords and whispered a couple of unintelligible words, then touched the wires clasping the handle of the door. The wire uncoiled itself and fell to the floor.

She whipped her sword back out in a fluid, practiced motion and ripped open the door so that Tegin could make a beeline rush into the room. Tegin entered the room in time to make eye contact with an unknown dwarf dressed in black leather armor holding the king's swords. Lelanda was just behind. Tegin rushed toward the assassin with weapons high, his axe crackling to life.

Corax turned and ran the last few steps to the balcony and leaped over the edge while turning in midair to get one last look at the captain of the guard with the amazing axe. He was thankful he wasn't dealing with that axe and instead was plummeting to what looked like a certain death.

In one hand, he held both of the king's longswords and, in the other, a small trinket that he crushed as he plummeted past the base of the castle and back into the pitch-black canyon. In an instant, his speed slowed to that of a feather falling through the air.

Tegin peered over the railing and into the darkness, not quite believing what he just saw. Lelanda pushed him to the side. She pressed her hands together while speaking, "firasatath!"

As she pulled them apart, a small orb of flame formed in her right hand. She whipped the orb straight down from where she last saw the dwarf leap. She assumed by his willingness to leap off the balcony that he had some sort of magical device that would slow his fall as he neared the bottom.

The castle's base led to a dead end one way and to a guard shack the other. If any magical fall was incurred, it would not dissipate until the person landed or until its duration ran out. She also knew that descent-reducing spells always kept the target descending straight down.

Tegin peered over the railing. "Was that a fireball spell?"

She said nothing as she kept her eyes on the

tiny dot falling into the darkness of the canyon below.

"In my experience, those have a limited range," Tegin quipped.

"Yes, a normal fireball spell does. This one is a spell of my own invention. More intense, but the big improvement is that its range is unlimited until it comes in contact with something other than the air it needs to survive. If it no longer has air, then the spell suffocates and dies. We use similar spells to create those magic lamps that light the streets and the castle."

Just then, they both saw the dot impact with the canyon floor and erupt into a huge fireball. "Do you think that had any chance of hitting him?"

"No, but at least the guards can locate the area he descended to and start searching from there. Besides, he's a dwarf. At best, he'll get some superficial burns and maybe lose some hair."

"I hope it burned off all of his hair. It'll be a lot easier to spot a hairless dwarf!" spit Tegin.

As both of them turned back toward the room, Thena came rushing in. The two guards were tending to the boy and the king as Thena rushed to help them. Stalken's eyes were partially open, and his breathing came in gasps. Thena put his head in her lap as Lelanda kneeled at his side.

"What is wrong with him!? Can you help him!?" she sputtered.

Lelanda spoke without looking up. "He looks to have been poisoned. Possibly some type of paralytic poison."

She pressed her palms to Stalken's chest. His gasps came slower and slower. Lelanda started muttering magical words unintelligible to anyone not trained in the arts.

Her hands started pulsing with power, first white, which faded darker and darker until it was an inky black. When the pulsing stopped and the dark light faded, so did the king's last breath.

"I'm sorry . . . I . . . I couldn't save him. The poison was very powerful, and I didn't have the correct incantation. I'll have to study his blood to know what kind of poison, but I'm guessing that it's the kind a rogue mage might deliver for the right price."

Tegin knelt down beside his king . . . his friend. He could feel the lump starting to rise in his throat, and his eyes became blurry.

He saw a flash of sorrow come across Lelanda's face as she closed Stalken's eyelids with her fingers. Tears streamed down Thena's face, dripping from her chin onto the king's forehead. Tegin blinked back the tears, and pain was soon replaced with rising anger.

"Time to lock down this city and squeeze that guild until it breathes its last breath!" he roared.

Tegin reached for the nearest guard and grabbed his breastplate, and pulled him eye to eye. The guard had tears in his eyes. Tegin's voice started in a whisper but gained volume as he spoke until he was roaring. "I want you to notify the runners. Every guard is to be called to their post. Nobody leaves the city until further notice! Anyone coming in will be warned that they cannot leave once they enter! Everyone trying to enter or leave will be searched!"

He half-tossed the guard into the hallway, and

the other guard rushed out after him. His eyes were wide in surprise at the sudden ferocity of the captain.

"And I want patrols sent out that stay within five hundred yards of the city, looking for anything suspicious!" he yelled after the guards.

He turned back toward his fallen friend and walked up to both Lelanda and Thena, putting a reassuring hand on their shoulders. Thena was sobbing uncontrollably. "Let's get him moved to an examination room. Lelanda, examine him while Thena and I equestion all of our contacts and any suspicious characters we come across." He knelt down on one knee next to Thena and whispered in her ear, "My friend, we have to act if we are to find his killer. Put aside your grief for now."

Thena looked over at him with tears streaming off her face. She nodded and lovingly took his head out of her lap, and rested it on a pillow. She got up from him and gritted her teeth. "Let's find them." Rage boiled in her eyes.

TWENTY-EIGHT

Corax was about seventy-five feet from the ground when what looked like a torch flew past him from above.

What are they planning on achieving by throwing torches? He thought to himself. He caught a chuckle in his throat as what looked like a torch impacted the ground, and a huge fireball erupted from its impact point.

He wriggled in the air like a fly caught in a spider's web as the magical flames enveloped him. The heat was intense but not unbearable and subsided quickly.

He looked at himself as best he could in the dark as he descended to the charred location below him. His dwarven resistance to magic proved itself invaluable yet again.

The captain of the guard has a magical axe he never knew about and what could only be explained as a half-naked dark elf mage wielding twin scimitars.

He knew of the captain and had heard of the dark elf. He had never seen her in person, yet she was half-naked, throwing fireballs at him. He loved this exciting life.

He patted himself down after reaching the ground and didn't seem to be the worse for wear, considering he just assassinated a king, and the whole kingdom was out to find him.

He scampered through the countryside in the general direction of his secret entrance while he focused on the next stage of his plan.

Reaching the guild, getting what few belongings he cared for, and getting out of town were top priorities.

He had been identified. His plan of being disguised as a visiting dwarf was not going to work now. Every dwarf within miles of the kingdom would be questioned. The easiest way to avoid questioning was to not be present for the questions in the first place.

Corax made it out of the crevice near the base of the castle walls into open terrain. He found an outcropping of boulders and scanned the city for anything that could help him determine his next move to get back to the guild hall.

Corax peered at the city from the shadows of the boulders. The city walls looked like a swarm of ants had invaded the city, looking for food. The captain must have rousted the entire guard. He would need to be careful on his approach.

TWENTY-NINE

Horsemen were sent out in packs of five, all positioned in a rough semi-circle about five hundred yards from the city while it was still dark.

Their orders were simple. Wait until the crack of dawn broke the horizon and then spread out and ride toward the city at a trot. Spotters from the city walls would also be scanning the area for suspicious movement and for alerts from the horsemen.

The location where Lelanda's fireball erupted had been located, and a few tracks had been found, but they were lost in the scrub nearby. The tracker seemed intent that the tracks indicated the assassin was headed east back toward the city.

Tegin and Thena both agreed that the assassin would not re-enter the city by any other means than a secret entrance if his plan was to re-enter the city at all.

East of the kingdom was a wild and untamed land that would be perfect for a killer like that to get lost in. But, for some reason, Tegin believed the assassin was not finished here yet.

Tegin theorized the assassin could not have predicted that he would be identified. Any plan he had would have been changed once that occurred. That profession meant he probably did not trust anyone else to meet him outside of the city with whatever materials and property he needed to gather before escaping.

Planting the items himself would be risky because there was always a chance the items could be found, or he could be followed by a fellow member and his items stolen. The one thing that could always be depended on by thieves is that they would stab each other in the back just as easily as they would any common person they met on the street.

Tegin knew that this was not a foolproof plan. The dwarf could have a person he trusted, might have stashed his things near the castle prior to climbing the wall, or any number of other things. This was their best guess, and they were not going to waste it if they had guessed right. Their friend was dead, and someone was going to pay.

Tegin and Thena stood near Thena's quarters, shouting orders to reporting guardsmen and guardswomen. Thena had not fared well in the hours since Stalken's murder. Her eyes were red and puffy, and her nose was runny from blinking back tears.

She occasionally had to go back into her quarters for small periods to regain her composure and had adorned her helmet and armor to shield her face from the other guards.

Word was spreading that something had happened to the king, but no official announcement had been offered publicly. As Tegin handed out the last of the orders to a group of latecomers, Thena had to excuse herself again. She scoffed at Tegin as she spun, entering her headquarters slamming the door behind her. A few nearby guards looked up from their duties.

Tegin turned and followed her. Thena ripped off her helmet and threw it against the wall. Tears were running down her face and dripping off her chin.

She looked at Tegin, "Why couldn't I have been there! I could have saved him!"

Tegin walked over toward her to console her, but she shoved him away.

"Why aren't you upset?! You stand there like a statue dolling out orders like it was any other day! How can you be so calm?" she screamed.

He reached out for her, and she attempted to shove him away again. This time he resisted. She smacked and pounded on his broad chest until his large, scarred arms wrapped around her. He shushed her without saying any words. She sobbed and sunk into his arms, tears pouring from her eyes.

"How can you be so cold while I cannot?" she whispered between sobs.

Tegin let her sink down into a nearby chair while not letting go of her. "I am as upset about this as you, girl. Make no mistake. I am quite distraught by his murder. Stalken and I are blood brothers, a bond shared and one that is not broken. It is not my way to show emotion in the face of tragedy, not when so much is required of me."

She listened to the rumbling of his voice through her own sniffles.

"It pains me to see my friend dead and to let the

killer within arm's reach to escape." He gently tilted her head so her tearful gaze was looking into his. "But it pains me even more to see my friends hurting as much as I am, and there is nothing I can do about it other than to hunt the offender causing that pain. Especially ones that were in love with each other."

She could see that his eyes were moist with tears now as well. Her secret was out, and part of her was thankful that it was Tegin who figured it out first.

"We owe it to our friend and each other to pursue this assassin until the end of his days. I will not let my friend's murder go unanswered, no matter how long it takes or what obstacles I am required to overcome to bring him down. That was my oath that I pledged to him when we became blood brothers."

As he spoke these words, Thena started finding new strength and a better control of her emotions. "You're right, there will be time for grieving. Now is the time for vengeance."

Tegin grabbed her by the arms and leaned down to her level. "Exactly!"

Just about then, a knock came at the door.

"Captain, the sun is about to dawn!" came a voice from the other side.

"We will be right there!" Thena shouted back. She jumped up and dried her eyes and then grabbed her helmet and her two-handed sword.

"I'm right behind you," she said to Tegin as he walked toward the door.

He nodded to her and proceeded outside. She walked to a mirror she had nearby and looked into it. "For vengeance's sake, I will take from him all that I can in return for taking you from me, from us, from your people."

She slipped her helmet on and proceeded outside behind Tegin.

The townsfolk were awaking to the terrible news. The king had been assassinated. The town criers were spreading word for everyone to stay indoors and that the guard would be doing a building-by-building search. As this was going on, the plan to try and tighten the noose around and snare the assassin was beginning.

CHAPTER

THIRTY

Corax had spent the precious few hours before dawn trying to avoid being tracked. It was a long process that required doubling back over his same footsteps in areas where the soil was loose enough to leave footprints, using brush to erase or obscure his tracks, and sticking to rocky outcroppings in the hills as much as possible. As dawn approached, he abstained from rocks since they would silhouette his body from a distance and make him easy to spot in the daylight.

He had been able to see the city's front gates for over an hour. He could hear the gate opening and closing, and at times, dared to peek up enough to catch glimpses of it. But for the most part, he was blind to what was going on inside or outside the immediate vicinity of the city walls. His only hope was that he had a clean shot to his secret entrance outside the walls and that no one saw him before he could enter.

What he didn't know, but could sense, was that a trap was in the works. He could feel it like a snake constricting around its prey. With the rocky out-croppings and rolling hills, it was nearly impossible to know what was nearby.

The problem with that was that he could walk straight into a patrol. He had no darts left for his blowgune, so that was nearly useless. That made him quite susceptible to ranged attacks. Even if he did have the advantage of seeing a patrol first, he couldn't do anything about it.

Dawn was now in full-effect, and Corax stuck out like a sore thumb in his black armor. He could shed the armor; however, he would still be left with black shirt and breeches.

He had managed to get within about one hundred yards of the entrance to the tunnel that led to the thief's guild. He could see the top of it from where he was. The big problem was that he spotted a line of scouts along the city walls that would be able to notice him as he approached the entrance. There was one angle that would provide him cover, but he would have to come in from the southeast to get to it.

Grumbling to himself, he slid back down to the small ditch that led between two bushes and some small boulders. He scratched his chin through his bushy beard. It was about an hour after dawn, so there was plenty of shadow left to utilize.

He made his way around to the southeast and got within fifty yards of the entrance. There was a small bit of cover from where he was to the entrance, which was a lot more than if he came from the west or east.

Just as he was about to make a move toward the entrance, the sound of hooves rang like a death knell in his head. He turned his head just in time to see three horsemen rounding an outcropping about seventy-five feet from him. His body tensed with panic, his heart jumped up into his throat, and he hurled himself over the top of the boulder he was perched behind toward the entrance to the tunnel.

Just as he moved, the scouts saw him. Two of them nocked arrows to their bows as the third blew a horn that he pulled from his saddle.

"Halt!" one of them shouted as Corax landed on the other side of the boulder.

Not even pausing to look back, he bolted toward the entrance of the hidden tunnel, his bracers giving him the strength that made him unnaturally fast for a dwarf.

"Stop him!" he heard one of the scouts say.

Within seconds of hearing the horn blast, the scouts on the wall located his dark shape darting toward a rock outcropping near the southeast part of the city wall. He was within thirty yards of the entrance when he heard an arrow zing past him to the left. He bounded up a rock and leaped into the air as another arrow ricocheted off the rock he had his hand on. The doors to the city were opening, and he could see armed men starting to pour out in his direction. Fifteen yards away from the entrance, he could hear the approach of hooves and another arrow flew over his head as he rolled through some brush. He slammed into the wall of the entrance and traced the symbol into the patch of rock that allowed the hidden door to open. He turned while brandishing his dagger and short sword at any would-be attackers while the rock slid open.

"Come on already," he said.

Just as the horsemen pulled up, he squeezed inside as another arrow missed his shoulder. One of the scouts leaped off his horse and sprinted inside the entrance in hot pursuit.

Corax threw his dagger into his pursuer's throat while he was disoriented in the darkness of the tunnel. He turned and sprinted a few feet to a rusty chain on the wall and pulled it hard. The other two scouts had dismounted together and pulled their dead comrade out of the entrance to the tunnel just as it started to collapse. Corax slid down a makeshift ladder through a hole near the chain about fifteen feet down to another section of the tunnel that led under the city walls. He could hear the earth falling in on itself behind him from the trap he triggered.

"That should hold them for a while."

Corax turned and sprinted down the tunnel as fast as he could, taking care not to trigger any of the other tunnel traps.

As he slipped into the empty guild hall toward his private room, he was hailed by a young lad about his height that specialized in pickpocketing.

"Did ya hear? The town is abuzz with the news about the king bein' killed!"

Corax knew that only a chosen group of men knew of the assault the guild did on the castle, and they should be dead by now. Corax thought to himself for a moment. An idea dawned on him.

"What idiot would kill the king?" Corax asked.

"Rumor has it the lieutenant did and that he is on the run!" the young lad exclaimed.

Corax stifled a chuckle and played the next part

as well as he could. "What? I never gave him the order for that!" he said.

He turned and flipped the nearest table across the room to smash against the far wall.

"Are you certain of this news?" Corax growled. The boy was scared stiff as a board by Corax's sudden reaction.

"The whole town will be coming down on us!" said Corax. "I have no choice. I'm disbanding the guild. I'm enacting command . . . black fog. Spread the word!"

He turned on his heel and stormed toward his private room while grinning through his beard the whole way. The boy, wide-eyed, let him leave, then ran off to tell the others.

Corax entered his private room and shed his armor and dark clothing. He slid open a secret wall and accessed a safe hidden there. He disabled the trap on the outside and then opened the door on the safe just a crack and disabled the trap he had on the inside. The outside trap fired darts from small, concealed holes in his weapons and armor wall coated with the same deadly poison he used in his assassination of the king. When triggered, the internal trap would shoot a powdered version of the poison he had dried then ground up. When inhaled, it had the same effect as if struck by his poisoned darts.

His magical portable hole was the only item in the safe. It could store many times the amount and fold up inside a pocket. He hadn't chanced taking it on his mission. It held all of his most precious items and currency.

He laid the cloth on the floor and opened it up.

When it was opened up entirely, he spoke the command word, and a storage area from another plane appeared that allowed all manner of items to be stored there.

He pulled out a mithril chain shirt and leggings. It didn't provide much protection against blunt trauma, but it did protect the wearer very well against slashing and piercing weapons. He dressed himself with the shirt and leggings, then put on some common clothing of a merchant from the south region that was common for dwarves.

He knew it was going to be very difficult to get out of the city now that his secret tunnel was no more. With guards lining the entire wall, it made it impossible to escape over the wall without being detected. The sewer was out of the question. It was frequented by the guard because the guild initially used it as a route of escape.

He could use the front they had in place in the market area to try and catch the word as to what the city was doing. Corax was certain the guards would be looking for a dwarf now that they believed him to be inside the city walls. Unlike merchant dwarves, Corax didn't groom his beard; in fact, he didn't groom himself much at all except for bathing to keep the body odor down.

Though some dwarves regularly came and went in Sandown, they were by no means a majority. It wouldn't be long until they picked up his trail. The front was a legitimate business specializing in various goods and spices shipped up from the south.

In reality, most of the goods were stolen and repackaged using the store's seal. They did just enough real business in the south to prevent the city from getting suspicious. Corax tossed a couple of weapons into his portable hole and grabbed his box of rare poison, his darts, blowgun, and some disguises. He closed the portable hole and tucked it securely into a hidden compartment in his jacket, leaving the rest of his possessions behind. It was time to make his way to the Spice Locker and start grabbing intel on the state of the city. His only regret is that he wouldn't get to see his traps at work on whomever came after him.

THIRTY-ONE

Tegin was patrolling the market when word came that the assassin had been spotted and pursued to a secret entrance just outside the walls of the city. One of the guards had been killed in the pursuit, and another injured when the tunnel caved in from a trap. Tegin had a runner find Thena and tell her to meet him at the tunnel's entrance so they could investigate it.

Thena arrived to find Tegin poking around the rubble over the tunnel, inspecting the ground. Dwarves had an amazing sense of the earth. They could make all sorts of interesting things out of stone. Traps and secret entrances were some of their most sought-after skills.

Thena watched Tegin poking about for a few minutes and then gave a slight whistle to get his attention.

"Aye lass, I know you're there."

He knelt on top of the rocky outcropping where the entrance was located. A ten-ton boulder was the last thing to crash down. It was blocking any attempt at him getting into the tunnel to inspect it.

"This trap was very well made and thought out," Tegin said. "It fits in with the suspect being a dwarf . . . it fits even better with it being a dark dwarf. Though I hate to admit it, they are the best at crafting stone traps and shifting walls. Their crafting rivals the best of any of the dwarven clans. If they weren't so conniving, they would have been involved in the tower projects way back when the four towers were being built for the Magi. But they could not be trusted."

He shook his head. "This . . . looks like the work of a master stone smith. He has noteworthy skills. Is there any way we could use a spell to get through this rubble?" he asked. "Maybe that spell you used against those brigands some years back? You know the one. It liquefied the rock."

"Well, in theory, I could. The problem with that is the spell is only active for about thirty seconds at the most. After that, the mud hardens back into rock. It wouldn't be possible to move the mud out of the way fast enough before it hardened again. It would be faster to dig it out than to try and use a spell to get past it. Maybe Lelanda has something more appropriate in her spell book than I do. We could ask her."

"We'll keep that plan as a backup. Even if we breach a tunnel from this location, it's bound to be trapped in multiple places. It could take days to bypass them all, depending on their complexity."

"Instead, let's see if Lelanda got anything out of the rogue we captured last night."

"You didn't mention anything about a captured rogue!" said Thena as she grabbed Tegin's arm.

He turned and looked her straight in the eye. "I

was afraid you might do something rash based on your emotional state. We're all crushed by his death, but until I spoke with you this morning, you were on the verge of a breakdown. Can you honestly tell me that if either of us had informed you that we captured one of the infiltrators alive that you wouldn't have wanted to skewer him before we had a chance to get any information out of him?

"If he knows anything, Lelanda is our best bet. She's sly, attractive, seductive, and innocent-looking all in one. We don't want to kill him based on our emotional states. We'll have no chance of getting any information then. At least with this scenario, we can track him if he resists our interrogation or really doesn't know anything. He won't give up the location of the guild, but he might lead us to it. That's why I'm not in there either—I would end up pummeling him into a mushy paste, and where would that leave us?"

Thena opened her mouth to respond but realized Tegin was right. Neither of them were thinking straight. Any information would be much more valuable than a dead thief. They had plenty of those after last night and just one that was still alive.

"Let's head back and see if she learned anything," Tegin prodded by putting his hand on her shoulder.

"You're right, it is the smartest move we have. Let's not waste it," she agreed.

CHAPTER

THIRTY-TWO

Braegen woke with a start. The last thing he remembered was holding off two guards in a far wing of the castle. The raid failed, and he was trying to escape. He remembered a sharp pain on the back of his head and everything going dark.

He calmed himself and tried to figure out his surroundings. He was tied to a chair in what felt like a small chamber with no light. All he could see was darkness. His clothes had been removed from the waist up, and his boots removed. His hands were tied behind him to the chair, and his ankles were tied to the front legs of the chair. He strained against his bonds to see how secure they were.

"I see you are awake," came Lelanda's smooth voice from the other side of the room. "I tied you up so you wouldn't hurt yourself when you woke."

Braegen strained his eyes in an effort to see anything at all in the darkness. It was pitch black. All he could do was listen to the seductive female voice coming from in front of him.

"If you ask it of me, I'll remove your bonds as

long as you promise not to do anything that might . . . endanger you."

Braegen stopped straining against his bonds. "Ok, as long as you tell me where I am and who you are."

He felt his bonds fall away without a sound.

"Fair enough. My name is Lelanda. What might yours be?" she purred.

"Braegen," he stated. "So, where am I, and why can't I see anything?"

"You are high up in the mountains at my retreat. You cannot see because it is too dark here for your human eyes to see."

"By your response, I'm guessing you are not human. Besides that, you can see me, and I can't see you . . . and your accent is definitely not from around here. Sounds more elf-like, but something a bit different than elvish."

"My, my, you aren't a common brute, are you? I am pleased to hear that," she replied. "You are correct. I am neither human nor common elf."

"May I see you?" asked Braegen.

"If you must."

Braegen heard Lelanda move. He was blinded by the flare from a match as she lit a tall thin candle next to her. As Braegen's eyes began to adjust, he found himself a mere ten feet away from what had to be a dark elf. He had never seen one in person. He had heard plenty of stories about them, all of them bad.

Lelanda sat cross-legged on a large sitting pillow on the floor. From the waist up, she was topless, and from the waist down, she wore a long white semi-transparent skirt that lay around her along the floor. The light danced along her ebony skin, hinting at what lay beneath the skirt.

Her perky breasts rose with each breath, causing Braegen to swallow hard. He had never seen such a beautiful creature in all his days. He followed her curves up until he came to her eyes, which he found closed. His heart started to race, and he caught himself thinking things he shouldn't.

He realized he was caught up in the moment and forgot for a minute that he was in grave danger right now. Held prisoner somewhere in the mountains, stripped of most of his clothing, sitting across from a dark elf in a small, dimly lit room, and he didn't yet know what she wanted from him or why he was even here. He remembered the guild code, *death before dishonor*. He moved his tongue to where the hollow tooth was supposed to be and found nothing there but a gap.

Had it fallen out or been removed by his captor? No point in worrying about it now that he didn't have the option of suicide.

LELANDA OPENED her eyes to the bright candlelight. It was bright to her kind, at any rate. Over the years, she had become more accustomed to the bright lights of the surface.

She had found a way to enhance her eyes to accept the brighter light on the surface but still possess the same dark vision inherent to her kind. The disadvantage to her was that they glowed.

It allowed her to be seen in the black of the underdark, but the advantages outweighed the one disadvantage. She wasn't as sensitive to light. Yet, she still kept her excellent dark vision. She was also resistant to cold and heat. It intimidated those who didn't know her and, at times, those that did know her. Once she opened her eyes to look at Braegen, that intimidation was very apparent.

BRAEGEN COULDN'T HELP but stare at Lelanda's eyes. One glowed red the other glowed blue. "I can't help but notice that your eyes are glowing. Is that some sort of trick to make me think you are all-powerful?"

Lelanda smirked. "When compared to what or whom? If you are comparing me to someone such as yourself, then yes, I'm all-powerful. But I'm nothing compared to other beings dwelling in our world, some of which you couldn't possibly imagine."

She shifted on her pillow a bit.

"But enough about me. Let us discuss your situation, shall we?"

Braegen started to sweat at the sound of that.

"Are you going to kill me?"

There was a long pause. Lelanda just stared at him. "Well, that depends upon you."

Braegen thought back to an incident he witnessed with Corax in the guild. He watched a savage beating of a guild member who crossed Corax and heard the screams of torture victims coming from the hallway to his quarters on multiple occasions.

The thought of being cuffed to Corax's wall and tortured for selling out the guild in exchange for his life was why he wished he had his hollow tooth in his mouth filled with poison. He could bite down on it, release the poison, and die a quick and relatively painless death.

Now he was stuck between Corax and this beautiful but deadly dark elf that could kill him in any number of ways. He didn't know if she was a fighter or caster. Her build was that of a fighter, but elves were known for their magic, and dark elves for their cruelty.

He could feel the sweat trickle down into the small of his back. "I will tell you whatever I can if it means I get to leave here alive and in good health," he said.

"I promise that if you can tell me any information that pertains to the king's assassination, you will be compensated." She lightly ran her fingers over her breasts.

Braegen felt his heart skip a beat. His brain was reeling at the thought of bedding this elf all while racing through thoughts of escaping this place and running as hard and as fast as his feet could take him, even half-dressed.

"W-what is it that you would like to know?" he stammered.

"We can start with everything you know about the attack and go from there. What was your involvement in the attack on the castle? Who is the assassin? Do you know where to find him? What is his name?" she asked.

"Umm, I wish I could tell you everything, but I don't know that much. My involvement was simple. I was told by the lieutenant of the guild to cause a ruckus in the wing of the castle that I was captured in. About two dozen of us were selected or asked to partake. I'd say a little more than half of that showed up. I knew going in that we were the distraction. I didn't know until you just said it that anyone was assassinated. I don't know who assassinated the king. I could offer a guess, though."

"Please do," Lelanda responded.

"Our leader is the only one with the tenacity, skill, and intelligence to even have a chance."

"And he is . . ." she prompted.

"I would be killed for even uttering his name in public, let alone tell it to an authority figure such as yourself . . . But circumstances being what they are, I think I'll take my chances."

"Wise choice," she purred.

"His name is Corax. When we do see him, it is because we screwed up something, and either someone is getting a beating or killed as an example. He is the strongest being I've ever seen."

"Can you elaborate on his strength?" asked Lelanda.

Breagen thought for a moment. "This one time, a brutish guy we had hired for a job was unhappy about his cut. Once everything was said and done, he decided to change the game. This guy was massive, but not that smart. He thought once the job was done that he could just muscle in on the cut and nobody would stand up to him. Back at the guild, a fight broke out over it, and he crushed a guy's head. The lieutenant tried to stop it, but he took the lieutenant and tossed him against a wall. That caused Corax to come out from his personal quarters to see what all the noise was about.

"We have strict policies about noise. Corax was

none-too-happy to see this guy trying to throw his weight around. I think his name was Kornash or something like that. Anyway, Corax wasn't too happy to see him making a mess of the guild. Kornash wasn't too impressed with Corax. Maybe that was because he had some orc blood in him or something. Anyway, he decided to challenge Corax for leadership of the guild. Bare-handed, no weapons. Corax agreed. Some of the guys had seen his strength in the past and knew Corax wasn't even going to break a sweat with this guy.

"To make a long story short, the fight was over in less than a minute. Kornash started right out of the gate trying to fight dirty. He tried hitting Corax with a solid oak chair. Corax blocked it with one arm while reaching out with the other to grab Kornash's leg. He crushed his ankle by just squeezing it. He yanked Kornash off his feet with a spin and slammed him against the same wall that Kornash had thrown the lieutenant against. Except, he just kept doing it over and over and over again until Kornash was no longer Kornash. He looked like a soggy lump of raw meat. I mean, I doubt Kornash felt much after the first impact with the wall. That first hit knocked him cold and had to have broken bones by the sound of it.

"That's the thing that scares us the most about Corax. If you draw his attention, your life is at stake. Rarely does someone disagree with him to his face and it ends well. He's like a predator. Once he's on you, he doesn't quit until he feels like quitting. I've seen him kill five people in the guild since I joined. That was a little over a year ago."

"Interesting," replied Lelanda. "I have to ask.

Why stay in a guild where your life is endangered all the time?"

Braegen chuckled. "You think our chances are any better trying to make an honest living in the world? Maybe you've had it easy in life, but the rest of us commoners struggle to make it every day. The guild means a bed, warm grub, and security. As long as we do the odd job for the guild when asked, give them a cut, and follow the rules, everyone wins. Plenty of the guys had been with the guild for years and said as long as you kept your nose clean and didn't make the mistake of crossing the boss, you could make a damn good life for yourself."

Lelanda shifted in her spot and ran her fingers through her long silver hair. "Can you tell me anything else about Corax?"

Braegen rubbed his hand across the stubble on his chin and crossed his leg.

"I can't say that I can. I heeded the veterans' advice and steered clear of any interaction with him. As I mentioned, we rarely saw him unless he was pissed off. The lieutenant ran the day-to-day affairs and led the attack on the castle. As for knowing where Corax is, I'm sorry, but I don't. I haven't seen him in the weeks prior to the job we pulled on the castle."

At that moment, he realized he made a mistake of getting too comfortable with his words. Lelanda went into a forward roll and came up under his crossed leg, lifted him by the throat, and slammed him into the wall behind him. He couldn't believe how strong she was. In the other hand, she held one of her razor-sharp scimitars.

She whispered at him, "The . . . job . . . you are

referring to is the one where my longtime friend was brutally assassinated because the country to our west wants what we have and doesn't have the strength to take it themselves. He was an honorable man that wanted everything for every one of his people, including the likes of you and those you represent.

"If it wasn't for your insidious little guild, he would still be alive, and we wouldn't be having this conversation. Now you and your crew have put everything in jeopardy. What do you think is going to happen when the source of the job finds out that the mission was a success? Do you think for one second they're going to sit back on their laurels and do nothing? They are waiting on this, and then they are going to try and take back their city and once again march on the gates of first Sandown and then Minsfet. After that, they'll slaughter half the population or more, killing anyone thought to be a threat, like an annoying thief's guild. Like your boss, I could crush you without a second thought. However—"

She pulled him back from the wall and released her hand from his neck. "I, unlike your boss, have honor guiding me. I promise you this, if I ever cross paths with him, he will come to know the meaning of revenge."

"I'm sorry, miss, I didn't mean to offend you by my callous remark," said Braegen while he rubbed his throat.

"Apology accepted. Now, by what you've told me and what I know through my agents, you are no more to blame than any other trying to scratch a living in this world."

She walked back to the other wall where she was sitting. "Please, take your seat."

Braegen picked up the overturned chair and sat back down.

"My last question, do you have an answer to it?" she said as she sat back down on her pillow.

"Um" he said. "I, uhh, don't remember the last question."

"The one about the guild's location," she replied.

"Ohhh yea, uhh."

He peered about as if looking for a hole to climb in. "You know I know it. If I give it to you, you'll just go there and destroy it, and then I'll be out of work and have no place to live."

"But, you'll be alive," she replied.

"Are you saying you are going to kill me if I don't tell you? What about all that honor crap you just spouted?" he exclaimed. "I've been forthcoming with everything."

"Everything but the location of the guild," she responded.

"Damnation, why did I have to lose my tooth? Please don't kill me," he pleaded.

Lelanda responded by outstretching her arms to either side of her with her hands forming a symbol Braegen couldn't recognize.

"You will find out if you don't answer by the time my hands touch each other."

She started moving her hands toward each other.

Braegen was sweating. *What to do?* he thought to himself. *Why couldn't I have been a simple farmer instead!* He watched as Lelanda's hands came together, forming what looked like a circle with a triangle above it held just about at her forehead. Her eyes closed, and the room filled with intense light. Braegen felt his eyes getting heavy and everything going dark as he slumped back into his chair. Once he was asleep, Lelanda prepped for the teleport back to Sandown in the morning.

THIRTY-THREE

Tegin, Thena, and Lelanda stood outside of the castle jail around a small table discussing what Lelanda was able to find out from the rogue, Braegen.

"So, that was everything he told you?" queried Tegin.

"Yes," replied Lelanda.

She was sporting her typical attire and scimitars. Tegin was equipped to fight as well as Thena. All looked ready for war.

"I don't believe there is any more to pull from him without torturing him half to death."

"I'm up for that!" piped Thena. She thumped the table with her fist.

"Easy, lass," returned Tegin. He laid his large hand on her arm. "Beating a worthless piece of scum to death isn't going to bring back our friend. Besides, I'd rather beat the actual murderer to death instead."

"We all would," followed Lelanda. "As I see it, he is still of use. If we let him go free and track him, it will be our best chance at finding the guild. Based on what he told me, it is his home. Most, if not all of them, shelter and live at the guild. At some point, he will attempt to return there to get his belongings."

"But won't he know we're following him?" asked Thena.

Lelanda shook her head. "Not in this case. The spell I evoked on him erased any memory of his entire conversation with me. He'll remember getting knocked out in the castle. As far as he will be concerned, he was thrown out and left for dead in an alleyway. He could walk right past me and not recognize me."

Tegin grumbled something and then spoke up as Lelanda and Thena glanced his way. "That's all well and good. Other than the tiny bit of information we gathered from him about Corax, how is letting him go and him having no memory going to help us find the guild? We've tried tracking these bastards before, and they always seem to slip away and disappear. You yourself have ascertained they are not using magic to teleport inside. My question is, how do we track this guy so the same thing doesn't happen, and we are back to square one?"

"I'm glad you asked," said Lelanda. "When I had him under interrogation, I removed his shirt and boots. I enchanted each heel of his boots as well as the hem of his shirt. If I am within a thousand feet of them, I will be able to tell how far away they are in any direction."

Thena smiled. "What are we waiting for? Let's get the ball rolling. The faster we find the guild, the faster we can hunt down the scum who killed this whole city's symbol of freedom."

"We have some time," she responded. "The sleep spell won't wear off for another few hours, and then he'll be groggy for a bit when he first wakes up. That gives us plenty of time to get some spotters on the walls and trackers near him. We can't have anyone following him because he'll spot that right away."

Tegin added to that by saying, "I'd bet my shiny axe here that he isn't going to attempt anything until dark. That means at least another day of lockdown for the city to try and keep the assassin within the walls. That also means Gunner can't come in from the field until then, either. He is our king now, though nobody is aware of that."

"Knowing Gunner, he would get tangled up in the plot and end up waist-deep in this mess, as we are. He just needs to keep focused on any attack by our overly friendly neighbors to the west."

"I'll figure out where to drop him while you two get spotters in place," said Lelanda. Thena and Tegin nodded in agreement and left Lelanda to attend to their duties.

CHAPTER

THIRTY-FOUR

Jonathan, a castle guard under Thena's command, headed down the stairs toward the castle jail. He was approached by Thena and told to report to Lelanda as soon as possible for a special task. He had never spoken to the dark elf in the three years assigned to his post.

He had seen her many times when he was on duty in various parts of the castle. She had free reign into any area that the king did. Jonathan had never even seen her face, just her eyes . . . they made him shudder just thinking about how they made him feel.

He came to the landing at the bottom of the stairs. Waiting for him was Lelanda in her typical attire—her hood up with her eyes shining their mystical red and blue.

"I was told to report to you, miss?" he said as he approached her.

"Yes, I have a special task for you. I heard that you used to be part of the city guard. I assume you know all the nooks and crannies in the city?"

"Yes, miss. I served for five good years under

Tegin. He promoted me to elite guard about three years back."

"Good, I need you to come with me atop the castle."

She reached out her hand toward him. After noticing his hesitation to take her hand, she spoke. "Where we are going, you cannot get to on foot."

"Ohh," he said as he grabbed her hand.

She muttered the teleportation spell that he heard the other mages say all the time in the communication wing, and in a blink, they were high atop the castle.

After getting his wits about him, he noticed they were on a specially built platform on top of the highest spire of the castle. It was big enough for maybe four people to stand on, with a wooden railing about three feet high surrounding it. A few spyglass boxes were resting on a makeshift table made of wooden boxes propped up in the corner. Before him was the entire city of Sandown.

Lelanda turned to him. "I need you to find me a spot to drop a live body."

Jonathan gave her a strange look.

She continued. "Tegin told me about the time you pursued a thief through the city for an hour before he finally lost you. That is many times longer than anybody else has ever managed to stay on their trail. To me, that means you are good at what you do and know the lay of the land. Where in the city would you feel most comfortable planting a body where we could have the easiest time tracking him from multiple vantage points around the city walls and at ground level?"

Jonathan flipped open one of the spyglass boxes

and pulled out a spyglass, extended it, and scanned a few locations. "That should do." He handed the spyglass to Lelanda and pointed north of the market. "Just north of the market, before you get to the higher-class inns and cottages, there is a network of alleys that the markets use for this and that. Some are used for storage throughout the day, and others for trash. A person could place a body back there for a few hours before the guards would notice it."

Lelanda peered through the spyglass for a few moments in that area. He was correct. There were a lot of alleys in that area. Funny that things like that are never obvious until pointed out. "We won't have to worry about the amount of time the body will be there. I will teleport the body into place just before he wakes. What I will need from you is to place a teleportation stone in one of those alleys prior to me teleporting the body. Otherwise, I will likely kill him without any knowledge of the area.

"People tend to not live very long when they are teleported into a solid object. But a teleportation stone allows me to have a focus point without having seen the area. Of course, if the person putting the stone in place doesn't take care, there could still be an accident. So, make certain you place the stone in an area where a body can appear. No one can be seen snooping around the area prior to the body being dumped; otherwise, suspicion will arise, and our target's life would be forfeit before we could use him.

"I will cast an illusion spell on you to make you look like one of our contacts in the market that is seen down there on a regular basis and at the castle. That should give you ample cover to plant the stone and get out of sight before the spell ends, and you look like yourself again."

Jonathan nodded in understanding. "What is our goal in this charade?"

Lelanda shook her head. "The less you know, the better. Just know that your success will be a great help to the city, in more ways than one. Now take my hand, and we'll get started."

CHAPTER

THIRTY-FIVE

An hour later, in the light of the midday sun, Thena, Tegin, and Lelanda all stood atop the castle peering through spyglasses toward the north area of the market, watching a heavy-set tradesman walk from the castle kitchen wing to the alleys.

Just behind them on the platform lay the unconscious Braegen, prepped and ready for teleportation. The three of them watched Jonathan wander into one of the storage alleys with a bag of grain. A few minutes later, he came out and knelt to adjust his shoe.

"Okay, there's the signal. So far, so good," said Tegin.

Lelanda turned and knelt by Braegen. She lay one hand on his chest and, with the other, made the symbol used for teleportation. He was gone in a blink.

"He should be in place. I made my focus some inches above the focus stone, so he should lightly plop down onto the ground."

THIRTY-SIX

Braegen moaned as he cracked his eyelids and peered around. His head was spinning, his stomach was doing flips in his gut, and his head pounded.

He could tell it was midday by the shadows in the alley. But, he had no inkling as to what alley he was in, how he got into the alley, or why he was even alive.

The last thing he remembered was fighting in the castle, then a sharp pain on the back of his head, and everything went dark. He rolled onto his side and cleared his nose and throat and spit on the ground. No blood. That was a good sign.

Braegen staggered to his feet using some bags of grain as a prop. He was dizzy and woozy—he assumed from getting hit on the head.

He took a moment to gather himself. Based on the sounds and smells, he must be north of the market. Not a bad place to wake up when you don't want to be noticed. He brushed himself off. All of his clothes were there, but his weapons were missing, and he left all his monetary possessions back at the guild.

First, he needed to find out how long he had been out. If he didn't check in within three days, all his possessions would be absorbed by the guild. He had built up a nice little nest egg for himself and needed to get back soon. He stretched his arms, legs, and back along with cracking his neck for good measure.

His primary goal would be to shake any tails that may be on him. Nobody ever went to the guild during the day, and for good reason. Any person off the street knew it was easier to slip a tail at night than it is during the day. He would have to lay low for a bit until it was more advantageous for him.

Braegen dug into the waistband of his trousers and found the silver that he always kept hidden there for emergencies. It was right where he put it, sewn into the waistband. He felt like he hadn't eaten in days.

Now that the foggy sensation was starting to leave him, his hunger was becoming more and more apparent. A pint and some stew sounded good right now. It would burn off some of the time until dark. He left the coin where it was so he wouldn't lose it and walked to the entrance of the alley.

The bright daylight blinded him, and he almost walked straight into a patrol.

"Hey, watch where you are walking, sir!" one of the guards rang out.

"My apologies, lads," he said as he stumbled back out of their way. The guards looked him up and down.

"You have someplace to be?" one of them shouted at him.

"Yes, I'm just heading over for some lunch at the pub," he replied.

"You best be on your way, then. We don't like seeing people just lollygaggin' near an alley, even when we don't have a city-wide lockdown in place. So, move on before you find yourself behind bars."

Braegen turned away from the guards and walked toward the pub. He had been on his feet for maybe ten minutes and was almost thrown in prison for just being outside. Probably had something to do with the action he was involved in at the castle. Whatever resulted must not have been good for the city. Time will tell if it was good for the guild.

He had spent time in a few guilds across Crescent Moon. None of them ever did anything to bring more attention to it than what was needed to stay profitable.

At most, they might corrupt an official or two and take over the dockyards or charge merchant fees. But never take on the head of state—that was just suicide. But, if Corax was involved, you could bet that anything was possible.

He was the fiercest leader he had ever seen and the most unforgiving. If he had brought the heat on the guild, then that would be the only way this could blow over. If he wasn't involved, then he was pretty sure that someone was going to die.

Braegen kept his head down and made it to the pub with no more incidents. This pub was one he used when he had a hankering for stew. They had the best stew around, and it felt great to get a nice bowl of it in the colder months to warm his bones.

The tavern was small and focused more toward blue-collar workers like miners and simple traders. It was great for blending in.

He ordered a pint of ale, a large bowl of stew, and some bread. He found a quiet corner and ate his fill. Then, he sat back and nursed his second ale and tried to remember anything from after he was knocked out.

Nothing was coming to him. Then, he started figuring out the route he was going to take to lose any tails he might have. Nobody suspicious came in after him, and nobody paid him any mind. That boosted his confidence.

THIRTY-SEVEN

Tegin and Thena were monitoring the progress of Braegen via the spotters and runners. They had lost track of him for a bit after he left the alley. Reports came in not long after that he made his way to a nearby pub and was eating.

They all agreed he was buying time until dark when he would be much more difficult to tail. Now it was a waiting game. All eyes were on the pub. When he made his move, they would be as ready as they could be.

Tegin knew it would come down to the tracking ability of Lelanda and not of the group of spotters and trackers. That never worked. Their ace up the sleeve was Lelanda. If everything worked out, Tegin and Thena would be kicking the crap out of a dwarf by morning and sticking his head on Skull Gate by mid-afternoon.

Thena saw Tegin smirking to himself. "What's so funny?"

He looked up at her. "Ahh, I was just thinking about what I'm going to do when we catch Corax."

"You too, huh?" she replied.

They went back to sitting in silence and waiting for dark.

THIRTY-EIGHT

It had been two days since the king had been assassinated. As dusk settled in on the mountain city of Sandown, all bets were on an unknowing rogue leading the king's avengers to the doorstep of the assassin.

Braegen had nursed his second and third drinks while he figured out his path. He knew now from listening in on bar conversations that there was a curfew in effect until further notice. Everyone was to be off the streets by 9:00 p.m. and not allowed back out until 5:00 a.m. the next morning.

It was dark by seven. That left him quite a bit of time to lose any would-be pursuers. The streets being clear would be a good and bad thing for him. It would be harder to follow someone without being noticed. It was also easier to be tracked from a further distance. However, the guild had ways around that.

Braegen paid his bar tab and headed for the door. He had yet to come upon anybody he knew. That part was sort of odd. He ran into fellow guildmates multiple times a day, and they did frequent the pub he just left.

He left the pub and walked a twisting, turning path. He never came across the same person twice. Another good sign. He tried to stay near the center of the city, away from the prying eyes of the city walls. With all the guards he saw lining the walls earlier in the day, he would be hard-pressed to evade their watchful eyes.

He turned down a blind alley and ducked into a front used by the guild to peddle random goods, like vases, chairs, and other furniture. A quick turn down the stairs led him to a secret underground hallway he accessed via a hidden shifting wall. That led to another front used by the guild. He came to the stairs leading up and ran face-first into Corax coming down the stairs.

Braegen didn't recognize him at first because he was in disguise, but the stature and beard couldn't be mistaken.

"Pardon me," he said as he continued by Corax.

Corax never said a word. He just watched Braegen go up the stairs and disappear around the corner. Braegen's hair was standing up on his neck. That was closer than he ever wanted to get to his guild master . . . ever.

He went up two flights above ground and peered around to make sure nobody was around. He pulled a knob on a coat rack on the second floor. That opened the wall to a hollow area with a long pole mounted in it. He grabbed the pole and closed the wall behind him. He made sure it slid into place. He waited for a minute and listened for anybody following him.

After listening for a minute or so, he didn't hear anything creaking on the floor. He slid down four floors, landing with a thump at the bottom and pushing the stone surface in front of him to the side, allowing access to an entry point at the guild.

The weird part was that nobody was guarding the entrance. He walked in and headed straight for storage to report in. The old man who ran it was sleeping in his chair when he came up. Braegen cleared his throat to wake him.

"I'm reporting in. Name's Braegen."

The old man snorted as he woke from his nap. He peered at him and started flipped through his checklist.

"I wasn't sure I'd be seeing anybody else. I stayed only because there are a few stashes left here unaccounted for. I get to keep them if nobody shows. You're lucky; you had little less than a day left before yours turned into mine," he said with a chuckle.

He dug around in the back and pulled up a small chest and a sack for Braegen.

"Yeah? So, what is going on around here? Why wasn't there anybody at the entrance when I came in?"

The old man peered at him. "You been under a rock? The boss disbanded the guild yesterday!"

Just as he said that, the old man's face became pale.

"I certainly did," a voice behind him replied.

The hair on Braegen's neck stood up again. *Shit!* How was he going to talk himself out of this? He turned to see Corax leaning against a chair maybe fifteen feet from him.

"I saw you in the stairwell and figured you were on your way in. Just doing the ol' tail check, I see." Corax stared at Braegen.

"Yes, I wanted to make certain I wasn't being followed as per the usual. Being hated and all makes you check your six often when coming home." Braegen shifted nervously.

"So, what's the rush? I mean other than the fact that the guild was disbanded. But you just said you didn't know that."

"Um, yeah . . . I wanted to make my time limit, and I didn't know how much time I had left."

"Why is that?" replied Corax.

Braegen scratched his head. "I . . . I woke in an alley late this morning, and I don't remember anything before that."

"Interesting." Corax took a couple of steps toward Braegen.

"Weren't you part of the group that entered the castle the other night?"

"Uhh, yeah. I was part of that group."

"Well, look at this. The only survivor to make it from the castle. Isn't that somethin', Ol' Pete?" Corax mused.

"Yea, boss, that is," Pete responded with a look of sympathy on his face.

"You know . . . nobody should have lived through that," said Corax as he came within a couple feet of Braegen and stopped.

He put his hand on Braegen's shoulder.

"I guess I was lucky," responded Braegen.

"Lucky? Noooo. See, I have a nose for these things. I have the lieutenant lead a squad for a suicide mission as a distraction. Nobody should live. If they live, then that means they were captured, or they fled."

Beads of sweat started to appear on Braegen's face.

"You come in here, no weapons, can't remember anything between the fight and waking up in some strange place. That can only mean one thing."

His grip tightened on Braegen's shoulder, causing him to scream out and drop to his knees. Corax leaned in close and whispered, "One of those bitch mages got their hooks in you and are probably tracking you right now."

Corax relaxed his grip on Braegen's shoulder and grabbed his neck. "Ol' Pete. What's he got in the chest?"

The old man grabbed a crowbar and pried open the small chest.

"Mix of gold and silver . . . maybe a hundred to hundred fifty silver and two hundred to three hundred gold," he replied.

Corax turned back to Braegen. "Nice haul you have there . . . you could live a simple life on that amount. Tell you what . . ."

Corax let Braegen get to his feet.

"I will give you one shot with your dagger. You hit the knob on the top of the nearest chair over there, and I'll let you see how far you can get with that nest egg of yours. If you miss . . . well, I'm sure you can fill in the bits there."

Braegen stood up straight and reached for his dagger . . . then remembered it was missing.

"I, uh, I don't have a dagger, boss."

Corax looked up at him. "Oh yeah? Here, use MINE!"

Corax whipped out his dagger and drove it toward Braegen's neck. Braegen was able to get his hand up in time in a feeble attempt to block the strike, but the dagger sank right through it and into his neck. Corax slammed him into the stone wall of the storage area, leaving him dangling off the floor by a couple of inches with the dagger sunk through his hand, neck, and into the stone wall.

Corax spit on him. "Idiot! You jeopardized everything I have for that worthless pile of gold and silver!"

Ol' Pete had disappeared under the desk he was at until he heard Corax's boots on the hard stone floor disappear in the distance. He poked his head out to see Braegen pinned to the wall, lifeless. Blood was still pouring from his mouth and throat onto the floor.

"Poor bastard. Well, I guess you won't be needin' this."

Pete poured the contents of Braegen's chest into his own. He flipped on his cloak and bid farewell to the hanging body of Braegen.

"Thanks for the retirement, chap. Better you than me."

He headed in the opposite direction Corax went.

THIRTY-NINE

Lelanda, Tegin, and Thena had all moved down to a small discreet staging area near the city guard headquarters while the trackers and spotters attempted to follow Braegen after his drop in the alley.

Word came in that he had moved from the pub. Soon after, he lost the trackers in an area of storefronts.

The trio stood over a map of the city.

"Our team said they lost him around here," Tegin said as he pointed to a row of storefronts on the map. "A few of these have had questionable dealings where lost belongings somehow found their way to their sales floors.

With Braegen's disappearance in this area, it seems we were correct in our suspicions that the guild owns a couple of storefronts here that they utilize for access to and from the guild," he continued. "We could spend days trying to find the entrances without dismantling the stores one by one."

Lelanda jumped in. "The spell I put on Braegen's clothing won't wear off for a few days. We need to move fast. If he happens to leave the guild again before we can pinpoint the guild's location, we'll lose our chance to find the entrance."

Just then, Lelanda's eyes closed as if she were listening to something far away. When she opened them, she turned to Thena and Tegin.

"I'm being requested to appear on the front. Gunner needs my assistance. He's never utilized my speaking stone before, so it must be urgent."

"Crap, that couldn't come at a worse time," Tegin responded. "How are we supposed to locate the guild when you have the tracking spell? I sure as blazing hell ain't going to cast it!" he exclaimed in frustration.

Lelanda turned to Thena. "You'll have to come with me. If it isn't something quick, then I'll instruct you on the spell so you can return and assist."

She laid her hand on Tegin's shoulder. "You know I have to go; our friend is in need."

Tegin nodded. "Aye, I know. Keep him safe, lass, and you two as well. I'll hold down the fort here and continue the search. I know you'll get back as soon as you can."

Thena grasped Lelanda's hand as she uttered words of magic. In a blink, both Thena and she were nothing but wisps of smoke. Tegin scratched his well-groomed beard and turned to a couple of guards nearby.

"Nothing left for tonight. I might as well get some rest and start fresh in the morning. Hold down the fort, boys. Rouse me if something changes. I will see everyone in the morn."

FORTY

The general stood in a spotting tower on the northern side of Solec when Lelanda and Thena appeared a few feet from him. Thena, not having teleported in quite a while, wobbled over to a nearby chair to catch her breath. Lelanda acknowledged the general with a wary glance.

"What is the emergency?" she asked.

"I apologize for requesting direct aid from you so suddenly. But we spotted what looks to be a small force coming in to counterattack. A scout spotted them less than a day out coming in from the west."

He pointed at his map on the table. Thena got up to join them both at the map now that she had her senses back.

"Were they able to get an accurate number of the size of the force?" asked Thena.

Lelanda just studied the map as the general spoke.

"We are estimating a force of five hundred with

a couple of giants. No word of any casters, elementals, or dragons. It could be a probing attack to see what fortifications we have put in place since we took the city. We know it isn't their counterattack, though I would expect a full force to attack sometime after we repel this one. Letharia has chaotic leadership, so it's hard to tell what they might do. Sandown and Minsfet are also on alert for anything suspicious. This is where we expect the attack to be. We insulted them by beating a larger force and by taking one of their cities."

The general gave a shrug. "The citizens seem to be quite content with our occupation. Though, I believe they want us to be here after seeing how we treat them versus how they had been treated."

He stepped back from the table, grinned, and sighed as he looked over Thena and Lelanda. "It does my heart good to see the both of you."

He reached out his big arm and pulled Thena in close while Lelanda stayed just out of reach. She smiled beneath her always-present hood. Thena hugged her friend hard as tears welled up in her eyes. She blinked them away as they separated. The general looked into her eyes.

"Don't worry, little one. We'll have time to grieve our king . . ." he sighed, "our friend . . . once this mess is cleaned up. For now, we must bear the weight of the world and, together, we will. Evil cannot win out over good; in the end, good will always overcome."

The general looked past Thena as memories of the past flitted into his head. He blinked them away.

"So, what news from the east?" he asked.

His plate armor grated against itself as he sat on a nearby stool. Lelanda leaned against the wall near the corner of the little twelve-by-eight-foot room. The general looked over at Lelanda, who always seemed to be thinking of defense even in a secure location by keeping her back to a wall.

Thena spoke up. "After . . . well . . . you know . . ." She cleared her throat. "We were able to capture a rogue that had raided the castle. Which, as it turned out, was a distraction to keep the castle guards away from the Royal Wing. The next morning, we sighted the assassin as he attempted to re-enter the city through a secret passage dug into a rock outcropping some distance from the city walls. In the attempt to slay or capture him, he caused a cave-in that sealed the entrance. Tegin surmised that he has to be trapped in the city due to the lockdown."

"If that doorway was all that existed, then I would agree that there is a good chance that he is still hiding out either in or near the guild. Since the lockdown, most moves by the guild have ceased. Though, we have seen a rise in pickpockets where people are camped out near the gates waiting to leave. We have added more guards on the streets for added protection." she said.

She looked over at Lelanda. "Lelanda?"

Lelanda leaned forward a bit. "As Thena said, we captured a single rogue who was attempting to escape the castle after we turned the tables on them. I personally interrogated him in my mountain home but wasn't able to glean much from him. He isn't important in the comings and goings of the guild. I would theorize that was a common ingredient amongst those that attacked us based on what they were wearing and how most of them smelled."

The general wrinkled his nose at the thought of that.

"What I did find out was not at all pleasant."

The general's eyebrow raised at the sound of that, but he kept quiet as Lelanda went on.

"The rogue, Braegen, told me that the guild leader's name is Corax. He is confirmed to be a dwarf. The abnormal thing about him is that he is unrealistically strong by the explanation I got out of our prisoner."

"How so?" inquired the general.

"He crushed a man's ankle just by squeezing it, then slammed him against a wall until he was nothing but a lump of flesh."

"You think he is augmented by magic?" Gunner asked. "I believe that is safe to assume. It would have to be something he wears or carries. Dwarves cannot cast magic or have spells cast on them. At best, they can be levitated. It would be the first time in the history of the world that one ever has practiced magic. All evidence points at something he's wearing. If I had to guess, I'd say boots, scabbard, gloves, or bracers. Those are the standard items chosen for enchantments, right?"

Lelanda nodded. "Rings and amulets are much rarer, primarily due to their size. It is difficult to get the power of the spell to take hold of a small bauble like a ring or amulet. Not saying it can't be done, but unlikely," she said as she held up her hands to show that she did not wear any rings.

"I wasn't able to get the location of the guild out of him. He would have taken it to the grave or, at the very least, provided the wrong location. He is quite afraid of his boss, Corax. I thought it better to put him to sleep and wipe his memories of being captured. I then enchanted his boots and the hem of his shirt with a spell I have been developing for this very thing. It still has many limitations, though. I should be able to feel a pull toward the enchanted object if I'm within range.

"The rogue was in an alley prior to him waking up. We tracked him as best we could, but he hid out in a pub until dusk. After that, we lost track of him in the dark alleys. We know the area we lost him in, and I was about to utilize my spell when your request for assistance came in."

The general ran his fingers through his fiery red beard.

"This is unfortunate. I need you here," he said as he motioned to Lelanda, "to stay and assist with repelling this attack and with a strategy for what will be a coming counterattack."

"I already thought of that. That is why Thena is with me instead of back in the city with Tegin. She knows her way around a spell book. The tracking spell isn't difficult to cast, so I should be able to teach her how to cast it within a couple of hours."

"That is going to cut it close," the general responded. "But it is what it is. Okay, you two get on with that. Thena, you and Tegin are doing a fine job back at the city. Keep up the pressure on the guild. Focus on learning Lelanda's spell. Then, get yourself back to Sandown and find that murdering bastard."

Lelanda nodded. "What about you?"

"What about me?"

"Stalken passed his legacy on to you. You should be headed back to the city as well," she stated.

"Don't get ahead of yourself, Lelanda," grumped the general as he leaped to his feet. "I'm needed here. Plus, with an assassin trapped in the city, I don't see that as the best strategy right now. Nobody other than our inner circle has any idea that I'm next in line. I'm worried enough about the rest of my friends having to combat this evil bastard without me. I'll be damned if I'm going to lock myself in a room just because I'm the next in line to rule!"

He shooed at them. "Now get on with what you need to get done and find me after so we can figure out how to deal with this rabble. I have to go find my second and see if he has anything new for me."

Lelanda and Thena both nodded. Thena gave the general a goodbye hug before she followed Lelanda out the door.

The general gazed out of the window to the north. He was quite fond of those two elves. They had become like sisters to him. Yet they both dealt with hardship in very different ways.

Lelanda was always closed off, probably due to her dark elf past and stereotyped race. She'd always been that way. Like a wise big sister who doesn't want to burden those around her with her troubles.

Thena was like a little sister. She was used to sharing her feelings and depending on her friends to help her through stressful times. Very un-mage-like. But she was a stout fighter and lightning-fast with a blade. Her spells centered around making her a better swordswoman rather than a wizard. He shook himself out of his gaze.

"Time to get moving," he commented to himself. He took one last glance at the map on the table and turned, and walked out.

FORTY-ONE

Lelanda and Thena found a quiet place to study so that Thena could learn the tracking spell Lelanda had developed. It wasn't a complicated spell to Lelanda.

However, Thena was having some trouble due to differences between the spell and the types of spells that she used.

She never bothered with non-combative spells. All of hers were either defensive or offensive in nature. But she was starting to grasp it.

While they worked together on that, the general headed over to find Captain McLeod, who was probably helping his men dig murder holes or shovel muck around for some reason or another.

He chuckled to himself at the thought. McLeod was very deserving of being his second. His men would follow him into the gaping maw of a dragon if he wished it. He always led by example, and his men loved him for it. He toiled with them in the trenches and fought with them shoulder to shoulder. Plus, he was a lifelong friend.

The general called for a runner to find the

colonel. He continued to wander toward the direction he thought his friend might be while he thought back to the paths that led them here.

Years before, the two wily swordsmen had met while escorting merchants from city to city as they roamed the land. They traveled all over and had become fast friends, like brothers.

Then they happened upon a dark elf and a dwarf, and their whole world was turned upside down. He chuckled again as the memories flooded him like a river. Some great times and some not-so-great times he had experienced with them.

All the while, his adopted brother McLeod had his back and would continue to do so. He came around a corner and saw McLeod with a group of his men. He stopped and watched them smiling all the while.

McLeod had his wooden training sword and his shield out. He circled one of his men left and then to the right in front of a small group of his soldiers.

"See how I keep my sight line just above my shield? If I hold the shield to the left or right of my sight line, then I am blind from the left or right. I always bring my shield back to this point after a block or parry."

The younger cadet waited for McLeod to shift his sight line to the incorrect vantage, and he rushed in with his training sword on McLeod's blind side. McLeod anticipated it and twirled to his left. He flicked his wooden sword up to parry the cadet's attack high. He continued with his spin to bring his sword around to slap the back of his cadet's neck with the flat of his sword.

"Never assume the opponent is blind just because his shield is to the left or right of his sight line. As you can see, that can get you killed. You must make every attack a chess move. Every attack followed by a defense; otherwise, you have nothing to counter with."

McLeod looked around to the other soldiers watching. "My parry left him with no way to defend himself. That's why I fight with a shield and sword. If you come up against a larger foe with a two-handed weapon, you can frustrate them by deflecting their blows with the shield. Then, attack with the sword or defend with both."

"What about another opponent with a sword and shield?" asked the cadet.

McLeod smiled. "Then you just have to be better at shieldwork than your opponent. This is why we . . . what?" he yelled.

"TRAIN!" yelled back the group in unison.

Just then, he saw the general watching them as they were practicing.

"Group, TEN-HUT!"

"At ease, boys," replied the general.

"Colonel, a word," said the general as he waved the captain over.

"All right, boys, grab some chow and jump on those tasks I handed out earlier. I'll join you when I can."

The group started off as the colonel joined the general by a small fire he had sat down near. Gunner started poking at the flames with a stick.

"I see you're sharing your years of wisdom with the men." The general smirked.

"I wish I had someone as handsome and forth-coming as myself to bestow upon me proper technique when I was their age," the colonel joked back.

The general chuckled, then looked up at him. "Lelanda has joined us. She brought news about the assassin. He's a dwarf and augmented with great strength. Sounds like he knows how to use it, too. Not unlike someone who stumbles upon such items and dies while trying to do something stupid. They are close to finding him, I believe. I pray that when they do, they do so as a group and not one on one. A being like that is not to be trifled with."

McLeod nodded.

"She is going to stay for the coming skirmish. We are going to get together tonight to strategize, and I'll need my *general* there," he stated with a smirk.

"Sure, sure, I'll be . . . wait, what did you call me?"

"General . . . you have a problem with that?"

"Ha! Me? Noooo. Just thought for a minute that I needed to get my hearing checked by a cleric. So, if I'm a general now, what does that make you? Stalken make you king?"

"He did. It hasn't been made official yet, but all those that matter know. Once this mess is dealt with, I'll have to attend some ceremony to inform the kingdom. Until then, just keep calling me by my name or general. Your status as of now is general, however. I've sent runners to inform the men. You'll have to appoint a colonel to replace you."

"I have someone in mind. If he survives the skirmish tomorrow, I'll let him know," replied McLeod.

"One last thing," Gunner said as he got up.

"Make certain your boys don't take those sticks onto the field of battle by mistake tomorrow."

Mcleod waved away his words. "Please, my boys are so good they could whip a giant with one!"

"They'll get the chance tomorrow, then."

"Hmm," McLeod replied. "No need showing off. I'll make sure they have metal ones tomorrow. I'll catch up with you after I get with my boys . . . sire," he said with a wink.

"Shut it!" Gunner replied as he walked off.

FORTY-TWO

That night Lelanda finished training Thena on her tracking spell. Thena found a place to get some rest while Lelanda, McLeod, and Gunner studied the map and laid plans for the skirmish that looked set to happen by afternoon of the next day.

The three sat at a small round table with a map in the center. Different colored stones allowed them to mark their units and the enemy units.

"Moving giants takes a lot of resources and slows the army's speed. You can only go as fast as your slowest unit. We have counted two hill giants. They'll either hold them back while the other units try and soften us up or send them in first. I suppose they could just charge in with all five hundred at once. You can never tell with these guys, so we have to plan for all three," said Gunner.

"What about option four?" Mcleod asked.

"What option four?" Gunner replied as he and Lelanda looked at McLeod.

"You know, the one where the hill giants get in

an argument and start fighting each other and kill their allies and each other while we look on."

Lelanda and Gunner looked at each other and then at McLeod, who was grinning from ear to ear. Gunner and Lelanda looked at each other and smiled.

"Anyway . . ." Gunner paused with a smirk. "Those are the three I would expect. If option four does happen, I'll order Lelanda to turn me into a chicken." Lelanda offered up a rare laugh.

"What defenses do we have?" Gunner looked over at McLeod.

McLeod started pointing at various points around the city walls. "We have nine catapults. Two north, two west, two east, two south, and the oddball we placed north-west. That is the direction we think they will come. We are building more, but those will not be close to ready before tomorrow afternoon.

"We have two ballistae. One south and one north. Ten more are expected when reinforcements arrive later in the week. The three trebuchets are deeper in the city, but we won't have experienced crews on them until we get men from Sandown to operate them.

"I'm leaving those inactive for the battle. We have about 1865 able-bodied soldiers ready to fight, give or take five or so. About four hundred are archers, which I spread as evenly as possible around the walls.

Speaking of walls, we have been able to restore all the walled sections around the entire city, including those areas destroyed when we took the city. We have murder holes dug about fifty yards out in front of the wall to slow normal-sized humanoids."

McLeod continued. "Giants are another concern. We could get lucky and catch one with the ballista, but they have to come from the south or north for us to get a shot at them. Hill giants' skin is resistant to arrows. Even if they pierce the skin, they won't even notice them. We've trained our soldiers in how to defend against giants. Simply put, lay down with your weapon braced against the ground when they stomp on you . . ."

Lelanda jumped in. "Easiest way will be to take the giants off their feet. I have some spells that should assist with that. The other mages we have here have been briefed as to what to do. My focus and theirs will be the giants. Since we don't have airborne attacks coming this time, that will free us up to focus on more dangerous ground units. That doesn't mean they won't have a mage or two tucked in that rabble, though. If I see that, I'll switch over and focus our mage attacks on them." McLeod nodded, and both he and Lelanda looked over at Gunner.

"All right, that seems like a solid defense. I'll be watching from a high perch and coordinating with our message flaggers as the skirmish progresses. I am hoping for the best result here. We will need every able body for the main battle later on. Getting those giants down fast will be top priority. Let's pray no mage slips through to get spells on the main body of our forces. Let's break off for tonight and get some good rest. I want everyone to be well-rested and well-fed before the battle. We're going to need it.

CHAPTER

FORTY-THREE

The embattlements were prepared the best they could, and the soldiers dug in at their positions hours prior to the first glimpse of the small attacking force. The lumbering hill giants were easy to pick out from miles away. They flanked either side of the attacking force.

Gunner had a great vantage point that Lelanda helped him locate and prepare. She cast an illusion over his position that would hide his presence from anyone looking that way.

It allowed him to see the battlefield without the danger of being noticed. This would help him to get word out if their battle tactics needed to be changed.

The city was situated on a flat plane, making it easy to see anything coming from far off. It looked as though the force was on a collision course with the northwest side of the city. This would allow five of the nine catapults to train their fire on the attacking force as long as they stayed the course. No sign of mages, but they tended to stay out of sight because of their high value.

The five or so mages onsite had created magical barriers that would disrupt any invisibilities passing through or over the city walls that extended up around fifty feet. At least, that was how Lelanda explained it.

He hadn't seen Lelanda since she said she was going to get into position. What position that was, he didn't know. He let her freelance in battles for a few reasons. One, she was so fluid and knowledgeable about battle that she made the right adjustments to assist whatever area needed the most aid. Two, she had a better grasp of the battlefield than he did. Of course, he would never admit to such a thing. Finally, she would not listen to anything he told her anyway, so it was pointless to try.

The tactics were quite simple. If the attacking force stayed grouped together, then the catapults would focus on the center mass of the oncoming force. The archers would also have an easier time hitting something clustered together at max range. If the enemy tried to disperse, then that would make it easier on the soldiers. They were well trained in overwhelming small groups.

The phalanx was an integral part of their battle plan. The army also utilized small groups of soldiers that preferred two-handed weapons such as the great sword, war axe, or heavy hammer. Those would be important against the giants to an extent. The phalanx was a style of combat that used shields locked together to form a wall. Even heavy horse had difficulty in breaking a well-trained phalanx.

The Sandown archers manning the walls were no mere run-of-the-mill archers. They trained under the most rigorous conditions to improve their aim and power and were not allowed into the main force until they passed their archery trials in both performance and mental aptitude. These archers rivaled any kingdom's, including that of the elves.

The foot soldiers also underwent rigorous training that tested their body, mind, and spirit to the breaking point. The best of the best were allowed to enter service in the elite guard that protected the castle grounds and the king. The best of those were allowed to protect the king himself. Some city guardsmen were also picked from time to time, though the majority came from the army ranks.

Gunner thought about all of this as the enemy approached. He had every confidence in his men and even the few women who chose to make the commitment. Stalken always wanted the best fighting force they could muster, and Gunner made it his duty to ensure that was so. It paid dividends when the war started.

Gunner watched the approaching force as it came within a mile of the city. They had not strayed from their course. The hill giants were starting to roar as they worked themselves up in anticipation of attacking the city. They each carried the typical tree-sized clubs that they preferred to smash and crush anything with that came into range. Hill giants were not known for their intelligence or battle prowess. By sheer size, they could sweep away entire groups of men. That didn't require a lot of tactical knowledge on their part.

He wondered where and when Lelanda and her small cadre of mages would strike. They would focus on the giants to try and get them down them as fast as possible. He guessed she would wait until the first volley of fire from catapults and archers so as to distract from their initial attack.

FORTY-FOUR

L elanda hovered about sixty feet above and a bit behind the defensive wall. An aggressive tactic, to be certain, but she took precautions.

She had an invisibility spell that would cover her until she attacked. A slow fall spell was ready if needed. If that failed, she was hovering above a large mound of hay that would cushion her fall. It would not feel good, but she would live. Better to be safe than sorry, she thought.

She watched and waited. The signal was to have three mages hit the hill giant to the west while she took on the larger one that flanked to the right. The other mages in the city were to monitor the city and check for other casters that might try and infiltrate their defenses.

Most kingdoms used their mages sparingly. A good mage took a lifetime to build up. It may take five to ten years to get a lesser mage like the ones Lelanda was leading.

Getting one killed in a skirmish could decimate

a kingdom's magical knowledge for years or even decades, depending on their system of training.

Lelanda was special. Being almost immortal compared to the lives of other beings, she had been studying magic for over a hundred years. She was at the point now where she understood the essence of magic and was developing her own spells and incantations.

Her first spell would require much concentration. It was the reason she preferred to use it on her initial attack. The enemy was getting close now. The one hundred or so dark riders riding black horses led the attack.

A mix of pikemen and swordsmen made up the girth of the force. She guessed their numbers coming in around three hundred strong. Crossbowmen made up the rest. They had a slower rate of fire but a greater range than the archers. That could be problematic if they were accurate. She would need to keep an eye on them.

FORTY-FIVE

General McLeod stood with his men. The heavy horse dark riders, as they called them, were starting to separate a bit from the main force as they gathered speed. Just as they did, he heard the sound of battle start as the closest catapult let loose a shot. He watched it arc out. The riders split open a gap that that boulder went through missing them and crushing just a few of the oncoming soldiers.

"They fired that one too soon," he said to his men. "They should have waited for the archers to release first."

The giants were howling and stomping as they started picking up speed. He could feel the ground shake with each stomp.

"Get ready, men!" he yelled.

All along the line, shields came up in preparation. Off in the distance, he saw little black lines erupt from the far end of the enemy's ranks.

"INCOMING!" he yelled almost in unison with others in their line.

Crossbow bolts started hitting their shields not

long after that, with a few screams coming from nearby.

"Steady, men!" he shouted.

He pulled his sword from its sheath just as a crossbow bolt whizzed past his ear and struck a soldier's shield behind him. He looked up as all the archers fired in unison, sending hundreds of arrows into the air.

Two more catapults fired, one from his far left and another far right. These shots were more effective. The hail of arrows distracted the would-be targets, who didn't see the large boulders coming until it was too late.

The soldiers roared in approval as both made direct hits into the center of the oncoming enemy. The horses were almost upon them when some of them started disappearing into the murder holes that were dug and the bottoms lined with barbed stakes. Those took down maybe a dozen riders. Another volley of arrows, this time directed at the riders, took down another dozen or so.

At that point, the riders fanned out in two directions, one heading east and another west.

"Stand fast, men!" came the call from McLeod and his sergeants.

The main force was in a dead sprint coming at the wall of shields.

"Fire at will!" came the call from the wall.

A steady stream of arrows started firing out. In came another volley of bolts from the enemy as screams of agony started filling the air.

The giants were getting quite close now. The giant to the west of McLeod's position had a mishap when his leading foot landed on a sudden patch of ice that formed out of nowhere.

A few mages became visible an instant later as faint wisps of white streamed from their hands toward the ground where the giant's lead foot landed. The giant had managed to do the splits as his lead foot slid forward on the ice while his back foot was firmly planted on the dry ground behind him.

He howled in pain as sinew strained and tore from the weight of his own body. Arrows started hitting him around the head as maybe five groups of ten berserkers sprinted toward the giant.

Just then, the main body of the force hit the line. McLeod braced himself as a body slammed into his shield. He slipped his sword out with lightning speed and sunk it into the man's ribs through an opening in his shield made for that very purpose. Bodies slammed into the line, and some flipped over the shield line as it became a mass of men and clashing steel. Those that had penetrated the first line were cut down, and the lines reformed as orders were called out to maintain the phalanx formation.

FORTY-SIX

Gunner watched the scene as it unfolded before him. The first catapult had fired too soon, but the first volley of arrows, along with the two catapults that fired after, must have taken out fifty or more of their numbers. They just kept coming. The mages had taken down the first giant. He had never seen a giant do the splits. The thought of the pain from that made him wince.

The giant was down, but not out. They'd have to keep an eye on it.

Berserkers were approaching that one to finish it off. The main force made contact with the phalanx, and the horsemen split into two groups heading in opposite directions around the perimeter of the city.

The injured giant swatted a few soldiers away but couldn't muster much of a threat in that position and was overwhelmed by about fifty of his finest, slashing and spearing the hill giant in the neck in an attempt to bleed him out.

His attention was drawn to the second hill giant when a white flash erupted near it. One of its legs was suddenly enveloped in ice. Lelanda appeared hovering in the sky just to the east. The hill giant howled in anger. He smacked and bashed the ice forming around his leg with his tree-sized club. It was forming much faster than he could smash it away.

Gunner watched as four small spheres flew from Lelanda's hand, three of which struck the giant in the head and exploded in a fiery cloud. The fourth one landed in the giant's mouth as he howled in pain and frustration. When it exploded, it took off the hill giant's jaw and part of his face.

Gunner watched in awe as the giant toppled over like a huge tree. It was dead before it hit the ground. Its leg shattered as the hardened ice around its foot prevented it from moving. It twisted at an odd angle as the giant fell.

"Yes!" exclaimed Gunner under his breath. "The giants are down!"

He couldn't have hoped for a better start. He wasn't afraid of losing the battle; he was afraid it would go on too long, and he would lose too many soldiers to the giants. The mages had managed to turn the battle into a one-sided affair right out of the gate.

He surveyed the field and noted that the dark riders were looking like they were attempting to flank the city and come in from another direction. He motioned to the flaggers to make certain the riders were tracked, and that forces would meet them wherever they attempted to commit. They had lost almost half their number and had moved out of bow and catapult range as they moved around each side of the city.

The main force had met the phalanx line, and the line held. Now it was turning into a rout.

"We need to get some men on those crossbowmen that are out of range of our bows!" Gunner bellowed at a flagger standing by.

Lelanda still floated in the air like some odd statue. Gunner was watching her when some kind of magical energy came from near the crossbowmen. She started to fall, and Gunner's breath caught in his throat. Then she slowed. Another ball of energy shot out and was about to strike her when she disappeared.

"She's a big girl; she can take care of herself," he tried to reassure himself. "Get some horsemen out to those crossbowmen and be on the lookout for a mage in their ranks!" he bellowed again.

FORTY-SEVEN

Lelanda had managed to get her feather fall spell off before hitting the ground. She was just able to complete her teleport spell before the next spell came in on her.

She popped out of the teleport about thirty yards behind the crossbowmen. Without hesitation, she drew a symbol on the ground and muttered the exact pronunciation of the incantation to put up a weather wind shield around her to prevent projectiles from striking her.

The crossbowmen were so distracted with the battle in front of them that they didn't notice she had appeared behind them. She spun a slow circle in an attempt to find the mage that attacked her, knowing it was a dangerous spot she to be in. Even an inexperienced mage could dispel levitation. It was an easy spell to learn and counter.

However dangerous it was, it usually worked in bringing out the mage. Leandra wasn't able to spot the mage at this point, so she stayed crouched to present less of a target. Mage fights tended to be short-lived. Whoever was the first to strike had the upper hand unless the mages were experienced and had a lot of defensive spells in their arsenal.

If the crossbowmen saw her fighting the mage, she would be in great danger. She had to move with a purpose. Since she didn't see the mage, she decided to strike hard and fast against the crossbowmen. They were firing a steady stream of bolts at the archers and the phalanx while being out of range of any return fire.

Staying low, Leandra reached down and dug up some dirt from the ground. She drew a magical symbol of a circle surrounding a triangle, then put the dirt inside the circle. She made a nice little mound out of the dirt, then poured a bit of water onto the dirt from the small water flask she carried.

Whispering a chant, she raised her hand, which started to glow until it was above her head. Then, she turned it palm-down and slammed it into the muddy pile. She continued to chant while not taking her eyes off the crossbowmen.

The men were so busy reloading their crossbows and firing bolts that they didn't notice the ground starting to get soggy. They realized something was wrong when they started sinking into the ground.

Some of them managed to scramble out of the growing muck. Around seventy of the one hundred were caught in the sticky muck that kept drawing them down quicker and quicker. Panic started setting in as men tried in vain to move their legs. Some fell over and suffocated in the gooey mud as they were drawn under.

The men that had escaped looked on in horror as their brethren were sucked down into the mud trap. Some tried to help by reaching out their weapons or pulling off their clothes to try and make a rope, but most just stood there in shock.

A couple of the crossbowmen that had escaped noticed Lelanda some twenty to thirty yards away and alerted the others. Some of them started firing shots at her. The ones that came close were knocked away by her wind shield.

In the meantime, the men in the muck sunk lower and lower every second. Some were reaching their chest. Others who had toppled over were gone, dragged down by the oozing sludge. Most were screaming as it reached their necks.

Just as the spell was nearing its end, Lelanda was blasted off her feet backward, sending her sprawling on her back. She felt a pain in her ribs where the blast had struck, but it wasn't a crossbow bolt that had struck her.

She looked around. She hadn't killed all of the crossbowmen, but her spell had done its job. A handful of crossbowmen were still trying to hit her with bolts, but most were either dead or stuck chest-to-neck-deep in the spell she had cast. Now that she had been interrupted, the ground had started hardening. The men were stuck in solid earth.

About twenty yards past the men, she found the culprit that hit her—the mage. He was a young man around his mid-twenties, wearing a dark gray cloak with dark windswept hair.

From this distance, not much else could be made out. She saw him start to gesture another spell. She countered with a reflective spell based on what she deciphered by his gesture as being a magic bolt.

It was what she must have been hit by from that range. A light blue, almost white bolt shot from his hand and raced toward her. She gestured and deflected the minor spell with a wave of her hand. The nearby men, realizing they were now caught in the middle of a mage duel, scrambled away. Some noticed the city gate had opened, and cavalry was now closing in on them.

The mage seemed confident and continued walking toward Lelanda, gesturing again as a prismatic bubble popped into existence around him.

Lelanda knew the spell. It was a minor spell barrier. It absorbed most minor spells and gave power to the caster in return.

Spells were divided into a multitude of categories, but they were also labeled by their expertise. Minor spells usually were fast-casting spells that required minor concentration. They could be dispelled or deflected with ease by experienced mages. The minor spell barrier was a common spell used in combat by mages.

Lelanda went through the counters she could use. There were a few. She could dispel the barrier, which would give the mage another shot at her while she prepped another spell. She could also use a higher spell than the bubble could absorb.

The mage might get off another quick spell before she could cast a more powerful spell, disrupting her casting. She could put up her own minor spell barrier and see if he knew anything more powerful. Those were all possibilities. However, she liked to improvise and, in the end, chose a method that would end the fight all together.

A catapult boulder had landed not too far away from their fray earlier in the battle. She gestured a telekinesis spell and locked onto the boulder. The mage laughed when he saw her gesture because he knew what spell it was. He started casting a longer spell.

"You'll need more than that minor spell to get through this!" he shouted at her with a mocking laugh.

He wasn't laughing after the full force of a two thousand-pound boulder smashed into him from behind, crushing him flat. The spell barrier flickered out of existence as his life drained away.

"I don't hear you laughing now," she replied.

The telekinesis spell was used by mages to levitate small objects. The spell extended the reach of the mage. That meant that the mage could only levitate an object that they could move on their own.

The mage couldn't have known that Lelanda was enhanced by her swords. That allowed the boulder to be well within her ability to lift. The benefit was easy to see since she didn't have to worry about physical contact with the boulder. Thus, she didn't rip her arms out of their sockets or break them when she threw the boulder at the mage. It was a trick she had used many times, and it had saved her on more than one occasion. It was becoming a favorite tactic of hers.

She surveyed the battle. The cavalry was chasing down the rest of the crossbowmen. The phalanx had held the foot soldiers off while the bowmen had rained death from the city's walls.

Now that the mage was dead, the leftovers were in full flight away from the city in the direction they had come. The dark riders had retreated after finding no easy way into the city and left the battle behind them.

Lelanda grabbed her hood and pulled it back up. She made the symbol for teleportation, spoke the incantation, and was back at the general's side. He winced at her sudden appearance.

"Sometimes you scare the wits out of me when you do that," he said with a smile.

"That is part of the fun," she replied.

"I have not heard reports of the damages and casualties, but I don't think the fight could have gone better. Though, you did give me a bit of a scare when I saw you fall."

Lelanda smiled. "I'm happy it went well for us. We need this good fortune to continue if we're to survive the might of their army."

The general fell silent for a moment.

"That is why it was crucial for use to win this battle with as little damage as possible," replied Gunner.

Lelanda nodded. "I'll let you get back to the cleanup. I need to check on Thena's progress with the spell so that she can depart, and we can continue preparing."

The general clasped her shoulder. "Remember, only a day or two, and our numbers will be bolstered by reinforcements from Sandown and Minsfet. Plus, I have a surprise I doubt even you know about." He gave her a sly wink.

He called for a runner. A young boy about thirteen years of age darted into the small room from outside. The general patted him on the shoulder.

"Let's go find McLeod and see about the soldiers."

The boy smiled. "Yes, sir!"

The boy made a point to stay out of arms reach of the dark elf with the strange eyes. Lelanda frowned a bit within the shadows of her cloak. Even after all these years, people treated her with suspicion. The general picked up on her body language.

"You know, maybe if you come out from under that rock more often and open up to others other than your closest friends, people would treat you less like an outcast and more like an ally."

She looked over at him. "What makes you think I want people to think of me at all?"

He sighed . . . "If we survive the main battle, then maybe I'll answer that question over a pint of ale. For now, we must make haste."

He brushed past her to follow the boy out. Lelanda stood there for a moment. She worked so hard to keep everyone out of arms reach, just as the boy had done with her.

Yet, deep inside, all she wanted was to be accepted by the town she loved. Maybe Gunner was right. Maybe she needed to change the way she acted around others. She shook away the feeling and rushed off to find Thena.

FORTY-EIGHT

Thena had spent much of the morning practicing the spell Lelanda had taught her the previous evening. While Lelanda was prepping the mages for the skirmish, she practiced casting the spell on items and having a runner go and hide the item around town, like a game of hide and seek.

The spell was interesting. It didn't point to the location like a compass needle. It urged the caster to go in a certain direction, almost like an instinct or sixth sense. When she needed to go up or down, she either felt a lighter sensation or a heavier sensation. It was quite unnerving at first, but she was able to find items with relative ease after a few hours of practice.

When Thena heard the horns sound the enemy's approach, she found a cozy location on a rooftop to watch from. Lelanda instructed her to stay out of the fight unless something went wrong.

She did as requested and watched the fight with her very acute elven vision. She saw Lelanda fall when her levitation was dispelled. She also watched the duel between Lelanda and the mage with great interest and knew Lelanda had been hit by a spell. Thena hoped she wasn't hurt, but she knew Lelanda wouldn't say anything if she was.

Thena was now waiting for Lelanda where she had taught her the spell, looking over a map of the city she had acquired in one of the shops in town.

He seemed quite happy that Sandown forces now occupied the city he lived in. She had used the map to mark all the locations she had found objects that had been hidden by her runner. She was just finishing jotting down a couple of notes when Lelanda walked in.

Lelanda was straight to business.

"How did your practice go?"

Thena turned and smiled. "I found every hidden object by being patient. As you said when you were instructing me, the more patient and calm I became, the faster I could pinpoint the hidden objects."

Lelanda nodded her head in agreement. "Remember that when you're trying to locate Braegen. Since you didn't incant the charm yourself, it will be more difficult to attune yourself to the item. Don't go stumbling into a trap because it points you in a certain direction."

Thena smiled and waved her hand. "You forget that I direct soldiers . . ."

"Yes, but we are dealing with an individual that thwarted your soldiers . . ." Lelanda caught herself before she finished.

Thena blushed with emotion and turned away from Lelanda.

"I'm sorry. I didn't mean to say it that way."

Lelanda reached out to put her hand on Thena's shoulder. She checked her hand before she made contact.

"I know. It was my fault the king was assassinated, no matter how you say it. I have full responsibility for protecting the king, and I failed."

Tears dripped from her eyes onto the map she had been looking at. Lelanda took on a sad but knowing expression and stepped closer to Thena.

"We all lost a dear friend—" she was cut off by Thena.

"He was more than my friend, we were . . ." she trailed off. Thena drew her dagger and slammed it into the table a few times.

"I know of you two," replied Lelanda.

Thena turned to face Lelanda, tears streaking her beautiful face. "Then you have an inkling of how I feel."

Lelanda took a deep breath and sighed, "I do."

Thena pocketed her dagger. "I'm headed back to Sandown to finish this," she said and stormed out. Thena shouted back over her shoulder as Lelanda followed her out. "Don't let the city fall, and don't let our new king die in the coming battle!" With that, she incanted a teleport spell and vanished.

FORTY-NINE

Tegin sat in his tavern, having a warm glass of mead. He had not heard from the two elves in close to a day. He hoped that they were okay. His thoughts went to Gunner.

Stalken couldn't have picked a better replacement than the general. Besides being a good friend, he had known Stalken longer than anyone else. They were lifelong friends.

He was an amazing strategist, swordsman, natural leader, and moral man, everything that was needed to be a good king. It didn't make sense for any of the rest of the group to be in that position. The city was primarily human, and though dwarves and elves were well received in Sandown, a human king being replaced by a non-human would be frowned upon by the majority populace. A human founded the city and the kingdom. It should remain as such.

Now it was even more important that the citizens of Sandown have a strong leader to look up to and could relate to in their time of need.

Tegin finished off the last gulp of his mead and

got up. He looked up at the late afternoon setting sun. The double moons were visible and high in the sky, even at this hour.

Everything was prepared and in place for the guild assault. The city was still on lockdown since Thena and Lelanda had left. The city morale had dropped over the days since, and those being kept in the city were starting to become angry at the lack of information.

It wouldn't be long until riots started. He hoped his friends wouldn't take much longer. Most of all, he hoped all was going as it should at the battlefield. Tegin walked back toward the city guard headquarters, kicking at the dirt and random rocks with his feet, his thoughts on his friends and the hard times yet to come.

FIFTY

Corax sat in the corner room of the shop the guild used as a front to launder their stolen items from cities and towns all over the northern coast.

It was a typical storefront with pine wallboards and an oak front counter. Most of the shelves and everything else was made from pine. That was the cheapest wood available in this part of the world.

He had a small fire going in the simple fireplace. He sat, still disguised as a gray-haired dwarf, and pondered how to escape. He had done so now for almost a day since eliminating the idiot Braegen.

He was lucky nobody had tracked him to an entrance, and his spies had reported nothing out of the ordinary since then. But none of that helped him get out of the city.

There were so many guards lining the walls now that he would have to kill half a dozen just to get to the wall.

Since the lockdown, nobody was allowed within fifty feet of the wall that wasn't a guard. He cursed himself for not completing a second tunnel out of the city for what, at the time, seemed too much of a hassle. Now he'd give one of his eyes to be able to have one at his disposal.

Corax continued staring into the small fire. The flames licked up around the small logs he had tossed onto them. He thought hard. He glanced over at a small mirror he used to set up his disguise.

"Hmm," he grumbled to himself.

He could try to disguise himself as a guard, but there were only two or three dwarves in the guard, not counting the captain. It was too dangerous to attempt. He stuck out as a dwarf who didn't groom his beard. The disguise only went so far to hide that. Close inspection would make it obvious he wasn't the well-groomed dwarf he was attempting to appear as.

A clip-in beard made from horsehair was the best he could do. Grooming his beard wasn't something he really had skill in, having never even attempted it before.

He looked back at the fire. The dry logs he tossed not long before had started to catch fire now. He watched the fire turn the dry timber black. Then, it turned red as it created an ember from the wood . . . his eyes widened.

"Fire! That's it!" he exclaimed.

Fire would be his release to freedom. It would have to be a very large fire, not just a simple house or two. He needed dozens of homes to be set ablaze. He wouldn't mind burning down the entire city if it meant he could get free of this blasted place.

He hurried over to a shelf and started ripping it apart, looking for a map of the city. He located one and started peering at it in the firelight. He would need to pull what was left of the guild back together one last time. Corax started smiling under his dyed beard. His eyes gleamed in the firelight. A plan was starting to form . . .

FIFTY-ONE

Thena appeared inside her little dwelling and caught her bearings for a moment. Everything had been as she had left it over a day ago.

She lit a nearby lamp and removed her clothes, and laid out some clean ones from her chest at the foot of her bed. Thena pulled her long straight hair back into a ponytail and tied it with a leather thong, then looked down at her dresser and noticed a cross carved from stone on her desk.

Stalken had carved it for her not long after they met. She picked it up and caressed it, feeling its rough edges. It represented love for Elohim. He gifted it to her to let her know his feelings for her. She felt the ache in her heart.

Nobody knew of their relationship, and none needed to. They started out as lovers, and it turned into love. She knew that she would live on for thousands of years longer than his life span. That is the funny thing about love. It didn't discriminate. It cares nothing about race, religion, or sex . . .

She closed her eyes and held the bauble to her

chest, seeing her love in her mind's eye. He stood tall with his graying hair, strong physique, and piercing eyes. Tears streamed down her face, dripping off her delicate chin and onto the table. Thena was soon pulled out of her daydream by a knock at her door.

"Thena, you in there, lass?" came Tegin's voice through the door.

Thena wiped away the tears from her eyes and face and cleared her throat.

"Yes, I'm here. Hold on," she said.

She put the cross back onto the desk and looked at it for a few seconds more. With a sigh, she threw on a nightgown to cover up and walked to the door. She opened the door to see her friend standing there. Tegin could see that she had been crying but didn't mention it to her.

"It's good to see you made it back!" he exclaimed with a grin.

They embraced.

"Yes, just returned . . . how did you know I was back?" she asked.

"I was hovering around this area, hoping you would be back soon. I was getting antsy to find out news of the general and, of course, the spell to dig out the filth beneath our city. I came here and saw a lamp was lit. I figured I would investigate. Sure enough, here you are."

"Yes, I was just about to get into some clean clothes."

Tegin ran his fingers through his beard. "So, that must mean we are ready to proceed?"

"Yes, I spent most of yesterday practicing the spell while Lelanda and the general set up for a skirmish. A small probing force attacked us earlier today. Lelanda was amazing; you should have seen her. She took out a hill giant by herself. Then, she had a mage duel in the middle of the battle. She killed him while taking out most of their crossbowmen. I think she did get hit with a magic attack, but it must have been minor because she didn't seem injured when I met with her after."

"If she were injured, she would never say. That isn't her way," he replied. "Probing attack, you say? Won't be long then before the main force gets there."

Thena nodded . . . "I'll catch you up on the details after I finish getting ready. I want to find that guild tonight before daybreak. Everyone will be on curfew, so we'll have free reign of the streets until then."

Twenty minutes later, Thena and Tegin were walking into the market square.

"This should be a good place to start, near where we lost Braegen's trail."

The street was empty. Some nearby oil lamps and a few magical lamps were casting shadows here and there. Thena pulled a very small scrap of cloth from her pocket.

"What's that?" She looked down at the piece no bigger than her thumb. "It is a piece of Breagen's shirt. It will allow me to link the spell with his clothes. Lelanda took it after she enchanted his boots and shirt while he was unconscious."

"Interesting thing, magic," Tegin responded. "Never been a fan of it myself, but if this works, then maybe I'll start coming around."

"Ready?" she asked.

"What do you think?" he said, smiling.

Thena looked over at him. He looked the part of a warrior dwarf. Shield on his back, twirling his wicked-looking axe in his right hand, and a short sword sheathed on his hip. A chainmail shirt and leather breeches completed the ensemble.

Thena, on the other hand, was carrying a special weapon. The handle of which was sticking up behind her head.

Thena was not a normal mage. Lelanda had taken her under her wing and taught her the ways of the Battlemage, but she didn't favor a two-weapon style like Lelanda. She preferred a two-handed weapon style.

Her primary spells were weapon enchantments and powerful auras that could boost or hinder those around her. She reached up and touched the handle while looking at Tegin.

"Looks to me like we're both ready for trouble."

"Aye, lass, you got that right," Tegin puffed.

Thena closed her eyes while muttering the spell of attenuation on the piece of cloth. Once that was finished, she cast the location spell that Lelanda had taught her over the past few days. She felt her senses come alive just like before. She started feeling a pull to move northeast.

She moved slower than she did when practicing; this was a real scenario, and she wanted to be certain. This time she wasn't going to find what she was looking for in a crevice of rock or under a basket lid in an alley.

She may be trying to locate something that was many feet under them. Tegin followed her as they moved along the road bordering the market's north side until they were nearing a street that left the market heading northeast.

Tegin stayed back some feet behind Thena so as not to disturb her. He kept watch about them, ready for anything to jump out of the darkness and try to strike at her while she was vulnerable.

They passed a few groups of guards patrolling during the lockdown. They nodded but otherwise kept to themselves so they wouldn't get chewed out by the captain of the guard and the captain of the castle guard for interrupting what was some sort of ritual or investigation.

They passed the last known location where Breagen had lost their spotters. They kept moving down the street to the northeast and kept moving like this for close to two hours, by Tegin's estimation.

Thena was in a total trance and was moving one small step at a time and would even pause at times for long periods to further attune herself to the spell.

The twin moons were getting lower in the sky. Thena had slowed her movements even further now. She stopped near the corner of a butcher's shop, then walked in a slow circle for about five minutes, then a smaller circle again. She came out of her trance and looked at Tegin.

"I believe he is right below where I am standing. I cannot tell how far, but I'm pretty certain this is where his clothes are, at any rate."

"Okay, then. Stand back."

Tegin walked up to the spot where Thena had been standing and brought his axe up over his head. In two hard strikes, he scored the cobblestone street with an X, burned into the stone by the lighting from his axe. Both strikes sent up blinding arcs of lightning that brought two nearby patrols to that area.

Tegin looked at them, "Okay, men. Secure this location. Wake up the store owner and lock down this street. I want this area marked off one hundred feet in either direction. I want a tent put up exactly where this mark is."

The gaggle of guards all nodded and started securing the area with two sergeants barking orders to their men.

Thena looked over at Tegin. "I'm going to get some mages from the tower to assist with this."

"It will be dawn soon, so there's no point in resting. Every minute we delay is another minute that he has to get away. You tend to those mages; I'll get more men into this area. I don't want what we are doing to get out. I think we'll just block and close this entire street prior to dawn," he said.

CHAPTER

FIFTY-TWO

The sun was coming up over the eastern mountains around the time that a contingent of city guards had closed the street between the market and uptown.

A tent was attached to the front of the butcher shop that took up about half of the street. The mages put up a fog layer at each end of the street to prevent curious people from catching glimpses of what was going on.

Tegin and Thena were putting the finishing touches on everything. Tegin stood in the street looking around with an approving nod. Thena popped out of the tent to stand next to him.

"Better to have gossip about this than for guild spies to communicate that we are digging in the middle of the street," she said.

"Aye."

He turned and walked back through the tent flap with Thena following behind. A makeshift table was made out of some crates they found in the butcher shop. The two mages stood there with some books that they were flipping through.

"Looks like you might have a plan for breaching the guild?" said Tegin. He looked at the mages with an eyebrow raised.

"Well, we could dig there with conventional methods. They would hear us coming, and we don't know how far we have to dig. My idea is to use a combination of spells. We would use the first to liquefy the ground. We use a telekinesis spell to move the liquefied dirt and stone out of the hole."

"That is blasted brilliant," Tegin responded.

Thena smiled. "I can't take complete credit for it. I saw Lelanda use a similar spell against some crossbowmen in the skirmish yesterday. The best part is that it is silent. The bad part is that we don't know how far down the guild is. We have to be prepared at any moment to burst through. It could take all day, hours, or minutes. Once we break through, we might face an untold number of guild members."

"I hope we meet some," Tegin growled. "I have some payback to dish out."

Thena's eyes had glazed over and were glistening with moisture. "Yes . . . yes we do," she hissed.

Tegin grabbed his axe and twirled it in his hand. "Are you ready?" he seemed to ask the axe.

He hung the axe back on his belt. He grabbed Thena by the arm, pulled her to the side, and forced her to look at him.

"I'll be ready to climb down this hole as soon as we break through. Remember, this dwarf is not to be trifled with. This isn't a sparring session with Lelanda or me. If we get separated, I want you to use all of your abilities to hold him off until I get there. Keep him at a distance and don't leave yourself open if at all possible," Tegin said.

"I won't let you down," Thena replied.

"I know you won't, lass."

FIFTY-THREE

When a boy they used as a runner and pickpocket showed himself to the dwarf, Corax informed him that he had a plan for the remaining guild members to escape the city and retreat to Minsfet.

He didn't care about the guild any longer. He needed bodies for the next stage of his plan. He wanted to use them to distract those hunting him while he escaped.

By early afternoon, he was able to scrape up about two dozen guild members. They all crowded into the back room of the store he was taking refuge in.

He sat in his chair, no longer as an aged dwarf. He was back in the black leathers he wore when assassinating the king. He sat there for a few minutes and listened to the murmuring of rumors flying around.

"So, what is this plan you've gathered us for?" said a portly fellow that, funnily enough, was nicknamed Slim. "We all risked a lot in coming here."

Corax rose from his seat and looked everyone

over. This was a motley crew. Young, old, fat, skinny, some dressed in disguises, and some not. These were the ones that had something to lose.

"You came because you are all looking for an opportunity to escape your deaths. I am your last chance to taste freedom before the noose tightens," he said as he raised a clenched fist.

He looked at the portly fellow. "I know the rumors about why the guild was disbanded. Don't try and point blame or put guilt on the one trying to save us all."

He looked back to the group as a whole. "I made many of you rich; is it my fault you squandered your wealth on food, wine, and women? I never told you how to spend your coin. I just enforced the rules and made certain you paid your dues for the protection I gave. As it is said, every good thing must come to an end. I built one of the wealthiest and most powerful guilds in this part of the world in one of the richest, least corrupted cities in the land."

He was laying it on thick now as he paced back and forth in front of the crowd of men. "I want to continue that legacy. To do so, we have to escape and relocate. Those that didn't show up were either too scared or have retired from the life after having a successful run. So be it. If that is their dream, then let them have it! In a year, we'll be stealing from them, too!"

That got a chuckle from the crowd.

"Now . . . before I get to the plan, are there any further questions or rumors that need to be quelled?"

The runner from earlier had poked his hand up so he could be seen.

"You there, boy." Corax pointed at him so the crowd would give way.

The boy stepped forward without fear. Corax kind of liked him. He always did as was asked without question and never whined about any-thing. Of course, fear has a tendency to do that. But here he was, stepping forward. "The road over by the market was closed off this morning by guards on both ends, and a magical fog blocks anyone from seeing what is going on."

Everyone turned to look at the boy. He was maybe twelve years old and on the cusp of puberty. He had seen death, poverty, and abuse. Lying was not tolerated, so nobody questioned what he said.

Slim piped up. "How do you know it's a magical fog?"

"Because I was watching as the mages cast the spell that created it," he said. He crossed his arms and stared back a Slim.

"They were erecting a tent over the front of the butcher shop at the same time. It looked like it was going to fill half the street."

Corax thought for a moment. "That isn't near any of our entrances. Maybe they're questioning someone they think is me." He gave a hearty laugh. "Regardless, that won't affect my plan in the slight-est. But if anything changes, I want you—" he pointed at the boy "—to let me know." The boy nodded and disappeared back into the crowd. Corax turned his attention back to the rest of the men.

"Anybody else? No? Okay then."

"If you'll turn your attention to the wall to your right, I've roughed out a map of the city with charcoal." He pointed a thick finger toward the wall. He had detailed out a majority of the city with the names of specific places written in for reference. "Those of you that can read, please fill in those who cannot. I've drawn out this map because my plan involves turning much of the city into that."

He picked up a large chunk of charcoal and tossed it at the nearest man. They all stared at it for a second. Then looked up at him with questioning glances.

Corax rolled his eyes. "We'll turn the city into charcoal by starting a bunch of those," he said as he pointed at the fire in the fireplace.

The men looked at the fire, then back at the charcoal. The lights were starting to come on.

"You want us to start a bunch of fires in the city?" asked Slim. "Other than starting a panic, how is that going to get us past the city gates?"

"Nobody is getting past the gates, so get that out of your head right now. That is the most protected point in the city, and only an imbecile would attempt that as a point of escape."

He turned back to his map on the wall. "If we start fires all around the market just as the sun is setting, that will draw the guard away from other more important areas we can start fires at. Food storage and other essential city management areas will be our primary targets. If we can start pulling guards away from the walls, then we have a chance to create an opening to escape. The more fires there are, the better our chance of escape. Even if we are spotted scaling the wall, it won't matter. We'll have the cover of darkness, and with the city burning, they won't have the bodies to spare in a pursuit. And before I have to smash one of you for bringing the matter up, yes, I'll be joining in on the fun and starting fires of my own."

Corax looked around the room. He saw many nods. He could see the gears turning. "Now I need to know who is in and who isn't so we can work out the details. Are you in?" he asked the crew of men standing before him.

"This could work," many of the men started saying.

Slim piped up. "Looks like we're in. Let's get crackin'. This will take some time, and dusk is not far off."

"Music to my ears," said Corax, grinning as he turned back toward the map.

FIFTY-FOUR

The digging process had been slow. The city was carved out of the mountain. After just a few inches of dirt and gravel, they ran into solid bedrock. It would have taken them days to progress this far with pickaxes and chisels.

The mages were working in one-hour shifts. One mage would cast the spell that would turn the stone into mud. Another encapsulated it in a bubble, and another levitated it out of the ground to the pile in the corner of the tent where it would harden back into stone after the spell ended.

They were digging a five-by-five-foot hole straight down on the spot that Thena sensed was Braegen's location. They hoped this would lead to them coming in through the ceiling of some room, but they couldn't be certain.

Every five feet they dug, Thena would climb down in the hole and verify that they were getting closer. Every time she had been in the hole, she confirmed the sensation was growing stronger from the spell. Based on her experience during training, she could tell they were getting close.

Tegin had pulled about twenty elite guards from reserves. Since the castle was empty of any real persons that needed to be protected, they had bodies to spare. The city guard was straining to keep the city under control and the walls manned in the three days since the lockdown started. Every day that the lockdown lasted, the closer they came to rioting. They were betting everything on this . . . everything.

Tegin kept a constant vigil on the hole being dug, as did Thena. Both of them were armed as if they were going to war. Tegin carried his lightning axe, sword, and shield.

Thena wielded her two-handed zhan-ma-dao style sword. The sword was used against cavalry to cut the horses' legs out from under them. The handle on the sword was nearly as long as the blade.

When Thena showed aptitude with the two-handed style, Lelanda suggested she use that style of sword so she could utilize the length of the handle. Tegin watched her sharpening the blade, and it made him think back.

He had surprised her with this sword after working on it for a year. It had an ironwood handle, which kept the diameter of the handle down to a size she could grasp.

However, it still had equal strength to handles the same size made of steel. It kept the weight balanced in the sword.

The blade was made of a rare metal called *mythril*, not seen often outside the dwarven kingdoms. Mythril was one of the strongest metals in existence. It was light, durable, and kept its edge. It was also expensive and difficult to shape.

When Tegin presented her with the sword, she fell in love with it. The metal, when polished, had a light gold to silver sheen to it. The weight of the sword made it easier for her to use than it was for someone with a short sword.

She hadn't had to take a life with it yet. It was still a pure sword, untarnished by blood. It had brought the two closer together as friends.

They both relished the opportunity to talk about weapons and spar with each other. Thena had even taught him a few things about how to combat an opponent faster than himself.

She learned how to counter one who was much stronger. Maybe soon, they would have to use their skills to take the lives of others. But for now, they took advantage of the calm before the storm.

FIFTY-FIVE

Dusk was settling over the restless city of Sandown. Shadows were getting long as the sun started sinking behind the mountains to the northwest.

Corax had laid out specific plans to the rest of the crew to start lighting fires just as the sun sunk behind the mountains.

It would still be before curfew, so it wouldn't be as hard to move around, and everyone could be in place to set their fire. With almost twenty fires being started at the same time, it should keep the town and the city guard busy while the guild moved to start others.

Corax had scouted the best location to scale the city wall hours before the meeting started. A group of houses nestled together to form the shape of a horseshoe. The middle of the horseshoe was a small garden and sitting area. He planned on setting all those houses on fire. Once he took out the guards on the wall with his blowgun, the houses would prevent anyone from locating him or following him due to the intense heat—unless they knew magic, in which case they shouldn't be much of a problem either since dwarves were resistant to most elemental spells and impervious to mental spells.

Corax was confident that his escape was imminent. He had prepped the houses an hour earlier. Now he just needed to go and retrieve his grappling hook set from his room.

He thought it to be a useless item when he was looking over his room for things to pack. *How ironic,* he thought. *The least valuable item now becomes the most valuable.* Without it, it could take him an hour to climb the smooth surface of the wall. With it, he could be up and over in thirty seconds.

He waited near an entrance to the guild. He was about to make his move inside when a patrol stopped outside the location, a storm sewer grate that led to a hidden entrance. They were standing just fifteen feet from it while he was hidden in shadows in a nearby alley.

Then he started to smell it . . . smoke! He grinned. It was starting.

One of the guards sniffed the air. "Hey, do you guys smell smoke?"

"A little, yeah," another replied.

Just then, Corax's runner came around the corner. As he passed them, he yelled, "Fire! Fire! Down at the market! I'm passing the word. Help if you can!" He ran off to find other city guards . . . just as he was instructed.

"Should we go help?" one of the guards suggested.

"We are not supposed to leave this sector of town during patrol under any circumstance. The captain would have our heads," replied another.

"There won't be much to guard if the city burns down around us," chimed in a third. "You guys go. I'll stay here," said the biggest of the five. "Nobody will mess with me."

"We'll be back as soon as we can," said the rest as they headed off in a trot toward the market.

That left just the one guard. Corax slipped on his pair of iron knuckles and looked around. Nobody was nearby since curfew was about to start. He sunk back into the shadows and clinked his knuckles together loud enough for the guard to hear.

"Huh?" The guard turned toward the small alley. "Is someone there? Guys? Is that you messing with me?"

He drew his sword and walked the twenty feet to the alley's entrance. He squinted his eyes and peered into the darkness.

"Is anybody in there?

Corax was on him in a flash, leaping with incredible speed from the alley and burying his left fist into the guard's gut. The guard fell to his knees and looked up in horror at the dwarf.

He had no breath and couldn't utter a word. Corax grabbed him by the throat with his left hand. The guard's head was about level with his own.

He whispered to him, "This is going to hurt you a lot more than it is going to hurt me." Corax grinned as he brought his right hand up. He brought it smashing down into the guard's temple with amazing power, crushing it in. He looked at the dead guard. "That's what you get for being an idiot."

He glanced around him and saw no others that

would have seen this encounter. He grabbed the guard by the leg and dragged his limp body into the farthest corner of the alley, then threw some rub-bish on top of him. He made his way back out and opened up the sewer grate, slipping in unnoticed.

After a few minutes of walking through a tight underground hallway, Corax came to a blank wall with a notch cut into it. He grabbed it and slid it out of the way. That allowed him access into one of the prime conduits that was used to access the guild. Three of his guild members were leaving the area when he came through.

"What are you three doing down here?"

They froze in their tracks. Slim happened to be one of the three. "We came to get some more fire-starting implements. We have fires started all over the lower half and the marketplace."

"Good . . . good . . ." he said. "Since you are here and gave me such great news, I'm going to return the favor."

They turned and followed him back into the guild hall toward what they called the guild bank. Braegen's body lay piled on the floor. The dagger was still covered in gore and embedded in the stone wall , but Braegen's head was half torn off due to the constant weight of the body pulling on the dagger.

"Don't mind that mess," Corax said.

The three stayed tight-lipped as they glanced at the body.

The bank was a stone chamber that Corax had a magic door installed into. He was the only one that could open the main door. Otherwise, the person manning this particular area had to slither through a small hole to prevent the place from being robbed in a snatch-and-grab attempt.

They approached the stone door, and Corax removed a medallion from around his neck.

"It is up to you to share with the others that don't leave right away. Otherwise, this is yours unless others lay claim."

He pushed the medallion into a slot that was made for it, and the stone door popped open. He swung it out, and the three men peered inside. Silver candlesticks, trays, golden goblets, and all manner of other shiny items that had not made it to being laundered yet were sitting like flowers in a field.

"Feel free to poke around. I need to get something from my room."

He turned and walked away. The urge to close the door on them after they entered the vault was tempting, but he had no time for simple games.

He turned the corner to the hallway that led to his room and found a dead body on the floor where it had sprung a trap of his.

He chuckled to himself. It didn't take long for someone to get brave enough to approach his room in his absence. They didn't make it past the first trap. Lucky sod, he would be in for a much more painful experience if he had gotten farther into the hallway.

He made it to his room and found it to be undisturbed, and his grapple and rope were right where he had left them.

He snatched them up and headed back out down the hall. He found the three hip-deep in the vault, trying to figure out how to take as much as they could without being suspicious. He was about to head back toward the entrance when he suddenly got a bad feeling.

He looked around but saw nothing but the three men in the vault occupied with their new reward. Everything else was quiet.

"Sshhh, quiet," he said.

The men fell silent and looked at each other. Corax thought he heard something from over by Braegen's body. The ceiling over Braegen looked like it started melting, then suddenly, it all turned to liquid and splashed onto the floor like gooey mud. Just as fast as it did that, it hardened back into stone.

"Intruders, boys!" Corax turned on his heel as the three men came scrambling out of the vault. A small figure fell from the new opening in the ceiling and landed without a sound on her feet. She wore brown leather armor and carried a long-handled cavalry sword. The three men paused, looked at her, and then at each other.

Slim spoke up. "Get her!"

The three rushed her with swords drawn. Her eyes locked onto Corax and never shifted from him. Corax took that as a sign to keep moving. He suspected something that his three companions did not. A lot more was coming through that hole in the ceiling besides a small elf.

FIFTY-SIX

Thena jumped into the shaft, not knowing what to expect but ready for anything. Tegin was going to be following her next. The twenty elite guards would follow him down rope ladders. She landed and caught sight of Corax.

It was him! She knew in an instant. Three men near the opening said something about her being an elf, and all three charged her. She slipped to the side as a two-hundred-pound dwarf slammed into them as they ran under the tunnel entrance. She never took her gaze off Corax.

Tegin and the three men were a jumbled mess of arms and legs. She noticed a body on the floor next to the wall.

She chanced a quick glance to see Braegen's lifeless body sitting next to the opening they had put in the stone ceiling. When she looked back to Corax, she saw him leaving through a secret door in a wall across the room. His hand flicked a small ball in their general direction as he slipped through the opening.

"Smoke bomb!" she yelled.

The entire room went black as night. She moved based on memory in the direction she saw him depart. She could hear soldiers coming through the shaft now, all of them tumbling into the pile of bodies at the bottom, not knowing or seeing what was going on. She would endanger herself or others if she approached them, so she made the decision to follow Corax.

She wanted justice, but a burning ember of revenge stirred inside her. She made it to the far side of the room near where the secret door was and could see a bit better. Smoke bombs were not made to last very long. They were just there as a distraction. Luckily, Thena was able to find the opening.

It was small and could have traps or still hold the assassin, so she decided to clear it first. She spoke two words of enchantment followed by a large inhalation of air.

Fire spewed from her mouth like dragon flame boiling into the opening for the hidden doorway. She climbed into the charred exit and found the passage led further in and up.

She followed it, and it led to a rope ladder that had been cut and left on the floor. She cast a spell of levitation and ascended the hole that came up into a closet of some store that sold imported items.

She exited the building and caught a glimpse of Corax slipping between two buildings and heading north. Smoke was heavy in the air, and even from here, she could hear and see some buildings on fire.

Fires that were probably started by the guild as a distraction while they all tried to slip away, she thought. Either that, or we are under attack. Catapults or dragons were the only things she could think of that could start this many fires this fast. It had to be the guild.

Thena picked up her pace as she darted between the buildings after the dwarf. She needed to remember that if she cornered him, he had to be fought as if she were fighting Tegin. He would have more power than her, but he wouldn't be as fast.

No fires were raging in this part of town, but the city wall guards were quite thin in this area. She stopped in a little square and looked around, thinking hard about where he could have gone. She saw he had a grapple on him back at the guild.

He was going to scale the walls, but where? "Think!" she muttered.

She knew this city like the back of her hand. What area up here would have the best seclusion for scaling the wall? Then it hit her. She took off at a dead sprint, weapon out.

FIFTY-SEVEN

orax took the chance after leaving the guild that he wouldn't run into any patrols. As luck would have it, he didn't. He made it to the group of houses, and no lights were lit. The residents must be out helping with the fires.

The thought of leaving the wretched town with a few more deaths on his hands would have been excellent.

He slipped between the two middle homes and peered into the garden area. It was thirty feet wide by forty feet deep, by his estimation. Two guards could be seen walking on top of the forty-foot-high wall.

Corax had to hurry. The elf may have been able to track him, and he wanted to get the fires going before she figured out where he might be. He slipped his blow gun from under his shoulder and loaded his poisoned dart, prepping two darts between his fingers. At this distance, he would likely miss once until he got an idea of the wind up there. He took careful aim at the guard that kept turning in toward the city to see how the fires were coming along.

He waited for the guard to turn his neck just so, and then . . . *pffft*. The dart hit the guard in the ear.

"What the . . . !" The guard exclaimed.

He drew his sword and grabbed the other guard by the shoulder in an attempt to warn him. The second dart was already on its way to the next guard, who turned to see what his companion was mumbling about, and the dart struck him in the cheek. Both guards attempted to signal for help but stumbled and fell from the wall with a yelp.

"Damn, I'm good," Corax whispered to himself.

He put the extra dart into the tube of the blowgun and slipped the blowgun back under his shoulder to hang from the makeshift hoop he always carried it with. He lit fires at each of the four houses and peeked through, seeing no one.

He unslung the grappling hook from his back with the forty feet of silk rope. He preferred silk rope because it was stronger, lighter, and smaller in diameter, which meant he could carry more. It was perfect for a job like this. Clearing the wall with it could prove difficult for anyone else.

His bracers allowed him the luxury of easily tossing it that far. In fact, he could throw the whole thing over the wall if he wasn't careful. He took practiced aim and lobbed a shot up over the wall. He tugged the rope until he felt the grapple catch and pulled it taught. He could see the fires throwing shadows against the wall as they started gorging on the houses behind him.

He gave the rope a few more yanks and then braced his feet against the wall, and started up.

About six feet up, the rope burst into flame right where he was about to grab with his outreached hand and snapped under his weight. He kicked off the wall as he fell, landing hard on his stomach and chest.

He had caught a glimpse of a humanoid form as he flipped. Corax got to his feet, pulled a dagger, turned, and whipped it in that direction. He heard a solid *TANG* sound in response.

As his eyes focused on the intense fire behind the person, he realized it was the elf, and she had deflected his dagger. He pulled his blowgun from his side, and before he could get it to his lips, it burst into flame and splintered.

"It isn't going to be that easy, murderer," Thena hissed at him. "You may be resistant to magic, but your weapons are not."

He dusted himself off and stood up straight. "Ah, so you've come to be the hero of Sandown by killing the assassin who took the life of your beloved king?"

"No," replied Thena. "I'm here to claim revenge for the murder of my king, our symbol of justice, and my friend. You wouldn't know anything about those."

Corax smirked. She was cocky for an elf. He was going to enjoy crushing her. He looked closer at her. She wore leather armor with the symbol of Stalken seared into it. But what caught his eye was the two-handed zhan-ma-dao sword. His eyes widened.

"What is someone as frail as you doing with a zhan-ma-dao sword? One that looks to be made of Mithril!"

She glanced at the sword and then back at

Corax. "A gift, which is something else you know nothing about."

Corax scratched his beard. "True enough. I've no need for friends. I have much bigger plans, and they don't involve any of those. Speaking of which, I don't see yours. You elves always roam in packs. Never fighting one on one, always cheating by ganging up on some poor soul trying to make a living."

Thena took a few steps toward the dwarf. The fire behind her was starting to rage, and she could feel the heat getting more intense.

Sweat was starting to trickle down her back, and she could feel the anger swelling in her. She wanted to charge him and cut his head off, but that would be instant death for her.

This was no sparring session with Tegin. This was the real deal, to the death. She could feel the tension in her muscles but accepted it and even welcomed the chance to give her life in response to the man she loved more than she had ever expected to love anyone.

Corax saw that she had switched from a relaxed position to a more combative one. He pulled his short sword and parrying dagger out of their scabbards. He gave a small bow to the elf as a taunt.

"Are you ready for your first and final lesson?"

"Are you?" Thena shot back.

As he circled the elf, Corax had to admit that the sword she carried was amazing. The craftsmanship and the beauty were something to behold. It would make an excellent trophy. However, all of that paled when it came to his escape. He needed to end this battle as soon as possible before real help arrived in the form of the captain of the guard. He carried an even deadlier weapon. One he didn't have an answer for.

Corax decided to see how talented the female was and led in with a feint to the left with his sword and a slash to the right with his dagger. Thena saw right through the ruse and parried the feint in a fluid movement, side-stepped the slashing dagger with ease, and came down and across in a spinning slash much quicker than Corax expected. He knocked the blade away with his sword at the last second.

Now that Thena had the advantage, she pressed on with a series of slashes that kept the dwarf on the defensive. Thena knew that every moment she could delay the dwarf was precious seconds Tegin needed to find them. He would undoubtedly find a way reach her; he always did. As long as she could keep the dwarf guessing, she had a chance.

Thena threw strike after vicious strike at Corax, but he flicked them away with a twitch of his wrists. Still, he had no time to counter before another sweeping strike came in.

He started growing frustrated at the length of time this was taking. It took all of his speed to keep up with the elf. He saw her coming around for another strike with her sword. He angled his parrying dagger to catch the blade.

He flicked open the dagger to spring the extra blades from the primary in a V shape on each side.

The zhan-ma-dao cut right through the blade, but the broken dagger delayed her next swing just long enough for him to slide inside her defense and kick her legs out from under her. As she fell, he tried to deliver a killing blow with his short sword. She brought her sword up in time to block, and his blade split in half as it came in contact with her blade.

She kicked him low in the leg, which allowed her to roll back and away. He growled in frustration and threw what was left of his sword at her with great ferocity.

She brought her zhan-ma-dao up to block, and the broken sword almost knocked hers out of her hand. She could tell he was enhanced by some magical item. The strength of that throw was completely off the scale of what she had ever felt. Dwarves couldn't cast magic and direct spells against them were mostly negated. They worked around this with alchemy and magical items.

She had taken Tegin's heaviest blows without losing her grip, and this was much stronger than anything he had delivered.

Corax stepped back and cocked his head at her in an attempt to hide his frustration.

"For a mage, you're pretty good at using that."

"I'm no simple mage. I'm a battle mage. Here, let me show you," she replied.

Corax was fuming on the inside. She hadn't even given him her best! This elf was showing him up, and he couldn't do anything about it. All he had left for weapons was his iron knuckles. He dropped his broken dagger and slipped those on while she signed some magic.

Suddenly her blade frosted up from the tip all the way down to the hilt. It was giving off a slight fog as the coldness of the blade came into contact with the warm night and the raging fire that was blasting them both with furnace-like heat.

Corax clanged his knuckles together and came howling at her. "Let's see what you've got, elf bitch!"

She hesitated at his sudden ferocity for a split second, and that was all he needed. She started to come down in a slashing strike to cut him in two, but he slid under the slash and stuck his boot up to catch the base of the pommel to prevent the blow from finishing while his other foot kicked out at her shin.

He heard a satisfying snap like a dry twig when he made contact, and she flew back, landing hard on her side with a loud scream.

She got up on her good leg before he could get to her and mumbled words of magic while taking a large breath.

"Yeah right, like that's going to hurt me," Corax said.

A gale-force stream of frost came blasting out of her mouth. He just stood there and took the blast. After a few seconds, the spell was over. Thena looked, and Corax was still standing there.

"Brrrrr, now that was refreshing! I think that gave me a second wind!" he scoffed at her. The ground all around him was slicked over with ice. Thena said nothing and started casting another spell. Corax started walking toward her but realized that his footing was unsure on the slick ground.

"Ahh, you tricky elf witch."

She finished her spell and started shimmering.

"That shield of protection won't help you," he said.

Thena said nothing and started spinning in place on her good leg. The other was broken and useless, dangling like a puppet from a string.

Corax was determined to end this. He gained speed with each step and attempted to charge her low. She was a blur as the haste spell she casted reached its crescendo and brought the weapon's handle hard into the dwarf's face, stunning him.

She followed with another hit to the gut. Corax stepped back on the slick ice, which was made worse as it melted. He lost his balance and flung up his arms. That saved him from her killing blow.

The mythril sword cut through the iron knuckles on his left hand and deep into the hand, cutting it open to the bone. Corax growled in pain. He rolled away to his feet and charged back in. Just as the haste spell was coming to an end, Thena used a move that got Tegin once in a sparring session.

She twirled the handle part of the sword around her neck, which looked like she was leaving herself open low again except that she bent in the middle of the twirl, which brought the leading edge of the sword around, catching Corax across the bridge of the nose and through his left eye

As the tip of the sword traveled through his left eye, he spun with the blow, bringing around his injured left hand to connect with the side of her head, sending Thena sprawling to the ground.

Thena lay semi-conscious while Corax howled in pain from her blow while flailing about on the ground. She started coming around when she heard a familiar voice screaming her name.

"Thena, are you there, lass?" screamed Tegin

through the raging fire. She started to move when she heard him again. "Thena! Talk to me, girl!"

"Yes! Over here!" she screamed with everything she had.

She heard crashing timber and looked over to see Corax still flailing around on the ground.

"You took my eye, you elf bitch!" Corax screamed.

With his good eye he looked at the blood pouring into his hands from his face. He was a mess, but he didn't care anymore—all bets were off.

All he saw was rage and blood. He could hear Thena's would-be rescuers trying to bust their way through an inferno to get to her. He didn't care if he died now. He just wanted to kill this elf and feel her bones crack in his hands while he watched the life fade from her eyes.

The ice from Thena's spell was nothing more than puddles now due to the heat coming from the house fires. Corax felt his muscles tighten to dangerous levels. He looked over at Thena, still woozy from his backhand, trying to stand by using her sword as a crutch. Blood dribbled from a gash on her head where Corax had struck her.

"I'm going to kill you!" he screamed in rage.

Tegin, meanwhile, was half on fire as he busted through the last part of one of the houses. He watched in what seemed like slow motion as Corax took two big strides and leaped up about four feet into the air. Thena attempted to put her sword up as a shield. However, Corax was not aiming for her. With all his power, he hammered the ground with his fists right at her feet. A massive cloud of dirt and mud blew up from the strike. This knocked Thena off balance and onto her back. Ignoring the searing pain in his hands, Corax grabbed for her. She kicked his face with her good leg, which did little to stop him.

Tegin tried to close the distance in time. He made it to about ten feet away. His leather armor was still smoking and his beard was half burned off before Corax had smacked Thena's sword away and grabbed her up by the throat with his good hand.

"Don't take another step," he said to Tegin.

Tegin stopped in his tracks. He didn't know what to do. His friend's life was hanging by a thread. She was in the clutches of a psychopath who could snap her neck in an instant. He was helpless.

"You trained this little one well."

Thena gasped under the strain of his grip on her throat. She could feel herself going in and out of consciousness. Tegin watched as her arms went limp.

"Let her go! Now!" Corax looked at Tegin for a long moment. "As you wish, captain."

He turned Thena toward Tegin and reached back, then punched her in the chest with a crushing blow that sent her flying into Tegin. Corax took the advantage and sprinted for the rope that dangled ten feet high up on the wall.

He jumped with all his strength and caught the rope with his right hand, the better of the two. He grunted as he almost ran up the wall.

Tegin watched him disappear over the wall but could do nothing to stop him. He turned Thena over. She was still alive but broken. She looked at him half-smiling, half-gritting her teeth with blood spattered on her lips. She managed to get out the words, "my sword."

Tegin raced over and grabbed the sword that he'd made for her and brought it back. He laid the sword across her and put her hand on it. Tears welled up in her eyes as she smiled in pain.

Blood trickled from her mouth as she mouthed the words,"Avenge us."

Tegin put his forehead to hers. "I will, I promise you on all that I am. I will avenge you both. She pulled his hand so it rested on the hilt of her sword. She sobbed for a few seconds, and he felt her spirit pass as her eyes glazed over and became dull.

The pent-up emotion from the loss of two of his best friends within the same week had become too much to bear. It felt like the whole world had come crashing down around him.

Tears dripped from his eyes onto her as he grieved with his dead friend in his arms. A low rumble started in the deepest parts of his chest, which turned into a screaming growl. He threw his head back, unleashing a terrifying roar of desperation that echoed off the burning homes and city wall.

FIFTY-EIGHT

Gunner and Lelanda had busied themselves positioning the reinforcements that arrived just after Thena left for Sandown. They lost very few soldiers in the skirmish.

Now they added another thousand phalanx soldiers, ten catapults, ten ballista, five elemental sorcerers, and one hundred and fifty berserkers. The berserkers were specialists in their field. Some thought they might be half-crazy, but in reality, they were all very well-trained and disciplined soldiers. It was in the thick of battle where they showed their true power.

They fought at one hundred percent of their body's physical ability the entire fight. Movement, agility, flexibility, and strength were all enhanced while they were enraged or berserking.

Gunner learned how to utilize the berserkers years ago. He met and befriended one years before during a clash of mercenary armies in his homeland on the south side of the continent and saw their potential first-hand.

They had to be used in situations that warranted their powers. Fighting at the level that they did for the entire battle has its repercussions, though. They require many days rest after fighting at that level to recover. If they do not, they can die from fatigue.

Lelanda also spoke of a special item that could be called upon if things turned against them. She didn't say much more than that. Reports of another small force of just a few hundred or so were coming in from scouts.

Preparations had been put in place for the approaching force. Though, something didn't make sense to Gunner as he looked over a map of the region. Why attack with another small force?

He knew that the first attack had survivors that escaped. Plus, they had scouts in the distance or even mages monitoring the battle nearby that would have reported the battle results. Yet here they were, attacking with another small force, albeit from a different direction. The more he thought about it, the more uneasy he felt.

Gunner had decided to use the same strategy as before and leave his catapults in place, utilizing the ones the attacking force came within range of. He had close to twenty catapults now and ten more ballistae positioned throughout the defenses.

The trebuchets were having problems. The kingdom didn't use them, which meant there were few who knew their operation let alone had any experience with them. The sergeants that came from Sandown knew catapults from the ground up. Trebuchets, though similar in function, were fundamentally different. Those would again be inactive for the coming battle.

However, the ballista would improve their defense against giants by a great deal. Though, none were reported in the recent accounts on the breakdown of the force that approached. The reports listed just crossbowmen and mercenaries. That reinforced his idea that something was amiss. They wouldn't have a chance against the defenses of the city by themselves.

At Lelanda's request, Gunner had distributed the reinforcements around the city. They were ordered not to leave their post unless told to do so by their superiors or when engaged at their location.

Meanwhile, Lelanda had set up a place of her own in an abandoned house that her contingent of mages could occupy. She learned many decades ago to trust her feelings, the second probing attack was making her uneasy as well.

She pulled out a small, folded silk piece of cloth and laid it on a rough-hewn table in the room she was in. She carefully unfolded it.

It was a circle that was about four feet in diameter. She formed a circular symbol with her hands and placed them on the edge of cloth, then chanted a series of command words. The piece of cloth flashed, and a large circular opening into another dimension flashed into existence. Gold, platinum, silver, armor, wands, scrolls, staves, and books of all kinds were placed therein.

She cast a spell of recall, and out popped a thick silver staff with a sharp point on the base and four points on the top. When she grasped it, the staff lit up with electric energy, and the four points on top arced with powerful pops as the energy shot between the four points.

She had come across this staff ages ago. It was useful when the time was right. It was cumbersome to carry at all times and even dangerous to do for long periods. In fact, it came close to killing her and the entire group of mercenaries she was with some years back when Tegin worked with her protecting shipments all across the continent.

She hoped to Elohim that she didn't need it. It was sort of an insurance plan in case the bad feeling she got came true. She spoke the command word again, and the magical hole became a simple piece of cloth. She commenced to folding it back up and tucking it into a hidden compartment inside her clothes.

FIFTY-NINE

Gunner lay in bed tossing and turning. He couldn't get the uneasy feeling out of his head about the impending battle. The enemy force was due to show itself sometime in the morning, which was fast approaching.

He rolled out of bed and walked over to a wash bowl. A cracked mirror hung above it. He stared into it for a few moments, looking at his fiery red hair and beard. He leaned forward and splashed some cool water from the bowl onto his face and dried it with a wash rag nearby.

"Bah," he snorted as he looked back at himself. "Might as well stay up; not going to get any sleep," he said out loud to himself.

He dressed and proceeded to the balcony that overlooked the previous battlefield. Just as he passed the entrance to the balcony, he saw someone out of the corner of his eye. He jumped back, fists up in a defensive posture.

"Gah! You scared the wits out of me!" he exclaimed.

Lelanda sat leaned back in one of the wooden

chairs on the balcony. She had her hood down, and her caltrop spell was not active on her hair that changed its natural color, which shown slivery white in the moonlight.

"My apologies. I couldn't sleep. I figured this was as good a place as any. I heard you tossing and turning and figured I would scare you if I walked in on you."

He smiled.

"Well, you scared me anyway." He paused. "But you do all the time. Maybe one of these years, I'll get used to it."

She smirked. "Nobody ever does. I still scare Tegin."

"That makes me feel all better," he said, laughing.

He settled into one of the chairs and leaned forward with his arms draped over the railing, looking down over the scarred walls that led out to the plains. He could see the night watches patrolling and even make out the horsemen past the walls in the moonlight.

"So, why couldn't you sleep?" he finally asked Lelanda.

"Something perplexes me about the approaching force. I have a feeling I know what it might be, but I'd hate to panic you for no reason if it doesn't come to fruition."

He turned his head toward her. "By all means, please panic me. If you know something or even feel the slightest hint of anything treacherous from our enemies, then I want to know."

She gave him a slight smile at the respect he just showed her.

"I suspect that the approaching force is the counterattack we have been expecting."

"But why such a small number?" he interrupted.

"Because I believe there is powerful magic being used to hide their true numbers." Gunner frowned. "How powerful? As powerful as you?"

Lelanda turned her head to look out on the plains surrounding the city. "Powerful enough to pose a serious threat. What worries me is that we don't know what they are hiding. It could be anything."

"What, like a dragon?" he mused.

She looked back at him and frowned. "Anything."

"Crap," Gunner replied. "I thought I was worrying for nothing."

"Better to worry and be relieved by overcompensating than to assume something and die for it," she said.

They both sat in silence for some minutes before Gunner spoke again.

"I think I might have an idea that could save many of our forces. Though, it might mean a death sentence for those who volunteer for this task."

Lelanda stood up, leaned against the railing, and crossed her arms. "What do you have in mind?"

He scratched his chin for a moment and then looked over at her. "Let's send out a couple of riders to scout the group up close to see if they are hiding their true numbers or not."

She smirked back at him. "I may have a spell or two that could assist them with detection and escape."

"This sounds like the makings of a plan!" he said. "I'll have McLeod pull his best two riders from the company. Of course, the daft bastard may try and go himself. I'll have to be explicit about him not being included in the two riders he pulls."

SIXTY

Dawn was fast approaching when the two selected riders left the safety of the city walls. They had both been given two chicken eggs. One was brown, the other white, with instructions on what to do with each of them once they were a distance from the city walls and in partial cover of the rolling hills of the plains.

They found a secluded area that shielded them from the lookouts of the city and any others that were watching. Bryain and Sheldin spoke in hushed tones as they sat upon their horses, looking at the eggs they were given by the dark elf mage.

"You think this is really going to work?" Bryain whispered to Sheldin.

Sheldin took out his brown egg and eyed it with a shrug.

Both riders wore green cloaks with mud, grass, and any other substance they hoped might blend them in with the shrubs and grasses of the plains. Their horses had been smeared with the same muck.

Bryain was just becoming a man. He wasn't far

past the age of seventeen, but he was a strapping lad that had shown his prowess in battle with bow and sword. He was chosen for this mission based on his knowledge of the area and skill with pushing a horse to extremes.

Sheldin seemed quite the opposite—graying hair and thin. He had been raised with horses since he was a child. He could make one sit and roll over like a dog if need be.

Sheldin looked over at his counterpart. "Let's get this over with."

They both took their brown eggs and crushed them over their heads. They expected to get doused with egg yolk. Instead, each egg burst into a glittery powder that drifted down on and around them and their horses. They started fading from sight.

"This is amazing!" Bryain whispered.

"Shh, keep quiet and get moving. Let's get into position and prepare for the enemy. With any luck, I'll see you back behind the walls of the city."

They split up and headed different ways. The only sign of their presence was the sound of the horse's hooves on the ground and the depressions they left behind in the dewy grass.

Bryain maneuvered his horse through the rolling hills in the direction he was told the approaching force would be coming from, knowing the spell he was given would last two hours. Though it wasn't an invisibility spell, it took the surrounding landscape and reflected it outward.

To anyone looking at him, it would seem like a shimmering outline. He still had to be cautious in his approach. He kept his horse and himself below the horizon so as to not silhouette himself too often to any scouts or lookouts that might be ahead of the approaching force.

He remembered what McLeod had told him. "Locate the approaching force and confirm up close that they are as they look. Be on the lookout for hidden forces like giants, mages, or worse. Once you detect their presence, return with all haste by utilizing the second enchanted egg."

He looked to the east and saw that the sun was getting close to cresting the horizon. After an hour had gone by, he had started fearing that he had missed the approaching force. He had not seen or detected their presence. He was just about to start second-guessing himself when he sensed his horse getting antsy.

He calmed the horse and looked around, yet heard nothing. Then he felt it. A thud that sounded like something heavy hitting the ground. It sent shivers up his spine because he had felt it before . . . a giant was getting close. He coaxed his horse a little farther up a nearby rise and caught a glimpse of the approaching forces.

He could not see any signs of giants. He got this bad sensation that something wasn't right, just like the elf had said back in town. He even started hearing horses in the distance. The only thing he could see was human foot soldiers marching in unison toward the city.

He calmed his horse that was starting to get startled by the noises it couldn't see but could feel and smell nearby. He decided to take a chance and prodded his horse into a gallop toward the enemy's left flank. He glanced over his shoulder and could see that the city was a good five miles out, and he had another half mile to the enemy.

He started pushing his horse into a harder gallop as the sun popped out from the horizon and threw rays of light in his direction. The sounds of the enemy were getting louder.

He could hear the loud thud of giants and many horses now. He could tell he was in the midst of them now and slowed to a trot. The shouts of alert were starting to go out, and he realized he was in grave danger. An arrow flew near his face as he reined up his horse and started heading back toward town.

"You are not invisible, just hard to see." The words echoed in his head.

He forced his horse into a full gallop as he started seeing crossbowmen appearing around him, firing their crossbows in his direction. His horse hit something that almost threw him from the saddle.

He was able to stay mounted and spun the horse around to realize that he had run into the leg of a giant. He looked up at a giant looking down at him. Bryain watched in horror as he realized that he was now as visible to the giant as the giant was to him. The giant raised his massive club over his head in preparation to bring it down on top of them both. Bryain watched an arrow sprout out of the hill giant's nose. It fazed the giant for just an instant.

Bryain looked over his shoulder to see the very visible Sheldin yelling and waving at him. Bryain shook the shock off himself and kicked his horse hard in the haunches while he fumbled to take out the white egg from his vest pocket. He watched Sheldin let loose another arrow and heard a roar from behind him as Sheldin's arrow hit something more sensitive than the giant's nose.

Moments later, he felt the "swoosh" of the giant's club as it hit nothing but air just above him. He was able to crush the white egg over the horse and himself. Everything seemed to slow down for him. He looked over at Sheldin. He was about fifty yards away, kicking his horse into a gallop when a lightning bolt came from behind him and struck the horse just behind Sheldin's leg. In a bright flash, they were gone, vaporized by a massive blast of a lightning bolt.

Adrenalin rushed into his system, and he pushed his horse as hard as it would go. He took a rise in a few bounds on his horse then down the other side. He had never moved this fast in all his life. The horse was covering ground so fast it felt like it could fly. He dared to look back to see what was trying to kill him. He saw a hill giant and an even larger giant that he had never seen before. But it was crackling with power. He turned back and focused on getting back to the city as fast as possible. He had seen enough to know that no mere force of five hundred was attacking the city in a few hours.

SIXTY-ONE

L elanda and Gunner sat looking out over the walls from their perch high up out of reach of any bow. It had been some hours since they dispatched the two riders.

Gunner ran his fingers through his fiery red beard. He was starting to worry that the scouts he sent out had been killed by the coming enemy's own scouts. He had called for a runner to give the word to McLeod to send another pair of riders.

The runner came in just as shouts from the walls started making their way up to his ears. He and Lelanda peered out to see a fast-moving dark shape coming straight toward the city.

"What can you make out, Lelanda?" Elven eyes were always better than human eyes. She looked out from under the hood of her cloak and squinted in an attempt to peer through the morning glare.

"It is one of our scouts," she replied after a moment.

They both watched as the scout approached at an unrealistic pace.

"He must have activated the charm. If he has

been pushing the horse for many miles, then the horse may die before he reaches the city walls."

As if on cue, the horse and rider collapsed just a mile from the walls. Gunner turned to the runner, who he had not dismissed.

"Send word to rescue that rider!" The runner disappeared through the doorway. the gates opened a moment later, and two riders went out toward the fallen scout.

"Looks like McLeod is one of your riders," said Lelanda.

Gunner turned to Lelanda. "What do you think of him as my second in command?"

She looked over at him for a moment and then back to the riders heading out to recover the scout.

"He'll do fine as long as he survives the coming battle," she said. "If the scout he is rescuing rode his horse to death, then there was a good reason. He must have seen something that scared him. I worry that we'll all share his fear once we get him inside the safety of the city walls."

Lelanda excused herself to go speak with the small group of mages sent to help defend the city. Gunner decided it was time to gear up and see what news the scout had.

SIXTY-TWO

McLeod stood with his men on the walls of the city, looking out at the small force of horsemen, bowmen, and foot soldiers that plodded toward them about a mile out.

The scout had relayed giants were among the attacking force, particularly one nasty giant that commanded lightning like a mage. None of those were to be seen. It seemed they had been cloaked in invisibility after the scout had made contact.

Lelanda had surmised as much. She also identified the larger giant to not be a hill giant but a storm giant. They stayed to themselves in the mountains.

They were a greedy lot and could be lured out with the promise of gold and gems. A storm giant had a natural affinity with lightning and could conjure it on command, along with changing weather to suit them.

No change in the weather had been noticed yet, but maybe they thought it would hinder their army more than help. McLeod had no idea how they were to fight a creature of that kind of power.

Lelanda even seemed more distant than normal in their briefing. She couldn't stand or sit still for any length of time. That worried him more than he was willing to admit. She had tried to ease everyone's minds that the mages would be able to handle the hill giants. When it was asked what they could do against one or more storm giants, she just muttered something about having faith and a bit of luck.

SIXTY-THREE

Lelanda stood on the defensive walls of the city this time instead of hovering above them, knowing what came for them would be an all-out rush. All the archers had orders to shoot for the eyes of any giant that got within reach of the walls.

The walls were not made to withstand a siege engine or even giants. They could bring down entire sections with one kick or swing of their clubs. If they were blinded, then that would give the men on the ground a fighting chance.

All the forces were behind the walls this time. This would help her plan when she decided it would be time to use it. Next to her, balancing itself on a single point, was the staff she pulled from storage. It sparkled like quicksilver in the morning light.

Atop the staff were prongs that came off a small round metal ball. Every now and then, they would arc electricity and make a loud pop.

This was effective at keeping the soldiers a fair distance between them and her section of wall.

Even after she made it clear that no harm would come to those who touched it, no soldier would get within ten feet of it.

It was slender but weighed a fair amount. It had taken her years to unlock its secrets. What she planned to use it for in the battle, she did not say. She didn't say because nobody would believe her except for Tegin.

He had seen it used by her once before. Also, she was worried about the damage it would cause if it were to absorb too much of the storm giant's energy. It could save the day, or it could annihilate the entire city. It was a chance she had to take for the sake of the kingdom. Either way, it would make the enemy think twice before attacking the kingdom again.

The enemy's horns and drums could be heard now. They were just a quarter of a mile out. He could feel the ground shake every now and then, but to look out at the rabble, one could not see what was causing it.

McLeod turned to a lieutenant and told them to fire all catapults and ballista at the flanks of the enemy once they were within range. Lelanda told the mages to cast dispels at the flanks in an attempt to break the invisibility she assured them to be hiding the enemy forces. Gunner stayed hidden in the small look-out as he did in the skirmish battle some days before, but he was dressed in full battle gear just in case the fight was brought to him. He was not used to being away from the front lines. Considering the new post he had inherited from the king, he promised McLeod and Lelanda to stay out of the fight.

SIXTY-FOUR

T he small force was coming within range of the city's archers and siege weapons. They were howling and laughing and pointing toward the men on the walls. Comprising of light foot soldiers and bowmen, they were no match for the forces they faced.

To the men on the wals, the large thumping sound was much clearer at this range. They could all hear it but couldn't see it. The four ballistas within range of the approaching force let loose their initial rounds of heavy arrows, followed by the six catapults that were within range as well. Archers let loose half a tic later. Everything was firing to the flanks of the small force of men taunting and screaming at the men on the walls of the city.

The ballistas' heavy arrows landed with no positive effects. However, four of the six heavy shots from the catapults hit things. A boulder ricocheted off of a hill giant, who appeared as if out of nowhere. Dozens of men appeared as the other boulders landed and rolled through the hidden force. Hundreds more appeared as nearly a thousand arrows came screeching down on the hidden force.

There was a slight pause from the small central force of a few hundred. Then, they broke into a charge. Seconds later, waves of magic flowed over the battlefield as the mages attempted to dispel the invisibility of the attacking force.

Invisibility could only be removed in a few ways —by physical contact that was initiated by the person who was invisible or something else that hit said invisible person.

It could also be removed by dispelling magic, forcing the spell to end by magical means. The more skilled the caster of the invisibility, the harder it was to dispel. However, the more mages dispelling, the easier it became to overcome an active spell.

Invisibility had a limited time it could be used. It took considerable energy to keep an object invisible for long periods. The larger the object or area, the more energy it took to maintain the invisibility.

When a mage tried to explain it, it all sounded like nonsense. But after seeing the powerful waves of magic flowing over the battlefield, one could see the mages doing battle with the enemy mages trying to keep the invisibility intact. It seemed to be a stalemate as the seconds passed and the charging force got closer.

Lelanda stepped in and fired off three orbs from her hands that landed like bombs on the battlefield. It was another type of dispelling that was much more powerful and localized. As the three orbs exploded in random areas, it was too much for the attacking force's mages to hold up against on top of the primary spell that Lelanda's mages were casting, and the entire invisibility came crashing down.

Instead of five hundred enemy soldiers visible on the battlefield, there were approximately five thousand from what Gunner could estimate from his vantage point high above the city walls. They were outnumbered almost two to one.

Gunner counted five hill giants and two other giants he had never seen before but heard about.

"How in Elohim's name did they recruit two storm giants?" he muttered to himself under his breath.

This must have been what Lelanda had been hinting at in their previous conversations. She didn't want to endanger the soldiers' morale by mentioning that their forces might have to take on something as dangerous as five hill giants, let alone two storm giants on top of the thousands of other troops marching toward the patched-up city walls.

The hill giants looked to be wearing their typical animal skins and wielding tree trunks for clubs. The storm giants, on the other hand, were decked out with what looked like copper or bronze plate mail and gigantic two-handed swords. They towered some twenty feet high.

They hung back from the front line and seemed to be lingering out toward the flanks with one to either side. The hill giants were all massed in the middle of the main force. They didn't seem to notice that they were now visible, or maybe they didn't care.

Stupid as most hill giants were, they were pointed in the direction of the enemy, and everyone hoped for the best. That was about the only thing

Gunner could see that his forces had an advantage on: intelligence and skill.

He didn't see any siege weapons, which meant the enemy was depending on the giants to breach the walls. He watched as signals were sent via flaggers from McLeod's position. He watched as three ballistae took aim at the hill giants along with five of the nearest catapults. They all let loose at the same time. That was a good strategy in his mind. It would keep the giants busy while the bowmen fired down on the now-charging enemy.

A hill giant caught one of the boulders from a catapult in his free hand and smacked another away with his huge club fashioned from a tree. It still had branches hanging off it.

The boulder he smacked ricocheted off and took out some soldiers nearby. The hill giant next to him tried to hit one of the boulders with his club. Just as the boulder got there, one of the ballista bolts hit him in the shoulder, spinning him around backward as he swung. That took out a few more nearby men. The other nearby forces took heed and moved away from the giants as the charge continued.

The five hundred light horsemen of the enemy stood outside of bow range and waited. Gunner ventured they were waiting for a hole to be made in the wall so that they could charge through and disrupt the city defenses from within to make it easier on the forces outside the wall. He had his flagger send a message to McLeod's position to make certain he was aware of that possible strategy.

The other rounds sent toward the hill giants missed. It would take a few minutes for the ballista and catapults to reload. By then, the giants would be at the walls. The storm giants were inching closer but still seemed to be placing themselves for something.

A wave of magic came from the city again; this time, it caused a heavy frost to appear on the ground between the charging force and the city walls. It kept growing thicker and thicker until it became a solid sheet of ice. Gunner watched as the approaching force attempted to cross the area with the ice, many of which fell or slowed to a walk in an attempt not to fall. The archers let loose another volley of arrows. Hundreds of arrows streaked away from the city walls, and Gunner saw dozens of men topple. The slowed charged would now be in the open for a few more volleys.

As he was taking that in, a commotion caught his attention down on a section of the city wall. A huge wall of flame erupted along a fifty-foot section, engulfing dozens of men that went screaming over the side, fell off backward to their deaths, or were burned alive where they stood.

He gripped his sword with his hand. He knew the enemy mages were within range of the city walls now, but his primary worry was the giants. He looked back over just in time to see another volley of ballista and catapult shots go out toward the hill giants. This time, three of the boulders were caught in midair by three of the giants. One of those took a ballista bolt to the face and fell backward, landing in a huge cloud of dust.

The giant that had taken a shot to the shoulder earlier returned fire by throwing the boulder he had just caught back in the direction it came. The boulder smacked into the city wall and came crashing straight through.

"Well, so much for the walls holding up," Gunner said to himself from his high perch.

The other hill giant that had caught one also threw his toward the wall. It landed short and thudded to a stop at the base of the wall. The hill giants all started into a plodding jog as they headed straight for the section that they just damaged. They were not slowed by the ice on the ground, their weight allowing them to crush through to the ground below.

The battle was in full swing now. The charging force had made it through the ice area and was taking heavy damage from the bowmen that still lined a majority of the walls. Clouds suddenly appeared over the city seemingly out of nowhere. Gunner glanced out toward the storm giants and noticed that both of them had their massive swords pointed toward the sky, and pulses of energy seemed to arc out from the tips of them.

"This can't be good."

The clouds deepened, and a cloud base was forming over the city in what was a clear sky. He didn't know what the storm giants were up to, but he knew it would not end well for this city, its inhabitants, or the men defending it.

He hoped Lelanda was going to make her move soon. He didn't know what she had up her sleeve, but he hoped it would turn what was a stalemate into something more advantageous to their side. A loss here would open the city of Sandown up to another siege.

SIXTY-FIVE

L elanda stayed put on the walls of the city, watching the clouds darken overhead as she expected they would. With the enemy's mages taxed from keeping the invisibility in place for so long and straining to keep it up while her mages dispelled it, it would be some time before they could pose a serious threat to the city. It would be up to the storm giants to be their magical arm in this battle.

Storm giants had a magical ability to change the weather around them. Multiple giants channeling together could create violent lightning storms out of thin air within just a few minutes' time.

It was an amazing display of power on their part and, unbeknownst to them, worked to her advantage. She anticipated something like this, and she planned on using her staff to harness the power of the storm and dissipate it at the same time.

She heard the first rumble of thunder and knew it was time. She grasped the gleaming staff in her left hand and closed her eyes while motioning with her right, and she disappeared from the wall in a blink, reappearing at the highest point in the city some blocks away. The highest point was a bit treacherous because it was a damaged tower at the city center. If lightning struck the tower instead of the staff, it could crumble beneath her, and she needed to save her magic for the fight with the giants.

Casting spells takes a toll on the mind, body, and spirit. Each mage has different levels of casting limits, which prevents them from casting spells indefinitely. Pushing too hard can mean death, or the spell could backfire at the mage or another un-intended target. The more experienced the caster, the more efficient they became with magic and, therefore, the more spells or the more powerful spells they could cast.

She could see the giants off in the distance channeling their power into the sky. The building clouds above the city started to spit raindrops, and the rumble of thunder was becoming almost con-stant. It started drowning out the battle outside of the walls.

The first lightning strike came streaking down from the heavens and smacked a building nearby, blowing a smoking hole through it. Another came down about a block away. Up in her tower, Lelanda had created a perch earlier for her to kneel on.

She knew it was time. She activated the staff with her power, and it came alive. Electricity crawled from the base to the top, and let loose loud pops as the electricity arced between the prongs on the top of the staff.

Another lightning bolt struck the building next

to the tower she was on in a huge blast that almost made her lose her concentration. She could feel the concussion from the strike, and screams rose from the building as the inhabitants started panicking.

After about a minute of her channeling, she initiated a spell that made her more attractive to electricity. The staff started pulsing in the opposite direction, now from the top to the bottom. As long as she held the staff, she would be immune to lightning of natural or magical means.

The sky lit up with multiple strikes that hit at random locations around the city. One landed near the wall facing the battle and blew half a dozen men right off of their feet. The sky opened up, and buckets of rain started coming down, drenching everything within the city walls.

The clouds started to spin as one big mass over the city, centralized over Lelanda's position on the tower. She and the staff were pulsing together now when three lightning strikes in a row hit her and the staff. No loud crash or pop or much of anything occurred. The staff grew a bit thicker and brighter in response to every strike.

Lelanda didn't move. She just continued channeling. She could feel the surge of energy entering the staff. She knew, based on its thickness and her past experience, at about what point she could still maintain a one-handed grip.

The staff was going to get heavy very fast. She hoped she could drain enough energy from the giants with this method that they would not have much left in them by the time she encountered them in battle.

Lightning strikes intensified around the city,

but most were hitting the staff and being absorbed. With every strike, the staff grew in size and weight. As the staff drew that power in, the cloud cover became smaller and not as dark. A couple of times, the storm strengthened a bit as the storm giants attempted to boost the power of the storm, but the steady and powerful absorption of magical energy into the staff was lessening the power of the storm.

Lelanda's plan was starting to work. It was too early to know for certain if she had absorbed too much power into the staff or if it was going to be enough. She had only seen the staff discharge its entire energy reserve once.

That was prior to her taking ownership of the staff. It destroyed an entire wing of a castle, and she and Tegin barely escaped with their lives. It took years of scrying to unlock the powers of the staff, and she had never attempted this devastating spell from the staff herself.

SIXTY-SIX

Gunner watched in disbelief as the clouds above the city started to dissipate. He saw the distant storm giants give up on their channeling and roar in frustration. He could feel their anger even from where he stood as they stomped about and smashed their massive swords into the ground.

At this point, the enemy was almost to the breach in the walls. Their whole strategy was wrapped around the giants bringing down sections of the wall. The giant that had taken the ballista bolt to the shoulder earlier was finally finished off by a boulder to the head and two ballista bolts to the chest as he approached the partially broken section of the wall.

That left three hill giants at this point, who had so many arrows sticking out of their thick skin that they looked like giant pin cushions.

The frost spell had been dispelled by the attacking force's mages with what energy that they had left, leaving the ground wet and muddy. That still was an obstacle for the enemy to charge through.

It had done its job well. The enemy had been decimated by the archers on the walls. The slight damage to the walls and low numbers of men lost were bringing the number into an even one-to-one by Gunner's estimation.

However, the three hill giants had made it to the damaged section of the wall. Each swung their giant clubs down onto areas near it while shielding their faces from arrows that were fired at them.

Arrows did little to slow or even stop giants due to the thickness of their skin. Siege weapons or magic was about the only way to bring them down fast. Gunner watched as the wall held for a couple of swings from their huge clubs. Then, it gave way, falling back into the city onto his soldiers, crushing dozens of them. He had his flaggers confirm for McLeod that the wall was breached.

He watched his berserkers move into action as the hill giants started forcing their way into the city, swinging their clubs this way and that with devastating results. Gunner noticed the enemy cavalry on the move as well. They were charging for the gap created by the hill giants in the city's wall. The battle would be decided by his army's ability to prevent the enemy from pouring through the gap. The fall of the wall was a morale boost to the enemy forces, and they shifted their assault to push in that direction. The storm giants were thundering toward the wall, too. In their anger, they decided to wade into battle with their armor and large two-handed swords in tow.

Another hill giant fell when the berserkers

swarmed the first one that came through the gap in the wall. They sliced the back of his legs, cutting into his tendons with their razor-sharp two-handed swords.

Watching them in action was incredible. The berserkers' ability to sustain one hundred percent of their intensity for a sustained period of time was amazing to watch. Once the giant was down on his back, they silenced his roar of defiance with quick slashes to the neck and stabs through the sides of its chest with their swords.

Another was killed a second later when a mage launched a huge ice spear through its chest. The final hill giant killed the mage and many of the berserkers with a few swipes of his club. Parts of the wall that he brought down crushed nearby soldiers from both sides. Then, the giant brought down another section of wall, allowing the main force of the army to start pouring through.

Those were met by McLeod's wall of shields set up in the phalanx. This brought the enemy to a standstill. Gunner's attention was brought back to the storm giants who had brought up the rear of the army and were some two hundred yards away from the gap in the wall just behind the cavalry charge that was brought to a standstill as well while the foot soldiers were trying to force their way through the gap and straight into the phalanx. This is when Lelanda struck.

Gunner saw her small form appear near the storm giants, who had been attempting to join the fray. Their stomping and roaring could be felt in the small room that Gunner occupied. He watched as she got their attention with a couple of well-placed frost spells to their codpieces.

He couldn't help but chuckle as the two of them grabbed at themselves. He could see she had something large in her hand that gleamed like a sliver of heaven in the sunlight.

He could see arcs of what looked like lightning coming from her, watching as one of the giants pointed at her with his hand. A huge ball of lightning flew from the giant's hand to her location, frying everything in a twenty-foot radius. Lelanda just stood there in the torrent, unfazed by the display of power from the giant.

Gunner could make out both giants' looks of disbelief from his vantage point above the city walls. They both paused for a moment and glanced at each other, then brandished their huge two-handed swords and started toward her.

SIXTY-SEVEN

Lelanda had gotten the attention of both giants and had absorbed even more electrical energy into the staff. The staff had grown in size to the point where her fingers could barely touch when hefting it in her hand. It was time. Now she needed to stay alive long enough to trigger the staff and pray that the energy released would not destroy her allies and half the city.

The two giants had realized she was immune to electrical attacks, and they were almost on top of her. She muttered an incantation and fired off a haste spell to increase her movement speed. The first giant swung at her with the flat of his blade in an attempt to swat her like a bug, but she was able to jump back in time to dodge the attack. The sword took a huge chunk out of the ground and sent it flying. The second giant did what she was hoping one of them would do.

He leaped into the air and came down in an attempt to squash her under one of his large armored boots. In anticipation, she lay down with the point of the staff aimed at the flat of his foot and fired off a teleportation spell. As the giant's foot came crashing down, the point of the staff penetrated partially into his foot and partially into the ground slick with mud from the earlier ice spell. Lelanda disappeared as the boot came crashing down into the wet ground, with the tip of the thick staff sticking out of the top of his boot.

The giant let out a roar of pain as Lelanda appeared just a few feet away from where she disappeared. Before either giant could react, she ran up and grabbed the top of the staff sticking out of the boot of the storm giant, who had dropped to one knee from the pain of the injury. She muttered a quick magical word that sounded unintelligible, and the staff started glowing and popping with power. Lelanda teleported away with what magical energy she had left. She appeared next to Gunner, who almost jumped out of his armor at her appearance.

The staff created an energy well that magnetized the armor of the first giant, turning him into an electromagnet. The other giant, still looking for Lelanda, wandered too close and slammed into the other giant.

Their armor bound together in a powerful bond that kept getting stronger and stronger. The light emanating from the staff grew so extreme that the giants had no choice but to close their eyes.

They both sooned roared in pain as their armor began crushing them. A large bubble of electrical energy started moving out away from the staff in an expanding radius in all directions. The crackling from the staff and the roar from the giants caused the enemy near the rear to stop and look back at the commotion.

Lelanda explained what was going to happen to Gunner as they left the confines of the perch to find a safer spot.

As they ran out of the room, he yelled over the sound of the battle below, "I hope you know what you are doing!"

McLeod's group could not see the commotion because they were still behind the standing section of the city's wall, but they could hear the bellowing from the giants getting crushed to death and the crackling roar from the staff getting louder.

They had no idea what was going on. McLeod hoped it was to the detriment of the enemy and not his men. The majority of the enemy was distracted by this event that was transpiring before them. The entire cavalry line had stopped and turned their mounts to look upon the scene.

The bubble was increasing in size and speed as it started racing outwards toward the rear flank of the enemy. When it reached the rear line of archers and horsemen, it passed right through them without any real effect. They could feel the energy pass through them, but it tickled more than anything.

The giants' own armor was crushing the life out of them. They both suffocated under the over-whelming pressure the electrical affect had on the armor. They both died with their mouths agape and eyes wide open in a painful grimace.

Lelanda and Gunner made it out of the building and down the street just as the dome of electrical energy made it to the city's wall. It passed through it by a few feet in one section and then stopped. The crackling sound was deafening, like hundreds of lightning strikes going off in rapid succession.

What happened next could only be described by those few who had a line of sight and were still out of the radius of the blast. The electrical dome collapsed inward toward the staff, and all at once, the crackling paused. For a moment, there wasn't a sound.

The explosion that followed tore a crater in the ground about four hundred yards in diameter. It came within fifteen yards of the walls of the city and was close to 150 feet deep at the center. The concussion wave moved faster than sound. Nobody heard it hit until it was already to them.

The blast was immense. It instantly killed eighty-five percent of the remaining enemy force and ten percent of the defending force. Those deaths were caused by the collapse of the outer wall and by the concussion wave. Citizens were killed when many of the outer buildings of the city that couldn't withstand the blast and fell.

The two dead storm giants were not vaporized because of their immunity to electricity, but they were thrown hundreds of feet into the air. Their bodies landed in different places around the city, causing some further damage and scaring the citizens.

Those that survived were blasted off their feet by the shockwave and knocked unconscious. After recovering from the incredible explosion, it took several minutes for McLeod to get his men back into a respectable formation.

In an instant, the tables were turned. The remaining enemy force had nowhere to go. They were made up of one hill giant and foot soldiers. Behind them was a cavernous smoking pit and McLeod's army to the front.

The mages and berserkers finished off the remaining hill giant that was still gathering himself after being thrown into a building. Once the hill giant was dispatched, the rest of the enemy surrendered.

Once they did, McLeod's army started cheering. None of them knew how the blast happened, but they were grateful that it did. Many more men would have been killed had it not been for the blast.

Some of the archers that survived remembered seeing the senior mage Lelanda fighting the storm giants by herself. It didn't take long for her name to start spreading through the remaining ranks.

The city came alive with activity after the battle was over. Crews were dispatched to clear out the dead and start repairs on the city.

Lelanda made her way down into the crater to see if the staff remained intact, not one to take credit for anything or want any acknowledgment from anyone. She slipped out of one of the side exits to stay clear of the troops.

It took her some time to reach the bottom of the crater. The interesting thing about it was how smooth the crater was. The blast had cut a perfect bowl into the earth. It was like someone scooped out the ground with a large spoon. She had to teleport down to an area level enough for her to walk on.

As she approached the deepest part of the crater, she found a small pool had started to form.

In the deepest section she could see something glimmering in the clear water being fed by a spring that had been cut into by the explosion. She waded in and was able to scoop the object up with her foot so she could grab it with her hand.

Sure enough, it was the staff. It had returned to its smallest size. That was about as thick as her thumb. When she grasped it, it electrified as it always did. She decided to take it back to her hideout and act like it was destroyed in the blast.

She didn't want it used as a weapon of war and hoped to never have to use it again. It was way too dangerous. She knew she was very lucky to not have destroyed or killed half the city.

They would give her more credit than she deserved, and nothing she said would prevent them from doing it. She looked at the staff with a wondering eye. What mind could think up and create such a devastating device as this? She muttered words of magic and disappeared.

SIXTY-EIGHT

A few hours later, she met back up with McLeod and Gunner along a section of wall that was still standing nearest the crater. The three of them stood there looking out at the devastated area. Huge blocks of earth and stone lay strewn about the area. It stood in stark contrast to the smooth crater that lay before them.

"Looks like we have a new lake to name." Gunner motioned at the crater. The pool of water could be seen growing in the bottom of the crater.

"Work will be needed to give the lake an outlet to a nearby creek; otherwise, it will flood the city," McLeod responded.

"I'll get some mages assigned here to assist in clearing a channel. It should take a long time to fill the crater. I think priority should be tasked to rebuild the city defenses, repair the buildings, and bury the dead," Lelanda mentioned.

Gunner looked over at her. "You did well, my friend. Though you were wise not to mention your plan to me. I would never have let you attempt such a maneuver. You are the advisor to the king and invaluable to the security of the kingdom. I hope you never have to attempt anything like that again to save our people."

Lelanda just kept looking out at the battlefield. McLeod prodded her in the side with his elbow. "Soon, we'll have Lake Lelanda to enhance the city."

"Please don't call it that."

"Too late, the men are already calling it Lelanda Crater. Once they realize it's going to fill with water, it won't take them long to change crater to lake."

The three of them stood there in silence for a few more moments until Gunner turned to the two of them. "We better get over to the rally to say some words to the troops and finalize things here. Then we'll head back to Sandown to find out how the hunt for the assassin goes and, if need be, finish business there." The three of them turned toward the stairs.

SIXTY-NINE

A couple of days later, the city of Sandown gathered to pay its respects to the fallen heroes of the kingdom of Stalken. Gunner, the newly crowned king, stood surrounded by his elite guard and his friends.

They were high up on a platform that overlooked the funeral pyres of their dead friends. Hundreds of pyres also surrounded the city to honor the dead that had been lost in battle in recent days.

William Stalken was displayed in his full plate armor on his pyre, with Thena on a pyre next to him and just a few inches lower, dressed in a beautiful white elven dress Tegin had found in her belongings.

Tegin had discovered letters between the king and Thena revealing a relationship that the two had been keeping secret for many years. He kept it to himself out of respect for his friends. He tucked the letters into a small pouch that he slipped into the king's armor. Tegin tried in vain to stifle back tears as Gunner began his speech.

"Citizens of the kingdom of Stalken, we are

gathered here today to say goodbye to our friends, our loved ones, and our leaders. They have paid the ultimate sacrifice to keep us safe and allow us to live as independent and free people. I had the pleasure of knowing many of the fallen that lay before us. Now is a time of mourning and sorrow. But don't be sad for those who have passed, as they now live in the kingdom of Elohim.

"Be sad because we do not get to experience the joy and love that they gave us every day. Let us honor them going forward. I promise you this day that I will not rest until those responsible pay for their wickedness! Let us remember our fallen for the laughter and love that they brought us and not for the way they died. Honor the fallen, honor the dead, honor life, and honor each other."

Lelanda has even taken her hood down and wore a gown of black. Though, she was barely recognizable with the illusion spell she had in place to hide her dark skin and silver hair. For the moment, she was Thena's sister, beautiful and pale like the rest of the above-ground elves.

During Gunner's speech, a single tear slid down her cheek as she stared at her friends' bodies. Her eye started twitching, and she quickly wiped the tear away and gritted her teeth to prevent a river of tears from betraying her emotion. She succeeded in protecting the kingdom. She failed to protect her friends. The kingdom was nothing without her friends who spent years and, in some cases, decades of their life breaking down her emotional walls to find the person within and accept her.

She swore right there she would die before allowing someone else she cared about have their life taken before their time.

After a short prayer by a priest, the funeral pyres were ignited. The fires lit up the sky for hours as night fell on the city. Tegin kept Thena's sword on his person at all times. He had tied a lock of her hair to it.

His friends could see the anger torturing him. They knew there was nothing that they would be able to do to console him. Time would have to pass before the wound in his heart would begin to heal. For now, rage was all he felt.

He had lost two of his closest friends in the same week. Lelanda knew that one thing would console her friend, and that was finding the person responsible for the death of them. Thena and Stalken were like kin to him, and Lelanda meant to help her friend avenge their fallen comrades. This was far from over.

Those responsible had awakened a warrior's rage in these two they thought they would never show again.

ACKNOWLEDGMENTS